REBELLION

Jay Taverner

Published in 2004 by Onlywomen Press, Limited.
Radical Feminist Lesbian Publishers
40 St. Lawrence Terrace, London W10 5ST

ISBN 0–906500–58–3

British Library/Cataloguing-in-Publication Data.
A catalogue record for this book is available from the British
Library.

Jay Taverner is the fiction-writing persona of a lesbian
partnership who both write under other names.

Disc conversion and typesetting by Seagull Books Private
Limited, 26 Circus Avenue, Calcutta 700 017, India.

Printed and bound in the UK

PROLOGUE

The candles leapt and guttered. And they were in the room.

Bell shivered. She had been afraid of the horned men all her life. When she was a tiny girl, Sir Walter had tossed her into the arms of their leader, laughing, asking a blessing on his youngest, and she had smelt the village smells of soot and dirt, and over them the strange acrid herbs of the face paints, and the rot of ancient fur. The horned man had grinned at her, and his teeth were huge as the antlers branching out of his eyes.

She looked for him now; but there was no man amongst them so large as Jack Smith. She had found out he was really the smith long ago, but it made no difference to the terror he carried in his horns and huge, ribboned skirts when he came at the turn of each New Year. Now the six dancers stamped their clogs on the flags, and horns and ribbons shook.

They were masked strangers.

Their piper stood in the doorway, and began the dancing tune; as they tilted their heads and brought stiff hands to their waists, the piper ran in small and lithe, and began to step a way between them, round them, and then out in a sinuous line to weave the spectators into their spell. The pipe shrilled. Bell watched the line pass behind the servants in the flickering dark under the gallery: Ben and Matt, John Dickson, Mistress Johnson, Dolly – the piper was no taller than the women of the household, but strange, in white breeches and shirt stiff with ancient embroidery; and flesh all green.

The inhuman face came slowly towards her, down the line of her kin, ducking in front of Sir Walter, but not with deference, no bow, more as if daring the family to answer the music's call. She tightened her hands in her lap. The piping tune came to her; passed close in a wisp of air warmed by the prancing body, danced behind her, shrilling, mocking. She held her neck rigid as a board. The little winding melody came close; in the corner of her eye the green head and hands reappeared – leaning over her shoulder, playing right into her face, then whisking away. Bell gasped; she had been holding her breath. As the tune retreated, the piper dancing, leading the others towards the far door, she found she wanted them to turn and come back. As if called, the green face turned towards her, and stood still. The dance was over, the stamping and the music stopped; the pipe was lowered.

Sir Walter applauded and called for drink for the Mossmen of the Moor. Benchley carried in the big old wassail bowl, and the Lord touched it to his lips, and handed it to the dancers. They were half themselves again now, villagers standing awkwardly in the Manor hall; but still the pride was in them and their horns. The piper drank last, and carried the bowl back to the household. Sir Walter said, 'Do you offer it to my family, Hobbinol: all mine shall drink with you.'

Bell saw James's lip twitch in disgust, but he could not refuse the custom; he smoothed his ruffles down and touched his fingers to the bowl, and his lip to the brim opposite the place where their paint had spread an oily half-moon. As he let go, his eyes flicked suddenly at the green face; the piper turned quickly and came to Bell. Their eyes met. The surge of response came up in her belly again; but it was not fright, as when the smith had enveloped her in his strangeness, nor did she share her brother's distaste. She put out her hands, and held those that held the bowl, drawing them towards her. She could scarcely swallow the warm cider.

The spell was quickly broken by James's snicker, and a whisper to Alistair at his side; the piper swiftly bowed, leaving the bowl in her hands, and darted away into the darkness outside the candles; the dancers with a final clatter of clogs trooped out. 'I see our sister is spellbound,' said James in his low voice, 'Perhaps a good thing Hobbinol was a wench this year.'

Bassett Moor was an open village; but Wiston Bassett belonged to My Lord. In Wiston Bassett no man or woman lived outside the shadow of the Manor. The village street wound round the home farm from the Manor gates to the church, snug as a cat's tail. Croft and cottage, appleground and barn all nestled and jostled along Sir Walter's path, when he walked in state each Sunday to the sermon preached by his poor cousin Patten, or rode out, every day but Sunday, to hunt his deer. Sir Walter Wiston was the fifteenth of his forefather's line, planted in the soil of Somerset since Domesday and before.

'I couldn't live down there,' Hope's mother declared, 'to be spied on by the gentry, and laughed at by their drunken swaggerers every day.'

By marrying John Bishop and coming to live in the keeper's cottage in the forest, she had escaped the craven bobbing and grinning of Wiston; and she had also escaped the dangers of the forge up at the Moor, where her family laboured in the flying sparks to make nails and latches, and sometimes barrels for guns, until their arms were pocked with red burns. Her Aunt Faith had lost an eye; her father had been killed by the shattering of a flawed cast. But if she had taken the singing gamekeeper Jack to save her pretty face, it had done her no good; the smallpox had left her as marked as any of them. And it had taken two of her children: her little Daniel, and a baby girl too new to have been named. It was God's providence, and she did not question His wisdom; but she loved her surviving children with a fierce protectiveness that often felt to them like no love at all.

Hope, her youngest child and only living daughter, had her mother's heartshaped face and her father's thick, corn coloured hair; a casual observer might take her for a pretty little thing. But she also inherited her father's sturdy frame, and her mother's determined will; she was not an easy child.

The Bishops' cottage stood at the foot of a bank, in a forest glade as green and secret as a deep well. Sir Walter allowed his keepers to fence their gardens. It took nine-foot hurdles to keep out the deer, who grazed over the plots and fields of the less privileged free foresters, So Hope's home was a fortress in the woods, and their fence trapped sunshine like sparkling water. Brilliant flowers grew, and apple trees blossomed along the path; rows of cabbages and peas flourished. A keeper's garden always grows well: buried carrion plumps the beanpods. The cottage stood back, its thatch running down over kennels, goatshed and henhouse. Bee skeps lined up along the fence. Behind, the bank rose away from the crumbling cob wall steep and dank with brambles; the great forest trees reached out over the thatch.

When she was small, Hope loved the forest. She played with it, hid in its skirts and climbed the great oaks to look down secretly on the forest people. She saw her brother Jack and his dog Benjy passing quietly, the little doe with the crumpled ear nuzzling her fawn, brother Eli with traps over his arm, and the noisy badgers who skirmished in the leaves and fired the blackbirds off in explosions of panic. Her brothers were much older than Hope; by the time she was six they were both working under her father in the forest, and Sir Walter counted Jack a man, when he was no more than seventeen. He could have taken a cottage and a wife, if he had wanted to.

'A good keeper,' Sir Walter had said to her father, 'worth a man's place – damned few good men to be found these days, and you bring me two, besides yourself, John Bishop; good man. Need anything from the house? Only to say. Come up and talk to the steward, any time; and harken - let the lad settle, soon as he's a mind, eh? Let 'em have the rope – they'll hobble

8

themselves,' and he laughed, so his huge black horse trampled backwards into her mother's cabbages. But Jack just smiled and looked aside; Hope knew he would not leave them.

Jack brought her nests from the forest, little speckled eggs in moss, frail white perfection, or brown spots on blue, lovely to see; he taught her how to blow them clean, and one spring the slopey beam over her bed had six nests at once; it was a wet season, and many birds deserted their first attempts at homes. When Jack or father brought home the bigger eggs of quail and pheasant, they were not for her, but kept warm against the skin, and quickly set under mother's hens.

With Eli it was different; his hands and feet were big, little creatures shied away from him, and any eggs he touched tended to break; but he was always sorry to do damage, and tried to go as softly as the others. He was kind to Hope when he remembered. The night a falling branch carved away half the thatch, and they all scrambled out into the drenching rain to rescue desperate goats while the dogs howled, it was Eli who crawled up the roof with ropes, sliding on wet straw and clinging on in the gale's teeth. He was a hero.

It was also Eli who brought home a dancing-man's antlered headgear, when Hope was nine, and stowed it in the back of the goatshed under the thatch. She found it when she was mucking out. All the forester's taboos clamouring in her throat, she ran to the kitchen.

'Whatever are you about, girl? Get that dungfork out of my house!'

'Mother – in the goatshed –'

Her mother pulled out the horns with an exclamation of anger, but dropped them on the path.

'How'll we hide them?'

'Hide them? Why should we hide them, child? Wicked mummings and prancings show themselves boldly in these latter days,' said her mother bitterly. She kicked the horns aside, and strode back to her work. Hope ran after.

9

'Isn't it poaching?'

'Poaching? Not it. Maybe it was a stolen buck, once on a time, but it's no recent kill, that one. It's a Mossman's headgear, child – you've seen them dancing, when your brother Eli took you up to Bassett Moor last winter, to my sorrow. Aye. Eli. It'll be his.' She plunged her hands into her dough trough, kneading fiercely. 'Go and throw it on the dunghill. Go on.'

It was Eli's. Eli was going to be a Mossman, a dancer. There would be a row. Hope went slowly out to the fallen crown; she could see now that the bone was old and yellowed, the cap of fur lying all ways, worn and smudged by many fingers. It had leather thongs. She lifted it for a moment onto her head, but the scratchy weight coming down over her eyes was disgusting, and she lifted it off. She took it back to the goatshed. Eli was grateful that it had not been on the dungheap; he forgave her for betraying him to mother.

'She'd have known it in the end, lass; don't fret. I's'll dance, anyhow. She cannot stop me, and there's no harm, I say. You saw them, last year? Jack the smith's leg is worse, and he's no boy or kin to take on; Uncle Joshua dances, thee knows, and he spoke for me. Father'd be a Mossman, but for her. He's the right.' He looked at her, pausing. 'I like it. The music, and the going round. It's neighbourly, that's all. How should we get to know folk, working always in the forest? How shall you find yourself a man, poppet, when the time comes, eh?' He picked her up and swung her, as if she were still a baby.

'Are there girl Mossmen, Eli?' she said, when he set her down. He just laughed; but when the mossmen's musician had an old pipe to give away, Eli remembered Hope and quietly brought it home to her, despite the fact that girls did not play for the dancing any more than they took a part.

It was always a mystery to Hope about what girls could do, and what only boys were allowed. She had no examples to copy. But she did not much care; she did not feel, like Eli, that they were lonely in the forest. When the work about the house was done, and her mother was dozing by the fire, she would slip away and go visiting. Her Uncle Joshua, who worked down at Wiston Bassett in My Lord's stables, spoiled her and gave her titbits from the kitchen; he let her ride round the yard with her legs stuck out across Daisy's back. Best of all she would go up to the Moor, to see her great grandmother.

Anticipation Liddell was very old, so old there seemed to be no reason why she should die at all. She still moved quietly round her granddaughters' garden, or sat in winter with the firelight folded into her face.

'Hope, my daughter's daughter's daughter,' she would say, welcoming, and gather her near to see some tiny flower or snail, or just the pictures in the hearth; one of Hope's earliest memories was of learning to read from the great Bible which Anticipation seemed to know by heart. When she was not reading from the scripture, the old woman would tell Hope brave stories of her own life, long ago. She remembered a time unimaginably strange, when the world was turned upside down, and the king – Charles Stuart, the uncle of poor Queen Anne – was executed, and the little people were promised their freedom from the cruelty of princes.

'But it never came to pass.' The old woman sighed. 'Troops and taxes, and lords of the church, oppressed us still.' So, when she was sixteen years old, and the prophet Anna Liddell had come to her village, preaching a new life of love and freedom, she had run away to follow her. Deep in the forest they built the new life, women and men, high-born and low, all working their fields together. They had all been baptised anew, all Liddell's Children, and that was when she became Anticipation, a token of their belief in the future where all could be free and equal in love. 'Love and have courage,' she told the little girl, 'for it is the loving that shall inherit the earth.'

Liddell's Children filled Hope's imagination with pictures of a perfect life; and her great-grandmother, who spoke little to others of those far-off days of glory, liked to tell her the story. For Hope was her most cherished child. Anticipation herself had named her, when she was born at the turn of the new century; a gesture of defiance, of hope against all appearances that there might still be a new dawn. 'For we were not defeated, little one,' she would say. 'even though the soldiers came and broke our fences and burned our cottages over our heads, and we were cast out, like Adam and Eve from the garden. We were scattered into the sinful world, but we carried our faith and our memories with us. And I came to live here, with the father and mother of your aunt Faith, bringing nothing with me but my sweet babe. That was your grandmother, who died the year that you were born.'

She would look round the room, with its whitewashed walls and swept floor, its pewter and plate, its pillows and footstools and solid presses, all the proud belongings of the years between; and she would sigh. Not for herself, Hope thought, because her memories are safe and her mind is free, but for us, the comers-after in a lesser time: for mother, or for me. Hope knew Anticipation grieved over her mother's marriage to one of the worldly; she had heard them speak, at the forge, about her father, and call him damned. Uncle Joshua called the horses damned, sometimes, or the stable clock; but that was not the same. When she was at the forge, Hope spoke their Bible tongue; at My Lord's house, she put it by. She was a clever child.

She had few friends of her own age; and no one to tell her what she should and should not do, until she began to spend more time with her cousin Dolly. She would go sometimes to help out in My Lord's fields at harvest, or in the kitchens at the Manor. Dolly took charge of her; she thought Hope was a little savage. She was forever sucking in her breath and saying 'Hope! You mustn't run like that' or 'show your legs so', or even

12

laugh at the jokes the men servants made together. Dolly was two years older; she took up with Hope when Noah the stable boy started walking out with a girl from over the Moor. Until then Hope's visits to the Manor stables had been to her uncle, and Dolly had ignored her as a mere baby; but now she made friends. Hope, at eleven, was ready to be led by the nose. Dolly told her all her secrets; all about boys and their ways, and what to expect when she was married. It did not sound too attractive.

'And then you have babies,' she finished, triumphantly, 'and you bleed ever so much more.'

'Goats don't bleed much when they have babies,' Hope objected.

'Goats! My dear!'

Dolly looked very grown up; she laced her bodice to push her breasts into a plump cushion, and made her skirts very full behind. She scoffed at what Hope could do most of the time; but she soon discovered a use for one of her cousin's skills.

'You can read, can't you? Look what I've got!' It was a little book, without a cover, but with a picture on the front of a man on a horse, and a pretty border round. The print was easy, though its lines were not very straight. Dolly snatched it back. 'Let's go up the forest, and you can read it to me.'

They read The History of Guy, Earl of Warwick many times. Dolly especially liked the bit where Guy fell sick with love of the fair Phillis.

'You be Guy,' she said one day, arranging herself fetchingly on a bank, 'and I'll be Phillis.'

Hope began to say the words. '*All hail, fair Phillis, flower of beauty and jewel of virtue –*'

'Kneel down, it says he saluted her on his bended knees.'

Hope knelt. 'What's saluted?'

'Kissed, of course. Don't you know anything?'

'Shall I kiss you then?'

'Of course, stupid.'

Dolly's cheek was soft; she smelled of baking. Hope warmed to her part. *'I know great princes seek to win thy love; yet may they come short of Guy's real affection; disdain me not for being a steward's son, one of thy father's servants.* Then she says –'

'I know it, shh. *Cease, bold youth, leave off this passionate address, you are but mean –'* Dolly tossed her head magnificently.

'Then Cupid shoots his dart, and she says she will offer herself up at his shrine, and Guy comes again and she sends him off on his noble actions.'

'Do it, go on!' Dolly stood up and clasped her hands to her bosom, like the picutre.

Hope threw herself at her knees. *'Phillis farewell –'*

'Accept of this kiss as signet of my heart,' cried Dolly, and enveloped Hope in her arms and kissed her. Then she curled up laughing.

And so Hope and Dolly found games to play together in the forest at an age when most girls were beginning to leave play behind. Soon they didn't need the book; Dolly kept it at home, in case Hope's mother should see it. Hope never tired of the game, but Dolly blew hot and cold, very much according to whether or not she was pursuing one or other of the men on the estate. They only played the game in the forest, when Dolly decided they should. Dolly was always Phillis, and was cruel or kind to Guy as the fancy took her; but Hope didn't mind being Guy.

The return of Captain James from London, with a fancy horse and a fashionable new serving-man, threatened to put an end to the passions of poor Guy for ever. It was the summer of 1714; Hope was fifteen, and shooting up to a sturdy woman's shape. Dolly no longer needed her as a make-believe hero; she set her cap at Godfrey. She laughed at Hope's plain homespun skirts, and tut-tutted at their shortness. Hope was irritated and moodily jealous; she refused to pretend to be a lady.

14

At least her family did not share Dolly's obsession with what was proper. At home, and up at the Moor forge, Hope had always been allowed to do anything that needed doing. Her mother had taught her to gut rabbits, to skin or pluck all that came into the house, and to make pelts clean and supple. Her hands and her stomach were steady: she had helped her aunt Faith to dress wounds and ease dislocated joints back in place, and learnt to feel for broken bones. Jack taught her to set snares. Her father gave her a slingshot to keep pigeons off the peas, and she practised to bring them down cleanly. Dolly thought this a particularly odd accomplishment.

'Killing pigeons!'

'But they eat the greens; and they're good for the pot.'

'But how can you bear to shoot them dead?'

They were resting, lying under the hedge, gazing out across the shimmering bronze of the wheatfield, to where the line of reapers moved slowly into the shadow under the far oaks. It was the second week of harvest; everyone either cut the corn or stacked and gleaned. Dolly looked dreadful, her face all swollen with hay fever.

'Best to shoot them dead, stupid, or you have to pull their necks when they come down. All soft and feathery.'

'Eech!' Dolly affected a ladylike shudder, but spoilt it with a sneeze. A distant bang and a shout went up from where the gentlemen stood under the oaks, ahead of the reapers.

'Captain James hit another rabbit. I'd like to use a gun; but father won't let me. Great-grandma Liddell knows how; but I suppose she's too old to teach me.'

'Your great-grandma can shoot a gun? Your mother's folk are dreadful. I can't think why a man of a decent family like ours took to one of them.'

That's Uncle Joshua speaking, thought Hope; or her silly mother. Certainly the Liddells were less concerned than the Bishops about her being a nice girl and knowing her place; but they had other prohibitions. She felt in her pocket.

'Would you like a tune?'

'Play me something dreamy. Affecting.' Dolly propped herself up and gazed into the distance, trying a pensive smile on the field gate. The other gleaners were spread out along the hedge to catch the shade; some had closed their eyes, but Hope's pipe was too soft to disturb them. A few turned towards the music. She played 'Waly Waly' for Dolly, and then tried a dancing tune she had heard a tinker playing on squeeze pipes under his arm; difficult in do, and interesting.

Dolly suddenly sat up. 'Shh! Put it away – it's Godfrey'.

Through the gate on which she had been practising her winsome looks came Captain James's spruce servingman, looking very hot and stumbling over the stubble in his high-heeled shoes.

'He mustn't see me. I look terrible. Do I look too bad, Hope?' She ran her hands over her hair, and licked her finger for her eyebrows. She wasn't going to make too much effort to stop him seeing her, it seemed. But he only waved vaguely to them all, and set off across the field, picking up his feet like Captain James's fancy mare.

'Come on – it's time to get back to work.' Dolly was up and shaking out her skirts. Resigned, Hope put away her pipe.

Far out into the field, one of the gentlemen saw Godfrey, and came running to him. They struck off across the stubble; they were going to leave the field by the far gate. Dolly flung herself down on her back, and started to sneeze with pure vexation.

The news that had brought Godfrey out into the harvest field flew round the village. Queen Anne was dead, and without an heir. Dolly heard all about it in church on Sunday, when the Reverend Patten preached a solemn sermon on the true succession and the House of David, and then told them that they were to have a new king called George.

'Vicar says he's a German and cannot speak a word of English,' she told Hope. 'He said King George cannot know anything about the true Church of the land, and besides he's already king somewhere else. So I can't see why he should care to come here where he can't even speak to anyone, can you? Godfrey says,' – here her voice dropped to an important whisper – 'that there are some among the gentry that would rather have seen Another on the throne of England. One who is now –' she looked around dramatically and silently mouthed, '– in France.'

Hope was mystified. Her knowledge of kings was sketchy, being in the main Biblical, and up to now it had led her to suppose that they were on the whole among the ranks of the ungodly. 'So did the Vicar bear witness against this George?' she asked with interest. Hope's family did not go to church; father and the boys had the excuse of forest duties – poachers might take advantage of church time – and of course she and her mother went to the Meeting at Bassett Moor, which was often held in the Liddells' house. She had several times heard older members of the meeting moved to rail against principalities and powers, and supposed this might be a feature common to all religion.

'Why no.' Dolly looked shocked. 'He said, whatever our misgivings, Sir Walter wished the people to be obedient in all things lawful, and render unto Caesar that which was Caesar's. But he was mighty solemn,' she added, 'and My Lord looked like thunder. The young gentlemen weren't there – I think Captain James has gone to London, he took his best horse and two more, and Master Alistair was away off too. There was only young Mistress, and Vicar Patten's simple maid with their baby. He cried at it, bless him; but he generally does cry, poor little mite, the church is that dank for him, and dark . . .'

17

Dolly loved babies, even the ever-increasing Patten brood; Hope knew she'd get no more from her about the new king. When she asked Jack, he just shrugged it off, as 'naught to do with them'; but up at the forge, she found, they were for calling it a blessing.

Anticipation, confined to her chair with pains which the sun and the forge fire together could not warm, and with a great shortage of breath, looked up at Hope with joy.

'They say he is a king that is a true believer; it is an end for ever to the pretences of the Men of Blood, the godless house of Stuart. Truly I have lived to be blessed. The Lord moves in mysterious ways. Lord, lettest thou thy servant depart in peace; Anticipation fulfilled.'

Her face shone, her eyes cleared wonderfully, but they did not seem to be fixed on Hope; Aunt Faith came and bustled her outside.

'You must not tire her, child; she has not much longer to spend amongst us. His will be done.'

It was clear to Hope that in this, as in so many other matters, her family – and the world at large – held conflicting opinions. So as not to disturb the house while Anticipation was so sick, the Liddells went more often to Meeting of a Sunday at the little Independent Chapel, five miles away at Carney Woodhouse. There Hope heard sermons denouncing all Jacobites and Papists, and fervently supporting the new King; but the family said little about it at home, preferring not to talk politics with the other keepers, who sat under Vicar Patten down at Wiston church. His sermons became more and more fiery every week against foreigners and wicked German innovations. At Advent he came out in a fine new purple vestment; Dolly admired it greatly. He was in favour, he said, of the good old customs of the people; the Mossmen were to dance in the church yard that year, as well as down the highway and in the houses. At Christmas the church was decked out in holly, and a new anthem sung; the Mossmen practised nights, up at Farmer Hardy's barn.

On December 30th Eli came home early, in a hurry. Everyone was at home, sitting round the fire, where the gaiters were nearly dry.

'Eli? Is all well?'

'Yes mother – well, no, not wholly. Thomas is took bad. He had to go home, go to his bed. A cough, he had, could hardly blow; and then he fell down in a swoon – clean out, on the threshing floor, and white as a wall.'

'God in his mercy grant you are not taken likewise – you and all your prancing crew. Here, take some cider – get those wet boots off.'

'There'll be no prancing, as you please to call it, unless we can find another piper overnight.' Eli looked sideways, under his brows. Hope felt his glance burn right through her. She handed him the jug.

She was lying waiting when he ducked under the curtain and came to her bedside.

'Hope?'

'Yes, Eli?'

'You're awake.' She waited. 'You heard about Thomas Piper?' She still waited. He was to say it; she wanted to hear it said.

'You can play the Mossmen's tune, Hope?'

'Yes, Eli.'

'Will you? For us?'

'To practise?'

'No – he'll not be fit. No. To go round, New Year's Night.'

'But I'm a girl.' She held her voice steady and low. It was Eli who got excited.

'No one would think it was you, little 'un, if you wear the breeches – and the green disguises wonderful, and Thomas is no bigger than you, the coat is woundy old, it fits all sorts, it takes to any that can play – and you can play, beautiful, good as a man.'

'But mother –'

'Aye. There's a snag, certain. But I've thought it out. You can get cousin Dolly to ask for you to go up the Manor a few days to help with the feasting – you can sleep there, with her, without anyone knowing when you come or go; Uncle Josh'll see you in and out.'

And so it was that Hope found herself standing, strung tight as a bow, in the dark kitchen passage outside the Manor hall. The green paint stiffened her lips and eyelids. The horned men drew together in a little silence. Then Leader struck the two at his sides on their shoulders, and they plunged through the door, letting out the candlelight and the waft of the great fire. They were all gone. She lurched forward, and stopped in the doorway to adjust her eyes.

In the pool of light across the echoing room, framed by the twinkling carved oak of the fire mantel, sat the Wistons. The two young men, tall and distant in their deep velvet coats, on one side of the hearth, and across from them their father, the Lord himself, sprawled in a great carved chair. A little apart from him sat the daughter of the house – Isabella Wiston. Clear as a flame, beautiful and remote as a hawk alone in a sunny sky. My lady, thought Hope. She caught her breath, compressing her lips to stop her heart from flying straight out of her body. She was on fire. Drawing a shuddering breath, she raised her pipe, and began to play.

Two

Bell dreamed of a masked ball at which all the dancers wore green. She was dancing with a partner whose face she could not see, to the sound of a silvery pipe. As the music quickened, Bell and her partner whirled faster and faster, closer and closer, until she woke up with a start. Outside her bed curtains the room was cold, and surprisingly light. She turned on her stomach. Oddly, the dream did not fade; her green-clad partner was not so much a picture as a sensation. Clasped hands, warmth. Then she remembered the piper, dancing round her, last night; and James's stunning remark. She flushed and wriggled out of the covers. James was a hateful cynic, always laughing his well-bred little laugh through closed lips, belittling what she felt. But it was true; the magical piper had been a girl. She got up quickly.

When she was dressed, she rubbed the frost from a diamond pane of her window, to see her father's only addition to the family mansion – the new stable block with its large-faced clock. It was after nine. Nobody was about, except Dolly the stable man's daughter, picking her way across the dirty cobbles ridiculously dressed in an old flounced morning gown she must have had from Aunt Patten at the vicarage. Dolly was not the kind of servant Bell liked; she was silly and forward, and fussed over her as if she were a child, when she was not fussing even more disgustingly over Rupert Patten.

There were no girls in the house that she did like, in fact; father kept too few serving maids. Bell was lonely. Her father, having buried two young wives, had not the heart to marry again. The wealthy and high-born Lady Belinda, the catch of his gallant youth, had rebelled and sickened when he brought her away from Town, and soon died, leaving her handsome, ill-tempered likeness in James, the Wiston heir. Sir Walter's second wife, Bell's own beloved mother, was altogether a more comfortable person, who had seemed set to make a long and happy family – until the fever carried her and her two youngest children off when Bell was eight years old and Alistair ten. He would not say as much, but Bell thought her father had never recovered from the loss; he would not risk being deserted again. He had an heir, and another lad, as he said, in case of accidents; and his dear little Bella was all the female company he needed.

Which was all very well, but how was she to manage on her own? She read and dawdled and dreamed of company; her ideas about growing up came mainly from her books. The few county families near enough to visit had no daughters near her own age. She had got on well enough for boys – there had always been her beloved Alistair, who had taught her to read and to cipher, though she could never share his love for figures and mechanical devices. With the cousins from the vicarage and Richard and Luke from Over Dean the two of them had tumbled into every brook and slough on the moor; and she had patiently helped him to dam every stream in the parish and to try out his inventions, for ever holding two bits of wood together while he measured and nailed and scribbled furiously on his designs. Even Alistair seemed lost to her now: back from Oxford after his first term, he was always being drawn into the urgent, secret men's talk with which the house had buzzed ever since Queen Anne had died. On the whole Bell looked after herself, and had time to think her own thoughts. Such as, who was the girl who played the pipe? What tale was there? She focussed again on the empty courtyard. Father would be on the moor for hours yet, and maybe James and Alistair with him. She turned away. Bread and milk in the kitchen? Dreams and mysteries were all very well, but she was rather hungry.

As she came to the end of the gallery, she heard her brothers talking, apparently still over their breakfast, in the great hall below. James's sneering voice cut into her consciousness. She slowed, unwilling to walk down and pass them if he was in one of his brutally teasing moods, when he preferred patronising her even to baiting poor Alistair. Then as she caught his words, she froze to the spot.

'You are such a damned precisian, Alistair. The girl shall get no harm from me – when have you known me cruel or neglectful to a good willing whore? She'll not thank you for protecting her from such a prospect. I believe you are become a secret Puritan, my boy – Oxford is a damned strange place to learn such sentimental notions.'

'Why should I betray the girl to you? You imagine all wenches die for your charms; but I tell you this one would not. It's the girl who is a Puritan, not me; she would not thank your lordship for the kind of condescension you have in mind, I assure you.'

'A Puritan – not she! Wearing breeches, playing and dancing in the devil's band – what do you imagine our local Bible-thumpers let their daughters do? We have no nests of Quakers or Tremblers here, they are good old-fashioned followers of Herr Calvin, and they do not dance in public. She's some village girl with an eye to showing her legs to best advantage – and here am I ready to buy her wares.'

He leant back, displaying his ruffled neckcloth and fashionable crimson coat, putting up a hand to touch his black-curled wig as he smirked down at his halfbrother. Alistair had never been a match for him physically, and now the contrast between them was exaggerated by James's fine clothes and grandly military bearing. James seemed to admire and enjoy his own body, while Alistair was impatient of the limitations of mere flesh and blood. Hardly knowing what she was doing, Bell took hold of the gallery rail and spoke in as clear and as cold a voice as she could command.

'I knew the London wenches painted their faces, brother, but the news had not yet reached us in the country that the fashion is for bright green. I must try it myself.'

She made for the stairs, bristling with dignity – it was a pity she had to surrender the advantage of height that the gallery gave her. She gathered her skirts furiously together, and descended upon them. Her brothers leapt up in such confusion that Alistair tipped his cider cup across the table. James seized the diversion, and flapped at the stream angrily.

'Mind my velvet, bumpkin! Your pardon, sister, we did not see you. Will you ride out? There's a good frost in the ground, the paths will be clean.'

'Cleaner than your conversation, at any rate.' She refused to see the chair Alistair offered.

'Come, Isabella – you disappoint me if you are still so childish or so rustic as to eavesdrop on the conversation of gentlemen and then be offended at what you hear.' James had coloured, and looked like their father in a rage; but she stood her ground.

'Gentlemen do not speak as you did.'

'On the contrary, most gentlemen speak exactly as I do. It is Alistair's foppery that gives cause for concern. I shall leave him to make lace and gossip with you. Good morning.'

Left staring at each other, Alistair and Bell were only embarrassed for a moment. Then he stuck out his tongue at James's retreating back, and they fell into the laughter they had shared from the nursery. He took her hand, and then hugged her.

'I miss you, Ali,' she said, into his ruffles.

'I'm here again now. Come, all's well. I won't tell him, and he'll soon forget about her . . . she's not a village girl.'

'How do you know?'

'I've seen her up at the forge, at Bassett Moor – when I used to get Elijah Liddell to hammer out iron bits and pieces that I needed for making things.' He smiled – as if he was amused at his childish self of six months ago, Bell thought. Then his face changed. 'Anyway, James has other things on his mind.'

'What other things?

He drew back, and turned away from her without answering. She followed him to the window.

'It's about King James, isn't it? Something is to happen soon?'

Alistair looked out, carefully, before he replied. 'Yes, he will be with us soon now, please God. Things are coming to a head. We expect news from the Duke of Ormonde – brother James's commander – who is to lead the uprising. James may be called to him. Or –' his voice dropped, and he turned towards her, like a conspirator – 'it may be that the king comes here, to us in the West Country, and that Ormonde comes to meet him.' He took her hand. 'You must say nothing, Isabella.'

'Of course not. I understand.'

He nodded. 'It could be any day. We have heard that support is coming in from abroad. The Spanish have sent funds, and the Swedish King Charles favours us. But here in England, we must all act together, that's the thing. We must pick our time. Some poor fellows down in Devon proclaimed King James last month, and they were roughly dealt with.'

'You'll take care, Ali, won't you?'

'Don't worry. Oxford is sound – we drink King James's health every day in my college. It was marvellous fortune for me, to arrive there at such a moment.' He turned back to the window. He is really excited, she thought. Despite his little new beard, glistening in the frosty sun, he looked just as he used to when one of his silly inventions finally began to ring the bell or pump pond water all over his feet. She went to hug him again, but he was off, heading for the door. 'James is riding out,' he said over his shoulder, 'there may be news.'

Eating her bowl of bread and milk in the window seat she watched as both her brothers, large and small, rode through the gates and away, going about the business of politics and wars. She sighed; despite all he said, she felt she did not really understand. What exactly were they doing? Why was it taking so long? They all seemed to be enjoying themselves, anyway. In no very good mood, she went back to her needlework.

Sleeping with Dolly had not been nearly as much fun as Hope imagined. There were three beds in the room over the stables, with Uncle Joshua and Aunt Cissy in one curtained off at the end, and Dolly's two little brothers in the other, right next to theirs. Dolly giggled a bit the first night and guided Hope's hand towards her, but she soon thrust it away, saying she tickled too much. The bed was lumpy flock, and narrow; only the idea of the dancing had remained as a consolation. And by the time the dancing was over, Hope had lost all interest in Dolly.

She could remember very little about the dancing itself, though she knew from the joking compliments of the Mossmen that she had played well enough. All she could think of was Isabella Wiston. Bell. Bell had cast a spell upon her which had still not broken. She had set eyes upon her and piped and danced for her alone. Then over the wassail cup their eyes had met. No longer the young mistress of the manor, glimpsed distantly in church or darkly on horseback against the sky, nor even the remote beauty that had stunned her as she entered the room, but a girl, less than her own height, a soft face candlelit and startled, big brown eyes, a faint flush. Hope thought she had never seen anyone so beautiful. She fell asleep thinking of that moment, and woke to the memory of candlelight and brown eyes. She wanted to be alone, but when she tried to find a reason to go home, Dolly would not hear of it.

'You can't go today – this is New Year, the day of the feast – Dame Johnson expects you to help out in the kitchen. That's what you're supposed to be here for, *if* you remember.'

So she found herself at noon sticking nuts into a whitish mound of sweet stuff, trying, pretty much in vain, to make it look like a hedgehog. The great kitchen was cold at her end, even though the venison was already turning before the distant hearth; a green gloom filtered in from the high windows, and a draught under the door was slowly sawing off her feet. Suddenly there was a clatter and stirring out in the court, and men shouting as they dismounted. Behind her, the door burst open and let in a howling gale; Sir Walter and Captain James stamped into the room and made for the fire.

'Hot cider, Mistress Mary, my darling,' bellowed Sir Walter, sprawling into a chair so that his footboy could get at his boots; at a signal from the housekeeper, Aunt Cissy rushed to bob and curtsy round him with the funnel-shaped shoe for heating the drink in the fire. Captain James sat down at the warm end of the kitchen table. Then he saw Hope. He gazed for a moment, still; his eyes were as cold as stones. Then he smiled.

'What have we here? Good day to you, my dear.' He turned his head, holding on to her with his eyes, and raised his voice. 'What have you been hiding here in the depths, Mistress Mary? Or is the secret one of yours, father, eh?'

Sir Walter stopped beating himself with his gloves, and peered at Hope. 'Never set eyes on her before,' he barked, 'Who's this, eh?'

Aunt Cissy bobbed about even on her knees, where she was tending the cider in the fire. 'My niece, if it please your lordship – come to help out with the New Year's dinner. Make your curtsy to My Lords, child, do.'

Hope got to her feet, but she could not bring herself to duck and weave like her aunt. Captain James also rose, his eyes fixed on hers. She took a step back.

'Your name, pretty one? But no. Don't tell me Doll or Bet or Sue – I shall name you. I shall call you Amaryllis. How's that for a beautiful name – for a fine pair of eyes?' His gaze flicked over her and to her horror, Hope saw the sudden flash of recognition. 'But wait! I do believe we met . . . last night.' He was walking casually down the length of the table towards her. She froze, like a mouse waiting for the owl to swoop.

At that moment Dolly, who had been washing cabbages at the pump when she saw the gentlemen arrive, rushed in. Pretending she had not seen them, she pushed by Hope to deposit her greenery on the table, right in front of Captain James. She produced a genteel start, and curtseyed low enough to show him what was in her bodice.

'Law, sir, you startled me, I do beg pardon. We are honoured by a kitchen visit, I'm sure.' She smiled up at him winningly.

Seizing the moment, Hope fled from the kitchen.

Bell had come down to the New Year's dinner half expecting to see some of the strangers from London who seemed to call more and more frequently. But there was only the rectory party: cousin Patten, his washed-out little wife and his eldest son William, a pale spotty youth of Bell's own age who tended to blush when she spoke to him. They all chewed their way through the fowls and the venison in a family silence; father soon sank into the fixed, dull-red look that meant he had had a hard day on the moor, and was now asleep with his eyes open. James amused himself now and then by instructing William waspishly about politics and his own delicate but important position.

'You may suppose, cousin, that I shall be recalled to my regiment; that may be, but I'll wager that the regiment is as likely to come to me. I say no more, but that the Cause may need its friends here in the west country before they are needed in London. I am in the confidence of Sir William Wyndham, our excellent member of parliament, and he is of my opinion also: we may yet see the sun rise in the west.' He smiled in self-satisfaction at poor gaping William, and turned his attention, with the courtesy he managed to make into such an insult, to wait upon his sister.

'Will you take a glass of wine, Isabella? I think it is

sweet enough for a lady's taste.' He beckoned, and old Benchley poured for her. James lifted his glass. 'To my delightful, mature little sister. William, surely you will drink to your beautiful cousin?' He sipped, and added, 'and of course, to your lady mother. Madam, your health.'

The Pattens drank obediently. James leant back. At last Sir Walter woke up and called for a glass. He creaked to his feet, and pronounced, 'The King.' He did not actually say, 'The King over the water,' but he waved his glass ostentatiously over the water in his fingerbowl. They all stood and drank, James and Alistair actually pronouncing 'King James' under their breaths; and Isabella turned away as the men sat down, to take Mrs Patten into the parlour. James called out after them.

'We shall not be long, Isabella – there is a matter on which I must speak with you.'

He was true to his word. Aunt Patten had only half completed the breathless monologue on her family's health which was her idea of conversation, when they heard the men's voices in the passage.

'Well, I say you should leave such decisions to our sister,' said Alistair, pushing open the door of the parlour. James, following close behind him, said nothing, but smiled at Bell as he held the door open for his father and the Pattens.

Sir Walter lowered himself into a brocade chair by the hearth and blinked appraisingly at his daughter. 'See what you mean,' he remarked eventually. 'Well-grown – yes. Lady of the house, what?' He shook his head. 'My little girl. Next thing you know she'll be marrying some fellow. Well, well.' Then to Bell, 'Want a maid servant, do you, Bella? Plenty of girls on the estate if you do. Ask Mistress Johnson to find one – two if you like – only have to ask, my dear.'

Bell looked at James. 'What is this about?' she asked coldly.

'Why, your own comfort, sister dear,' he replied

smoothly. 'I was reminding our father of what he so often forgets – that you are no longer a child, but a young lady, and need a lady's little attentions. This is altogether too masculine a household, eh?' he appealed to his brother and cousin. 'We men grow uncouth with too few maidens to check us, and our sister lacks for female company. A nice girl from the village –'

'Of your choosing, James?' put in Alistair quietly.

Suddenly Bell understood. They were still talking about the girl who had played the pipe for the dancing. How dare James try this trick to get the girl into the house!

She rose and went to her father and leant winningly on his arm.

'Oh papa, no, must I ? Be made into a fine lady and turned out of my father's house? For all my brother says, I am but a child at home. Mistress Johnson helps me to look after my linens and other things; and if I need a maid, why, there is Dolly Bishop already around the house. But I would rather stay your little girl, and warm your nightcap by the fire and bring you your posset, than have twenty fine lady's maids to teach me airs and graces. You would not have me grow up so soon, would you, father?'

She wondered for a moment if she had overdone it; but he smiled and reached an arm round to draw her with some difficulty onto his knees.

'There there, sweeting, never take on so. Of course you need not leave us. James did not mean to say that you should. She shall never be too fine a lady to make her old father happy, eh?' He chucked her under the chin, delighted; Bell turned her eyes on James and wrinkled her nose ever so slightly.

Alistair caught her eye, and she could see he was amused; Aunt Patten, moved by a display of family feeling, threw her arms round Bell and called her a good girl. James said nothing. As soon as politeness allowed, he excused himself on pretence of business. Only the slam of the door betrayed his fury.

Three

Hope's mother beat her for going with the Mossmen; but she didn't care much. All her pain was centred on Isabella Wiston. Like Guy of Warwick, she was in love with a nobleman's daughter; but Guy had been lucky – he could do something about it. Hope was raging and helpless. The old squire was not going to make her his trusty steward; no noble adventures with foreign princesses were going to come her way. She spent weeks in a haze of misery, re-living the scene in the candlelit hall, the green and crimson richness of the family grouped round their father. Bell had sat there so still, so tensely upright, like a bird about to fly away, while the Mossmen stamped and pranced and Hope played, her pipe like a live creature moved by the beat of the dance. But then, when she carried the bowl to Isabella and looked into her eyes, and touched her hand – then she knew she had fallen in love. Even that sweet agony had lasted only a moment before the magic faded as Sir Walter came laughing and booming at them, and snake-eyed Captain James had fixed her again in his glittering stare. She did not play her pipe much any more. Eli had saved it from their mother's wrath, and quietly hidden it in the thatch over the goathouse, where he used to keep his Mossman's horns. Those he hung over his bed, now; he was too big for mother to beat.

As the winter darkness began to recede, and the cottagers came out to dig their gardens and spread them thickly from the dungheaps at the doors, there was another sharp whiff in the air, a whiff of excitement, edging into anger. The dispute over who should be king trickled down from the great ones to the villagers, and divided the two Bassetts along predictable lines. My Lord's men from the home farms and the parish church were Jacobites, all for My Lord's king, the gallant exile James, while the stout Independents up on the Moor found themselves on the side of the protestant succession, and law and order. The idlers round the cider house at Wiston Bassett talked loudly of the good old times, and shouted after Abel the cobbler 'No foreigners', though foreign he was not, only known to be of levelling opinions, and no churchman; a group of boys and one or two of the wilder young men of Wiston even went up to the Moor, one wet and murky February day, when they had had nothing to do all the morning but drink, and set fire to the hovel next door to the higglers' house. It was easily put out – would, as Aunt Faith said, no doubt have gone out of itself since they had been so handless as to try to fire wet thatch without so much as a scrap of oily rag – but their cries of 'No dissent! The Good Old Cause!' disturbed the village, and Jacob Marsh, whose thatch had been burnt, was with difficulty restrained from taking a gang of friends down to Wiston, to root out, as he said, the growing nest of traitors. Bassett Moor was well armed, and blood might have been shed. At the Moor forge they were deeply troubled, and saw to the fastening of their doors. A stock of pikes and swords and even crossbow bolts had lain undisturbed in the furthest shippen for many years; no-one mentioned it, but Elijah fitted it with a new lock, and then smeared his fresh and shiny work with mud and clinging dung.

Hope was often at the forge. The light and warmth, and the purposeful bustle of it all, drew her when she was soaked through with striding wildly about the forest in the mists; and she came especially to Anticipation, whose talk had soothed and straightened her mind since she was a child. But the old woman was increasingly sleepy and far away, and even when she was awake she was chiefly interested to hear tell of the goings-on down at Wiston, eager for the discomfiture of the great ones and their Stuart pretender. Hope ached to ask her for reassurance, to talk to her about her love for Isabella. Her great great grandmother had lived so long and seen so much, Hope thought, that nothing surprised or frightened her any more. Hope knew that

32

the community of Liddell's Children had held all people to be equal before God; and that this had caused them to cast aside many of the rules by which people like Hope's mother lived their lives. All her life, Hope had gone to Anticipation about everything, sure she would be taken seriously.

One late winter's afternoon she begged her again for the old story she knew almost by heart, the story of Liddell's Children. Her great great grandmother smiled indulgently. 'It was ever your favourite tale. I do believe, should the prophet Anna Liddell come again in these days, you would follow to the Kingdom with us.'

Hope wondered. What would it be like to know so surely, to believe so fiercely, that you could leave home and family to follow that belief? She thought, I would go if it were Isabella who called me; and then felt guilty. Anticipation had been fired with the love of God, not of Anna Liddell. Hope tried to picture Anticipation as a young woman, scarcely older than herself, who had walked away from all she knew on that spring morning long ago. 'Were you not afraid?' she asked.

The old woman considered. 'My mother was afraid for me, I think. But then, there were so many hungry mouths in that house, I believe she would have called any chance a blessing that took me from under her roof. And I? No, I was not afraid. You know what Saint Paul tells us.'

She paused expectantly. Since Hope could first talk, her conversations with Anticipation had been threaded with lessons in the scriptures. She took the thin old hand in hers. 'Perfect love casted out fear,' she quoted obediently.

'And so it was. Truly to love God, and to love each other, is to bring the kingdom of Heaven down to earth. In Liddell's Kingdom we all loved equally, and in love all are equal. Love levels all; high and low, man and woman, we are equal in the sight of God.'

'But you loved some above others? You loved Exultation most?" Hope felt herself begin to blush.

The reply was patient. 'Exultation, that was Joseph in the life before, joined the Kingdom with me; we were not then married in the world's eyes, nor was there marrying or giving in marriage in the Kingdom. Our children were Liddell's Children, and all Liddell's Children were my kin.' She paused, watching the past in the fire.

'But Exultation died in the burning?'

'He did. And in our house four children with him: three of mine, and little Anticipation that was daughter to my beloved friend.' She shook her head. 'Then I knew, truly, what it was to be alone and afraid. And so I came here.'

This was more than Hope had heard before. 'Your friend?' she urged. 'Who was she? Did she come here with you?'

'She did not. We had no choice, for we had nothing on which to live in the world, and must needs part and go back to our families. She did not live long after, sitting idle in her mighty father's house in London.' She patted Hope's hand, answering before she spoke. 'Oh yes, child, we were of all degrees in the world, low and high, though we had lived equal in the Kingdom. What God had joined only the greed and hatred of men dared to put asunder.' She turned her head aside and closed her eyes. After a little while, when she did not open them again, Hope kissed her and crept away.

Spring came early, and by Shrovetide it was warm enough some days for Hope to take the goats with her, to browse an hour or two in the long arm of the forest which lay between Wiston and Bassett Moor. This was Sir Walter's hunting ground: a broad ride ran through it, rutted by the wheels of carts bringing cut timber down to the Manor or to the river quays on the Frome. The goats were glad to be out; Old Billy, the patriarch of the small family, would often have disappeared into the distance had Hope not restrained him. Leading them off the broad ride and into the trees, she sought out sunny glades where she could keep them under her eye and think her own thoughts at the same time.

On the Saturday before Shrove Tuesday, Hope took care to lead her charges deeper than usual into the forest. It was the day of the Shrovetide Ball Game, and like most of the girls of both villages, she kept well away from the fray. Jack and Eli had risen before dawn to join their fellows at the cider house in Wiston; they had on their strongest breeches and boots, and Eli had bound his head and arms with old cloths for protection. By sun-up, the men and boys of Wiston and of the Moor were massed in two shouldering droves under the Trysting Tree in the centre of the ride, waiting for the Ball Man to throw the leather-bound bundle which was the ball up into the branches. As it fell, the two villages fell on it and on each other, and fought and bellowed and kicked all day, up and down the ride, until the ball, slimy by then with mud and blood, could be planted by some breathless hero either at the standing cross at Bassett Moor or at Wiston church door.

From time to time during the day Hope heard the distant shouts, and wondered if her brothers were still whole; heads, and sometimes arms and legs were broken in the ball game, and epic deeds done which raised a man's standing in field and cider house for years to come. She found it hard to be very interested; the battles of her own life were more absorbing. She took her pipe from her pocket and began to play halfheartedly with the Mossmen's tune, bending it from its jaunty beat to a haunting lover's plaint. The blast of the Ball Man's horn, the signal that the game was ending, shook her from her reverie and she saw to her concern that the light was failing. To get home before dark she would have to cross the ride while they were straggling back to the Tree. She listened carefully as she came up to the ride, restraining Old Billy from bustling ahead up the familar path; but there was no immediate sign of the players. She emerged slowly, and peered up towards the Moor. The evening mist had closed in, and she could see nothing that way. She stepped out, and as she did so the horn rang out again, down to her left. It was followed by a ragged cheer. As she crossed the ride, half a dozen of the smaller players, shame faced and spattered, who must have been keeping their distance from the last desperate efforts round the ball, came down towards her from the Moor.

Billy took flight at them looming out of the mist. He jerked his rope from Hope's hands and, calling shrilly to his family to follow, set off down hill towards the Trysting Tree. Hope plunged through the mud after them, calling helplessly, and a couple of the players behind shouted too, egging on both goats and girl. They all stumbled down the ride in the deepening gloom. More figures appeared in the mist between the trees ahead; at the sight of them Billy, slowed, and cast sideways, but found he was up against an impenetrable bank. He stopped, head down; the six other goats caught up and milled round him. Hope was able to grab his nearer horn, and get the rope tight round his neck, that being the only way to hold him when he was in truculent mood. At that moment, as the Moor boys from behind cheered her and the little goats bleated plaintively, the mass of players milling under the Tree ahead parted, and a procession appeared. They carried torches, and some were on horseback. It was the Wistons, Captain James and Isabella, escorted by two of their servants.

The players cheered again, losing interest in Hope and scrambling to respond to the steward, Benchley, who came striding ahead of the family, ushering the villagers into a suitably deferential line. Under the ancient oak the family stopped. Benchley brought the Ball Man forward, clutching his horn and the ragged ball under his other arm, and Captain James leaned down to speak with him. The flickering torchlight gave his pale face unaccustomed colour, and threw his heavy features into sharp relief. The teams shuffled, and attempted to sort themselves into two. Hope shrank back against the bank, and sank on her knees, behind

Billy, one arm round his neck. In the darkness she might not be seen. At last Captain James straightened up, and walked his horse out into the ride, between the teams, holding up a hand to silence them. His voice came thinly down the wind to Hope, a foreign, sharp-cut twang.

'A good game, my lads,' he said, 'well played, well played indeed. You show us what you are made of – what fine stuff are all the lads of Somerset, like their fathers before them.'

The players all cheered; even the Bassett Moor lads did not mind the heir of the Wistons calling them complimentary names. James smiled, encouraged. 'Good lads, for peace and war,' he went on, through their shouting. His horse stirred a little to and fro, as he added, 'And I hope that if a time should come, soon, before very long, where you may show your mettle in another way – in a bigger game, but one equally timehonoured, and grand in its design, as this customary game of ball – when you may all show up as well and play as heartily, for the right – for the good old cause – as you have done here today.' As he developed this climax, Hope saw, as clearly as if they were a flock of running sheep that meets a fence or a wall, the two sides of his audience part. The Moor lads fell silent, and stood still; and when he reached 'the good old cause,' the Wiston boys cheered, and stamped and broke around him offering their caps, their hands – their hearts; and one shouted 'Captain Wiston – and King James!' and he pretended to hush them, smiling all the while.

Then he beckoned behind him, and held out his hand for quiet. 'I hear from the Ball Man, Master Fletcher, that Bassett Moor won the game today,' he said, and talked on through a dissenting voice or two. 'Where is their leader, their Captain? My sister, Mistress Wiston, has something to present to him, on your behalf.'

Hope crouched lower as the torchlit group opened again, moving aside to allow Isabella, on Captain James's beautiful mare, to ride forward. Hope caught her breath;

37

it was the first time she had seen Bell this close since New Year. Bell held herself very erect, guiding the mare with one hand, while in the other she held up a pole, with some kind of bulky cross-bar at its head. She stopped beside her brother, who handed her another thing – Hope could not see what. After a moment's pause John Barton, the Moor's master wheelwright, who had played more than a dozen ball games and was their leading expert, walked sturdily up to her horse's head. Hope, one hand twisted firmly in Billy's headrope, crouched spell-bound, her heart hammering, her eyes greedily taking Bell in.

Bell looked down past Beauty's shoulder. The torches showed her another of the village men she secretly feared; this one looked more like a walking mud-slide than a person, head to toe in caked clay, with blood on his left eyebrow; his clothes were invisible, stuck to him under the coating of earth. He did not touch his forelock, but at least he bowed slightly; and then stood four square, hands hanging, as if he were a huge molehill, an earthy eruption out of the trodden bracken at his feet. She suppressed a desperate giggle. She was a fool to have allowed James to persuade her into this. Being allowed to ride Beauty was not nearly worth it. She swallowed hard. There was no way but to go through with his little pageant. James prompted her, introducing the man and the scene. 'This is Master Barton, if I mistake not,' he said.

'Master Barton,' she began, and stopped to take her voice down half an octave. 'Master Barton, here is a purse of silver,' she held it out, 'for all the players to drink the health of the king.'

Under cover of the shout that went up, she glanced at James, who smiled tightly. The man took the purse gently from her hand, and bowed again, about to step back. James nodded at her urgently. She went on quickly, 'And here is a trophy for you – for the winning team, this year and in future. It is a painted banner.' James had said she must tell them exactly, and she repeated his words, as she pulled on the tassel which, to her relief, released the roll as it was meant to do, and the thing fell open. It revealed the picture she had spent several hours painting, after James's design. She looked at it, aside. She had been quite pleased with her handiwork, but now she was glad that it was too dark for any critical eye to judge its art. She lifted the pole from its resting-place on her stirrup, and held it out, awkward with the weight. She must complete the speech.

'I hope it will remind you all, as you play for it in years to come, of the great Shrovetide match of the year 1715.'

As the man reached up and took it, she ventured to look beyond him, at the crowd. Only their whitish faces still glowed through the gathering dark. They were craning to see the banner Barton now held, and he turned it out towards them, squinting up at it himself. They are surprised, she thought. The family had not taken this sort of interest in the two villages for many years, since her own mother died. But they were willing to be pleased, and a smattering of cheers greeted her, and a voice shouted for 'the young mistress.' But they were too quiet. With a flush of embarrassment, she realised that she had not got the speech right – she had not told them the subject of the picture; and they could not properly see it, in the dark. Before she could speak again, a second man from the Bassett Moor crowd, a small, dark youth less dirtied than the other, suddenly stepped forward and grabbed Barton's arm.

'John – put it away!' he cried, 'See – it is a trick! See the picture! Treason!'

Barton resisted manhandling, and pulled back; the other grabbed one of the torches and thrust it at the banner. Bell's painstaking efforts sprang out in lurid colour, flickering in the flame.

'It is a Jacobite picture!' he shouted, 'see – the oak tree, and in its branches the grinning face of the damned Charles Stuart, the Man of Blood! See!' He wrenched it from Barton's startled grasp, and thrust it back at Bell.

'Take your damned treasonable banner, Mistress! We will have none of it!'

James started forward, but the two horses jostled, and the pole was in Bell's hand. She grasped it firmly; she had to put things right.

'No, look – you are wrong,' she shouted back, matching his tone with her own, then steadying her voice again as best she could. 'It is not King Charles's oak – it is yours, your oak, the Trysting Tree here – see! and in it, the ball, that's all! Look, and see!'

The sea of dirty faces surged round, and many voices began to mutter in disputation. Then a lad at the back called clearly above the murmuring, 'Trysting Tree, oak tree – what matter? Hurrah for the rightful King! Jemmy's the lad! Hurrah!'

There was a moment's dreadful silence. Bell saw all the faces round her clearly – James, and Dickson their groom, and below them Barton and Jacob Marsh – she recognised him now, Marsh the higgler – and all the men within the little torchlit circle; all with the same, terrifying expression, an expression of ferocity, of pure, bloodthirsty hate. There would be murder done. The wave of tenor that swept over Bell set the mare, Beauty, trembling too.

Then from up the hill somewhere, beyond the light, there was a a frenzied noise – not of people, but of goats. A huge old billy goat, galloping like an army charger, erupted into the midst of the crowd, bowling men over right and left on the slippery ground, and behind him came, apparently, dozens more – every goat in the two villages seemed to be milling about bleating wildly, under their feet. Men fell, cursing, as goats cannoned into the backs of their knees; others tried to catch them, giving chase, beginning to whoop and laugh; and Beauty's nerve finally broke. She reared and whinnied, lashed out and missed a passing head, and dashed off down the ride, with Bell clinging ignominiously to her back.

40

The banner was found next day by a Wiston boy, who tried to wash off the mud; but it was so trampled by men and horses, ball-players and goats, that he could never make it out.

Four

The faces full of violence haunted Bell. She could not talk to James about the encounter in the ride. She felt angry with him for teasing her into going, and guilty about making such a mess of it; and at the best of times she could not really talk to James. The next day he affected to find it all vastly amusing, and to have dismissed it as of no importance.

'I have more vital affairs on hand, I assure you, than my beautiful sister's failure to manage beasts – whether the country bumpkins or the mare. At least the beast Beauty was not hurt. She was clearly the most intelligent animal involved.'

Then he was gone, anyway, back to London to see his commander the Duke of Ormonde, and to report on the situation in the West. Bell wondered bitterly if he would tell him all was going well. She realised that she had not properly understood, until Shrovetide, what the restoration of the rightful king would mean; really mean, to the people who went out to fight for it. The stomach-churning tension came back to her again and again, the dangerous excitement in the crowd, and the sense of fear – theirs and her own. She wished Alistair were home; or that she had someone else of her own age to talk to.

More than once she remembered the girl piper, who might have been her maid. Alistair said she was called Hope Bishop; what would she have been like as a companion? A lady's maid was often, she knew, more of a friend and confidante than a servant: someone to talk to and spend time with while the men were about their business, to share your daily concerns. Mary Johnson, Sir Walter's housekeeper, had once been lady's maid to Bell's own mother: she had come with her to Wiston, and had grieved so sorely when her lady died that Sir Walter had not been able to find it in his heart to dismiss her. Johnson had dressed her mistress' hair and tended her clothes, known her secrets better than Sir Walter, and shared her bed on the cold winter nights when he was away, or had drunk too well to need her company. Bell, who had never had sisters, and had slept alone all her life, wondered what it would be like to have such a friend.

The glimmering days indoors seemed endless; her books were all dull and her needlework did not occupy her mind as well as her hands. She sat over it in the cold window of her room re-living the humiliation of the ball-game, speculating about how she might have done it better, what would have happened if she had said the right thing, or if Wiston Bassett had been the winners, or, worse, if the goats had not appeared. She did wonder, also, about the goats. As far as she knew the villagers never let their goats out on their own; certainly not at night. But the chaos in which it had all ended was nothing compared with the vivid stain on her mind's eye of those angry, frightened, hate-filled faces.

One day in mid March, she rose to find the sky lifted from the chimney-tops into a giant bell of clear daffodil-yellow, sun already sparkling on the wet cobbles in the courtyard. It was cold, but not frosty; the air was like a draught of fresh white wine. She could not stay indoors on such a day; she put on her strong boots and a cloak and ran down to the still-room, to Mistress Johnson. The housekeeper smiled to see her.

'Now then, young lady, what are you about? Looking for an errand in the sunshine?'

'Yes, if you please. Could I not take some of the marigold salve to Widow Bellwood? She must be wanting it – we have sent none since we put up that batch at Michaelmas.'

'What a thoughtful child.' Mistress Johnson, for all her fierce exterior, was fond of Bell; her ironical praise was kindly meant. They understood each other; Bell had learnt much household and medicinal lore from her.

Carrying the pot, she ran down the village street. The smell of wet, but also of green growing things filled the air. An insect whined by. As she came to the clergy-house a different aroma met her – a slightly rancid, steamy smell; the smell, as clear as anything, of salt pork broth. Aunt Patten was making charity soup again. Bell stopped, and impulsively turned down the track beside the churchyard gate to visit her.

She was greeted by the usual volley of spaniels, yelping and slobbering her hands, and the usual thick fug of the Pattens' kitchen. The steam hung under the beams of the ceiling, where only a few bunches of withered herbs remained from last year. The cauldron stood on the hearth, its greenish surface gleaming with slowly rolling fat. May, the Pattens' maid, stood over it, stirring awkwardly with a wooden bat, her front hair dripping steam and sweat into the brew. She smiled her wide, loving, empty smile at Bell, and shouted her greeting over the clamour of the dogs.

'Missis gone up to Maister Rupert,' she said.

'Thank you May, that's all right. Are you making something good?'

'Poor broth. Missis say to use up smelly ends that old pig,' May bawled cheerfully, and picked up the ladle to sniff. 'Smell's not so bad now. Missis put stuff in. Taste?' Bell backed off from the dripping ladle.

'Not now, thank you.' She perched on the end of the table fighting off the dogs. Aunt Patten scurried in, Rupert on her shoulder, and the next two up tagging on her skirts. The children flung themselves at Bell, who knelt in the deep rushes to hug them. Her aunt swung the baby to the opposite hip, and dashed at the fireplace, throwing greetings at Bell in passing.

'Isabella, how kind! I have not seen you these three weeks. Your father is well? May, take your master's boots out to Peter. Patch, good dog, no. Down! Leave him alone, Charlotte, do. Sit down, Isabella – I am busy, as you see, as always busy. The hungry days are here again, no work in the village and plenty of empty bellies, tell your father. I have been doing my best here are usual, not much but it may help someone, as I always say, may come to some poor soul just in time to fend away despair. A little thing may help at such times, as indeed I know myself. Thank you, May, do go, good girl, I will stir if I can just—'

Bell left the children to the dogs, and took the stirring stick.

'Thank you, dear,' said her aunt. 'Now Charlotte, where is your sewing? All astray I expect. No, no arguing child, go and get it – you may come back here.' She sat down abruptly and prepared to feed Rupert. Little John, the three-year-old, started to howl.

'Is the soup nearly done?' Isabella asked, trying to peer in without sniffing up the rank steam.

'It must be four hours boiled by now. Yes, my dear, you are right, it will be done. But May's gone out – it will bear another boiling yet, I dare say; unless you would portion it? No, no, not in that habit – oh well, if you are careful –'

She began feeding, as Bell took up the ladle and began gingerly to fill the row of pottles on the edge of the table. John ran out, dragging his special spaniel. There was a momentary silence as both women concentrated on dispensing nourishment. On impulse, and because she was not obliged to look at her aunt as she said it, Bell asked, 'Aunt Patten, what do you think about the Cause?'

'Do take care, dear, that nearly went down your skirts. The dog will trip you, move it nearer, that's better.'

'Aunt Patten? King James is the rightful king, is he not?'

'If you say so, my dear. Though what we have to do with such things I cannot for the life of me see, for my part I'm sure it is better to concern ourselves with our needs and obligations nearer home, and to see to our duty to our neighbours as best we can, as is given to us, and never trouble with matters so far away as London.'

46

'But it will not be London, Aunt – they say he will land in the West, down at Bristol or Plymouth, and our countrymen will lead him to his rightful throne.'

Just for a moment Aunt Patten was entirely still. Her head was turned sharply towards Bell, one hand to her throat, the other clutching the sleepy Rupert to her breast, spread fingers digging into his bunched skirts. Bell though, she is surprised, she does not know. Has no-one talked to her of it? Have I done wrong? And then she thought, she is afraid.

Then the little woman tut-tutted and shook the baby; wiped his eyes and dabbed at her own.

'We shall see, no doubt we shall see. Look in the kist by your left, there, will you, Isabella, and get me out a clean breech-clout for him? There then, Rupert, will that do? Wake up child, do. Here comes Charlotte. Good girl, sit by the light there. I'll see to your work in a moment.'

She laid Rupert down by the pottles of fast-cooling soup. Bell felt she had to get away. What she sought was not in this welter of domestic busyness.

'Is some of the soup for Widow Bellwood, Aunt?' she asked, 'I will take it.'

'Yes, yes, she always needs what we can spare. There is her basket ready behind the door there, cover a pottle and pop it in, and your salve, I see, good girl. That's right, wrap it well, that flannel piece is for her leg, tell her to use the tincture for at least another month yet. No, Charlotte, before you ask, you may not go with Isabella. Bring me your work. Goodbye, Isabella, goodbye, thank you for your call.'

Bell breathed deeply in the green-wood-scented air of the forest ride. The restlessness was growing in her like a mighty sneeze. She ran a few steps, and stopped, reluctantly, when the soup slopped in the basket. Gladly turning aside before she came in sight of the Trysting Tree, she took the mile or so deep into the forest to Dame Bellwood's as rapidly as the narrow way between the brambles allowed. The old lady clutched her hand in a skinny claw, and it was all Bell could do to escape without a view of the ulcerated leg; she ran back towards the village until the cottage was out of sight, fervently wishing for freedom from old age and sour smells, babies and cookery. She was no good to herself alone, she thought, and no good to anyone else either.

Seeing an opening unexpectedly, between two willows that were beginning to show a haze of gold about them, she left the track and plunged into the forest itself. Anywhere to be free of it all. She fought her way through the underbrush for perhaps a quarter of a mile, getting her skirts well snagged and completely soaked; water began to ooze between her toes inside her boots. Then she saw more light ahead, sunshine between the trunks, and she burst out into a perfect glade, full of stillness and clear light. She stopped, gazing round, and saw a fallen log where she could sit and be a little dry. As she sat there, the sun pressed on her face and hands with a tiny but unmistakeable warmth. She breathed deeply, and shut her eyes.

She must have been sitting there for ten minutes, tranced by the sun, emptying her mind, when she heard a movement. She opened her eyes and saw a big jack rabbit, running fast, pop out from the opposite undergrowth. Abruptly, half way across the clearing, it let out a single scream and turned unnaturally head over heels, fell and lay still. Something stuck up from behind its head. Suddenly aware of being alone and unprotected, Bell jumped up, looking round for the hunter.

Fifty yards away across the glade a figure was poised in a frame of golden willows, A huntress; her eye was on the rabbit, a short bow sinking slowly to her side. Her skirt was kilted high on her thighs, long, strong legs bracing bare feet on the uneven ground. She was smiling; absorbed in her hunting, she had not seen that she was not alone. Suddenly Bell recognised the Mossmen's strange piper – but here, in the forest, she seemed entirely natural and at home.

Then Hope leapt forward with a little whoop of satisfaction, throwing up her arms and bounding out into the sun. She dropped down beside the rabbit on one knee, her skirts pushed out of her way as she pulled out a little knife and expertly slit open her prize. She turned her head – a heavy blonde plait lay down her back – and called softly 'Benjy!' A lurcher trotted out into the clearing; but it saw Bell, and hesitated, whining.

Hope raised her head, and she saw Bell too. She stood up slowly, not quite believing. The rabbit dangled from her hand.

Her first words made no sense to Bell. 'We have rights of warren,' she said.

'What?'

Hope held up the rabbit. 'My family have the right to shoot and snare. Father is one of My Lord's huntsmen – Jack Bishop.'

'I know, yes. You are Hope Bishop.'

'Yes.' A flush of pleasure warmed her face.

Benjy whined, and Hope, looking down, realized she was showing her legs. She dropped the rabbit and hurriedly made herself decent. Benjy stood over the fallen prey growling. He had obviously decided that Bell was challenging them for possession of it. Hope bent to take it up, to quiet him, and once it was in her hands she felt she might as well give him his share. She crouched again, and set about to clean it neatly.

'It is not good to kill in March, it lessens the flock, but it is for my grandmother who is not thriving.' She turned the rabbit over, deft and quick, Bell thought, admiring the economical flicks of the sharp knife.

'What ails her?' Bell said.

'Old age, is all it is,' said Hope, 'she has been with us too long, she says. Now she does not fancy her food, and salt meat least of all. Her mind goes back. She says Liddell's Children did not kill, and ate no meat, and it is like eating rotting corpses. But it angers

49

mother to see her so weak and so stubborn, and she said if I were to get a fresh titbit, it might tempt her.' She paused, and Bell saw the look of pain. 'But I doubt it. She is tired, and ready to go.' Hope turned slightly away, and called to Benjy. The dog came on his belly, tongue out, whining with excitement at the smell of blood.

'Good dog – yours, Benjy,' Hope said and stood up, leaving the offal. He pounced, stern waving. Still not looking at Bell, she said, 'The dogs do not fare well this time of year. He is hungry for it.'

Bell had caught up with herself sufficiently to move; she walked towards them. Her boots squished inside. She wanted to say, 'Barefoot like you is better,' but she was too embarrassed. Hope was looking at her now. She must say something fitting.

'Have you practised long, with the bow?' she tried.

Hope looked down again, watching the dog. 'No. Only this winter. I used a sling, when I was a child. This is better.' She began fiddling with her knife, cleaning it on a bunch of grass, fitting it into a buckskin sheath at her waist. 'A bow is quicker to fire, straighter over a distance, and the size of the stones is important.' Hope was aware that she was not making sense. She ventured to look up. Their eyes met. Hope caught her breath.

'I should go now,' she said roughly. 'Benjy!'

The dog pretended he had not heard. Bell, suddenly desperate to hold on to her, said, 'Let him eat it all, at least he will get some benefit from your skilful shot.'

That won her a smile, but no more words. Then the wretched dog barked once, and ran up to them, grinning the way hounds do.

'He's finished,' said Hope.

'Yes,' said Bell. They laughed together.

'Goodbye, then, my lady,' said Hope, and turning, she lifted her skirts in her free hand, and ran away, Benjy bounding at her heels. At the trees, she turned her head; but then she was gone.

Bell was surprised, after that, at how often they chanced to meet. There was no reason why they should. Hope was passing outside the church as service ended the very next Sunday, and curtsied to Bell, grinning shyly; Bell nodded and smiled in return. Then one morning Bell heard Dolly say that the ballad singer was at the tavern with a new batch of songs, and she put on her hat with the peacock feather and ran out, and there was Hope, on the edge of the crowd. They listened to the motley fellow sing, and as he finished, Hope was by her side. They stood together on the edge of the pack of villagers haggling for the broadsides.

'Has he good songs? I only heard the last,' Bell said.

'Not very – the tunes are old, and the words not much, apart from the one the Wiston lads there are buying; and that's for one reason only.'

'Is it indecent?' Bell was determined to keep up the cool, adult level of the conversation.

'Oh no, my lady, worse – it is treasonable – a Jacobite song,' Hope answered.

Bell flushed scarlet, and wished the earth would swallow her up. Hope knew about the disaster in the ride? Then she saw that Hope was smiling – laughing at her. Teasing her. She smiled back.

'Perhaps I should buy it, in that case,' she said solemnly, 'to sing at the next ball game.'

They parted laughing.

The Spring warmed into April, the green buds came and burst, and Hope was becoming as expert in tracking Bell's movements as ever she had been in the ways of rabbit or deer. As Easter approached, she saw that Bell walked more and more in the forest; and so it was not long before they met again, in the rabbit glade. They sat down side by side on Bell's log.

'Can you hear the goldfinches?' said Hope, cocking her head.

'Yes, there.' Bell pointed as the bright little birds

dipped through the trees before them, carolling their distinctive melody. They watched until they were gone. 'Do you still play the pipe?' Bell asked.

'Sometimes. I don't always have much time; and Thomas Piper is well again now, for the dancers.'

'Thomas Piper?'

'Did you not know? I was standing in for him. He had an inflammation of the lungs at the turn of the year, and could not blow. He is the real piper for the Mossmen.'

'Oh, no,' said Bell impulsively, 'I'm sure he could not be as good as you were! It was like – magic. I still think of it,' she added shyly.

'Do you? Do you truly?' The intensity of Hope's response was disconcerting; Bell hurriedly turned the conversation to other things. They talked for an hour, without saying anything important. They had lived in the same place all their lives, not meeting; there were things enough to say, matching their lives and fingering the places where they touched. They laughed about Dolly. Several times Bell thought, if she had come to live with me we could talk like this every day; but she did not say it. Hope devoured Bell with her eyes, longing to take her in her arms and kiss her; but of course she did not. Bell spoke of Alistair's absence, and Hope talked a little of the slow fading of her great-grandmother, and the old woman's heroic history.

'Did she eat any of the rabbit?' Bell asked.

'No. I don't think so. Mother was angry, I didn't ask twice.'

'You will miss her.'

'Yes, my lady.'

'You need not call me that.'

'What else should I call you?' There was a shadow of trouble behind the broad blue gaze. Bell had no answer.

'I must go,' said Hope suddenly. 'I have work today, fetching wool for carding from Carney. It's a bit of a step.' She seemed to speak deliberately rustic, broad.

I'll come too,' said Bell, springing up.

'No, my lady,' said Hope. She turned quickly away, and only looked back from the edge of the dell. 'I'll be here again tomorrow,' she said.

And so she was; but when Bell burst into the glade, carrying a bunch of primroses she had gathered on her walk, she found Hope face down in the grass, her clenched hands pressing the ground beside her head.

'Hope?' she said, standing over her.

After a moment Hope rolled over onto her back. She did not get up. She was not crying; but her face was flushed and her jaw set. She hid her face in her hands for a moment, then stared up at Bell. Her voice was thick.

'She has gone,' she said, and made as if to get up. Instinctively Bell fell on her knees, and put out her hands; Hope flinched away. They sat, close but not touching, side by side on the damp grass.

After a while Hope said, 'She died while I was away, yesterday; and I don't know what she would have said to me, after all.' She sobbed once, hard.

Bell searched frantically for some word of comfort, something that would ease this raw pain. 'She spoke to you only a few hours before, Hope – you said so. She told you the story of Liddell's Children that you told me. You had her blessing then, surely you did.'

'But I wasn't there at the end. So I don't know.' The crying burst out of her; she squirmed away, to hide her face.

Bell had no idea what to say or do, even whether Hope knew what she was saying; she could only pursue the logic of the strangled words. 'What was it you needed to know?' she asked gently.

Hope looked up at the sweet face all puzzled and puckered with concern for her; the brown eyes brimming, the little posy of primroses spilt in the grass. How could she speak to her? What could she say? That was what she did not know, what Anticipation might have told her, if she had only had the time – and the

53

courage – to ask: what was right for her to say or do, about her love for Bell? But at least she must not hurt her like this, imposing on her with grief. She wiped her sleeve across her face, then leapt up and away, to stop herself from catching hold of Bell and never letting go. As she stood, unable to speak or to go, she realised that Bell too was crying, the tears running silently down her cheeks.

'Don't cry, my lady.' She reached out a hand, and Bell clasped it. Without speaking, they walked together across the glade; and parted, helplessly.

Five

'Does the household go Maying tonight, Dolly?'

Bell had gone into the kitchen to collect her father's posset cup, so she could add a little ginger, just as he liked it. Mistress Johnson did not bother, as he had sometimes complained. She measured the spoonful carefully.

'Yes, my lady, so we do. We go with the folk from the clergy-house, and gather boughs for both.' Dolly was pert; Bell felt she was looking at her slyly, but she could not back out now.

'The weather is set fair for it,' she said.

'Yes, my lady, proper warm nights we've been having already.'

'Is it so warm afield, though?'

'Never fear for that – we keep each other warm, May morning.' Dolly giggled. Bell moved a step away, but Dolly was not to be stopped now. 'The family from the clergy-house are coming – Master William, at least. Won't you come with us, my lady?'

William was not good news. But he could probably be avoided, in the woods, in the dawn; he was a slow awkward youth at the best of times.

'I? I don't know. I had not thought of it.' Dolly smirked, and Bell went on, 'I must take father his posset, before it cools. What time do you go out?'

'About an hour before the dawn, my lady – you'll be able to see us, in the yard.'

It was not difficult to convince her father that it was a good idea. The maidens of his family had often done it, he said; he went himself, and his own sister went a-Maying many a time, before she married poor Fortescue. But –

'Cousin William will be there, Papa,' Bell said demurely.

He pinched her cheek. 'Take care then, pigeon. Don't fall over any tree roots, eh? – especially next to your cousin, you rascal!' He buried his face in his posset, his pink, ridgy scalp gleaming. She slipped away.

She could not have said why she was so set on going maying this year. Whatever her father's fancy, there was no-one she specially looked to meet in the woods – unless it was Hope. She did want to see Hope, she admitted to herself – but what she expected of such a meeting, or why she was so drawn to her, she could not have put into words. And anyway, she told herself, there was no reason why Hope should go a-maying; from what she had gathered of Hope's family, they would condemn such junketings as the devil's work.

She dressed in her green habit, with the white lace kerchief that James had brought her from his soldiering in the Low Countries. She discarded each of her hats and hoods in turn, and ended up with her little jockey hat over the very old lace cap her mother had left her, a fine filigree frill, soft round her face in the black reflection of the window pane. She could not see into the yard, but she heard them come out from the kitchen, the door clap to, a suppressed laugh, clogs echoing on the cobbles. When she ran down, they greeted her quietly, almost off-hand; there was no hint of dawn yet, and in the softly failing moonlight the house servants looked like travellers from a distant land, mysterious faces hidden in their hoods. They left the gates wide open behind them, as was the custom, welcoming in the May.

The clergy-house party were waiting at their lane end: Cousin William, with little Peter and another serving man, and simple May, who beamed delightedly at Bell. William did not look best pleased to see her.

'Isabella! I had not thought–' he moved to walk beside her. She sidestepped, and took May's arm.

'I won't trouble you, William. He should not speak to me at all, should he, May, not until we are in the wood?'

May hugged Bell's arm, like the child she was. 'Right you are, Miss Bell, menfolk and girls shouldn't speak, May

Morning, 'cept in the woods. 'Tis bad luck, so 'tis. Go your ways, Maister William, do!' Bell patted her arm to quiet her – she was too excited already.

William soon fell behind as the little procession moved on. He was empty-handed, but Bell saw the curved pruning-knives glint in the hands of the servingmen of both houses, and the maids carried baskets, with ribbons wound in their hair, and round their wrists and waists. May was playing with hers.

'See, Miss Bell, pretty!' she pulled them out in front of her, from her waist. 'Where be your pretty ribbons, Miss Bell?'

'Oh, Dolly's carrying mine,' Bell said. 'Where did you get yours, May? Aren't they fine?'

'Mistress gave them me, said for my birthday – 'tis my birthday, you know, that's why I'm named for it. Queen of the May, my mother used to say I'd be.' She paused, her face clouded. 'I never have, though.'

'We must be quiet, now, May, mustn't we?' said Bell in a hurry, to stop the descent to tears.

'Yes, Miss Bell,' said May, trustingly.

As they left the houses for the broad green lane, Peter the Pattens' footboy began to beat on a little tabor, tap-tap, tap-tap, a soft insistent heartbeat rhythm, for walking; there was a skip in it, every now and then; too slow for dancing, but the dance lay at its heart. From somewhere in the darkness, another drumbeat sounded; and a little way off a song began. From far ahead, up the forest ride, another, stronger chorus of the ancient Maytime carol came down towards them on the dawn wind.

They came to the skirts of the forest, still dark and looming, with only here and there the white glimmer of blossom along the branches. The young men cut boughs, to carry at their head, and they walked on, singing, between the first trees, under the forest eaves into the ride. In the distance ahead the clear moon rode low in a net of branches. They came by a stand of pines, and a rich waft of honey and bee-gum washed over

57

them. The breeze was warming, and silky with the smells of spring. Excitement bubbled up into their singing voices, and walking feet began to skip and dance to time. They came to the Trysting Tree, and sticking the may houghs in its branches they swung into their first dancing circle, joining hands in a wide ring round the Tree, fifteen or so of them, swinging, stamping left and right, moving into the dancing song –

'Heel and toe!

Jointly round we go!

We were up

Way before the day-ay-o . . .'

Bell stepped a little aside and stood still, her head up, looking for the first colours, the first light; listening. All round them in the woods it seemed there were people stirring; distant voices called or sang. And then, not very far away up the wind, the music of a pipe.

'Bell, will you dance?' William was pawing doggily at her elbow. Irritated, she felt a great urge to push him over. The pipe music called faintly on the breeze.

'Not yet, cousin. I want to gather some flowers.' She shook him off her arm, and ran into the trees.

The piping eluded her. As she pushed through the undergrowth, she could not hear it for the noise she made herself; and when she stood still, it seemed no nearer. After a quarter of an hour she rounded a huge may bush, glowing in the first light, and came back unexpectedly into the ride. In the distance a larger group were gathered under the Tree, beginning, now they could see a little, to collect and fashion the boughs and the garlands. Several girls had already gathered baskets of yellow flowers, primroses and buttercups, even some cowslips taken up on their way through the meadows; they were sitting in the roots of the tree plaiting and twisting them with their ribbons. Boys ran from group to group trying to snatch the ribbons from the girls, amidst shrieks and scuffling. Defeated, she walked reluctantly up towards them.

William caught sight of her, and came galloping up, a

ribbon in his hand.

'Where are your flowers, Bell? I thought you were so eager to be a-gathering – you'll be left behind!' He was over-excited, she thought; by the time they returned he would be thoroughly objectionable.

'I'm just going to a good place I know. Don't follow me,' she added quickly, 'it's a girls' secret.' Hopping about trying to wind the ribbon round his left leg, he grinned up at her. She gave way to her baser instincts, and gave him a push that sent him sprawling in the grass. She was gone before he could get up.

She followed the music of the pipe towards the line of the dawn light, where the trees overhead were thinnest and grass and flowers showed at her feet, glimmering into colour with the glowing blue dots of forget-me-not. Now that she could see, she could step more quietly; but then the fiddle and drum started up again in the ride, and she could no longer hear the pipe. Rounding a tree, she all but fell over a couple in the grass. Their threshing legs and buttocks shone white in the morning light. She backed away hurriedly out of sight, her heart hammering – she had not seen people coupling before. She began to run, and after a moment struck a clear path she recognised, between two willows. She was panting with effort as well as fright by me time she came out into the rabbit glade.

Hope was waiting. She had been sitting alone for an hour, sometimes playing her pipe to keep her company, sometimes watching the birds and rabbits beginning to feed, sometimes just thinking about Bell. At a deep level she had not stopped thinking about Bell at all, since they had parted in this place three weeks before; and her thoughts about Bell were inextricably entwined with her thoughts about her great grandmother. Anticipation, who believed in the holiness of the heart's affection as strongly as she believed in God, had been the only one wise enough to help her, and she was gone. But at last, only a day or so before, she had been sure what Anticipation's answer would have been. She could hear the old, serenely certain voice saying 'there is no fear in love, child; perfect love casteth out fear': the watchword of Liddell's Children.

The only remaining problem was how to take Bell with her; obviously she had to woo and win her. She recalled the ill-fated rabbit, and grinned to herself. This hunting might not be so easy. She cocked her head at the sound of someone rustling through the bracken. My first step at least was right, she thought. Here she comes. Her heart leapt as she stood up to greet her.

Bell crashed out of the trees headlong, as if she were indeed hunted, and came to a stop amidst the bluebells. They were both suspended for a moment; then Bell drew a panting breath and spoke. 'A good morning to you, Hope, and a happy Maytide.'

'Thank you, Mistress Bell,' said Hope gravely, mocking, 'Is that how they greet the May, in Wiston Great House?'

'What?' It took Bell a moment to understand that she was being teased.

'So formal a thing is it, down your way?'

Beginning to smile, Bell shook her head. 'No, it's not a formal thing, down my way. We dance. Listen, you can hear the fiddle even from your woodland retreat.' She held up her hand. The dancing tune trickled through the trees, thin and high, a little waterfall of bright sound. Hope bowed.

'Will you dance with me then, my lady?' she said gravely.

Bell smiled, and dropped a profound curtsey. Hope's blood pounded as they stepped closer together, and took hands. It was not a girlish ring dance, pulling and breathless; they moved into each other's reach, and then apart, to and fro, up and down upon the grass, with formal movements and clasped hands as the music led them; they danced a pattern around their private green space, an exquisite quadrille. Bell was in the ballroom of her dreams; Hope, following and improvising round her to the tune, was Guy of Warwick with his lady love. Then the fiddle stopped and started again, the tune changed and quickened. They confronted each other in an older rhythm, stamping and leaping and posturing at each other, hands on hips, laughing. They moved urgently together in time. The music finished with a flourish, and they heard the distant dancers cheer. They stood still for a moment, breathing hard from the dance, looking in each other's faces; then Hope took Bell in her arms.

She felt little shoulderblades through the soft net of lace, tense, thin as a bird; the stiffened bodice of the green gown pressed against her breasts. She could feel the thud of Bell's heart. Hope held her still; with her other hand, after a moment, she cupped the back of Bell's head and turned her face up. Their lips were scarcely a breath apart. After a lifetime, it seemed to Hope, while their warmth seeped into each other, the violin started the May carol in the distance, and they pulled apart.

'They will be going soon – look how high the sun is,' Bell said.

'Do you want to go?' There was a brief silence.

'No,' said Bell, 'I like it here in the forest – with you. Hope–' She stopped, as if she had suddenly thought better of what she was going to say next.

'Yes?'

'Have you ever thought – since I have known you – that is – I was thinking of engaging a maid, and I wondered if you might consider – if your parents might allow –' she dried up again, looking at Hope.

Hope spoke very carefully. 'Are you asking me if I would come and live with you?'

'Well, yes, I suppose I am. But if you don't want–'

'Oh, but I do,' said Hope. 'I do.'

Ten days later Hope stood in the courtyard at the Manor, looking up at the L-shaped back of the house. The great kitchen chimney was smoking, but all else seemed still asleep; all the doors were shut. She massaged her left shoulder thoughtfully; even her few possessions made a heavy weight over three miles of forest track. She had left the cottage before it was light. She had expected to go without speaking to anyone; but as she roped her box, on the hearth before the raked-over fire, her mother had come down. Standing tall, wrapped in her blanket, she had looked like a vengeful prophet; but all she said was, 'You'll have to ask your Aunt Cissy about your washing.' Hope had gone on pulling the knots. When she was actually outside the door, her mother spoke again. 'I will pray for you.' But she would not kiss her goodbye, and went indoors, not watching her depart.

It was no good dwelling on that. They were all better off now she was gone. For a week, ever since Sir Walter had spoken for her to her father, the house had been unbearable as they battled over her. Jack and Benjy had more or less left home. Her mother's angry accusations of worldly pride and lust, of bowing down in the house of Mammon, had stung her father into defending the gentry, and it had set off all their old divisions. But when he was alone with Hope, the two of them splitting and stacking logs, he had tried to tell her his own worries about her going into service.

'You'll take care, my lass. It's all right for a lad, a fine thing to go to serve; not that there's anything wrong with Sir Walter, with the gentry, whatever you mother says. But a lass; you have to have a care. You may speak to your Uncle Joshua – any time, you understand me?' He put down his axe as if it cumbered him, and scratched the back of his neck.

'Don't trouble about it, father. I know how to look out

for myself. I'm not a child; maids younger than me by far go into service, and make their fortunes – and come to no harm.'

'Aye, but you? I wonder what you are about, with this maggot, to be a lady's maid. You never seemed that sort of little girl – I never thought of it. You never hankered after finery and ribbons, you like to be a-doing, out of doors. And you've always been so set on your mother's people's ways, up at the Forge, at the Meeting, all that; I thought you scorned the gentry. She looks down on the Wistons, your mother, for all their wealth and standing, and I thought you took after her, upon my word.' He seemed less than happy to find her so unexpectedly on his side.

'It's all right, father; truly, I know what I'm about.'

Standing there in the Wiston stable yard, she wished she could have parted from both of them more at ease. She flinched from the memory of her father's puzzled, almost guilty face, avoiding her eye as well as her mother's, when he returned from his formal visit to shake hands over her wages with Sir Walter. But what could she have said? Don't worry, father; forgive me, mother; I will not be corrupted by the wicked ways of the gentry, I care nothing for the pomps and vanities of reach-me-down fine dresses, I will not be led astray by Captain James's treacle breath and wandering hands; for I am in love, I go to woo my mistress Isabella? Nonsense. She sat down abruptly on her box.

As she gazed at the massive oak corner-post above her head, the kitchen door clapped back, and her Aunt Cissy appeared. She was already talking as she came, grumbling under her breath as she bustled out on high pattens, to gather Hope up.

'Bring your box, girl – come into the kitchen, no use standing about like a post, come. Too much to do without a helpless girl like you to run after. And my poor Dolly –'

Hope picked up her trunk and caught up with her.

'Dolly? What's the matter with her?'

'You may well ask what's the matter with her, poor child. You of all people! Her own cousin, a wild trollop from the forest.'

Hope was not catching the drift of this. She held open the door for her aunt, and followed her into the scented, slightly smoky dimness of the kitchen, putting her box down just inside on the flags.

'I'm sorry, aunt?'

'So you should be. Yes, indeed!' Aunt Cissy was working herself into a rage, hissing at Hope like an affronted cat, and flouncing. She came up very close. 'What's at the back of it, that's what I'd like to know! A lady's maid! My poor Dolly!'

Hope at last grasped what it was about. She had got a coveted place – my lady's maid – over Dolly's head. She looked round a little apprehensively for her cousin, but she was not there; gone off in offence, perhaps. Old Benchley sat on the settle by the fire, dozing.

An inner door opened, and the housekeeper – Mistress Johnson, was she? – appeared, carrying a whole tray of glassware. She was a dignified woman, in a large no-nonsense cap and an enveloping holland apron. She put her tray on the table, and smiled a little at Hope and her aunt.

'Hope Bishop? You are not very like your kin here, to look at. A much bigger build: we must take thought for fitting you. Your own clothes must serve you for a few weeks; Miss Isabella will no doubt put up with you as you are, since you are her choice.' She had taken a cloth as she looked Hope up and down, and was polishing as she talked, and stacking the glasses into a little cupboard; no movements wasted. Her hands were old, bony but strong. 'If she had a mother, now, there would be other waiting-women for you to learn of; but if she had a mother, of course, she would not have made her own choice of a lass from the woods for her maid. But don't fret, girl; you'll shape, I make no doubt. I have seen wilder things than you turned into useful and

65

respected heads of substantial households.' She shut the cupboard with a click, shook out the cloth with a snap, and headed for the door. 'I will show you your duties now, and you are to come to me when you are astray. Mind,' she turned back, and addressed the room at large, 'there'll be no foul play.' She fixed Aunt Cissy with her eye. 'Tell Dolly to mind her manners with her cousin, or I shall hear of it, and so will she.'

Mistress Johnson towed Hope away into a tour of little rooms where things were kept or done; closets and boxes and irons and hooks, presses full of linens and racks of bottles and jars. Hope was impressed, which was perhaps all that the housekeeper expected; there was little chance of her remembering a tithe of what she was told about goffering lace or turning down beds, mixing face washes and making clear starch. Eventually they were back in the kitchen. Dolly was there, pounding something in a large basin and humming to herself. She did not look to Hope like someone whose nose was seriously out of joint. She sang out, 'Mistress Johnson, shall I take my cousin to our room now?'

The housekeeper resigned Hope to her, with instructions not to be long and to come back to her in the stillroom, when she was settled in. Dolly was bursting with her news, as they made off.

'Silly old stick, don't take any notice of her. Round this way, we go up the old stairs. Nor mother neither – I bet she said I was dying of jealousy of you! That's all she knows. I don't envy you looking after that puffed-up little thing, you may be sure. I shan't be a lady's maid, thank you very much. I shan't be here at all much longer. Come on, one more landing. No – I'm glad you've come. Look!'

They seemed to have climbed up into the roof – it was hot, although it was not yet mid-morning, and the passage was too narrow for Hope to carry her box beside her. Huge roof timbers sloped from over their heads almost into the floor. Dolly brushed heedlessly through ancient dust, and flung open a little wicket door, only about four feet high. Hope peered in. Beyond was hardly a room, more a slightly wider continuation of the passage. One little window at floor level let in sunlight, showing her a rough, low bedstead, piled with folded sheets and blankets and a newly-stuffed straw mattress. There was a lingering smell of apples.

'Isn't it fine? I said to mother, there's no room for us all over the stable, not if Hope is to be called to my lady, coming and going late and early, and you won't want to be disturbed, and what about her clothes; and it will salve my broken heart if I can go along with her, into the house, and keep her company!' She flung herself onto the mattress, shrieking with laughter. 'She's no trouble, mother.'

'You mean this is for you and me – we are to sleep here?'

'That's right! All on our own! No one to bother us – or to know what we get up to!'

If she had not had so many other things to think about, Dolly and the bedroom would have given Hope some trouble during the rest of the day. But as soon as they went down, Mistress Johnson told her that Bell wanted her, and led her up a wide staircase and along a dark corridor with woven matting down its centre, to a polished oaken door, on which she tapped sharply. Bell's voice answered; Hope lifted the latch and went in.

Bell was sitting in the window, but now she jumped up, fumbling at the sewing that slid from her lap, and said quickly, 'Hope; I am glad to see you. Mistress Johnson has made you welcome, I trust? It is a pleasant day, is it not? And you are not too tired from your walk? Then I will show you my things, and we can talk about what you are to do.' Without looking at Hope, she walked quickly away across the room.

Hope stood helpless. Bell was acting like a stranger; the little lady in her bower, bright, gracious – nervous? – Hope looked round to see if Mistress Johnson was still at the door. She was not. Before she could speak, Bell rushed on.

'This is my own chamber, as you see; and here, in this chest, are my gowns and petticoats; the press is for my linen, I'll show you that later.' She started to burrow in the chest, taking out clothes and putting them back, talking all the time, still not looking at Hope. There seemed little prospect that she would ever do so again.

It was a difficult day. Bell continued to be bright but distant, and she talked in brittle spurts, about her brother Alistair, about her dresses, her needlework, her grey gelding – anything, apparently, to avoid a silence. Hope dared not touch her, but she knew no other way to make her stop. She wanted to smooth and soothe her, like a nervous animal, to tell her it was all right; but she dared not, and anyway Bell was never still for long enough.

They got on best over Bell's books; she showed Hope all her store, more than a dozen fine large volumes in proper bindings, with titles and the Wiston arms tooled in gold. There was a beautiful bible, feeling curiously stiff and unopened to Hope's hands. Bell was more pleased with the little papers she had from her beloved Alistair, full of the latest news and polite conversation, she said. Hope explored all the books with pleasure. Two of them were poetry, like ballads she had read on broadsides, but without verses – five-beat lines, going on and on, and in one book even without any rhymes.

'How do you fit the tune?' she asked, and was puzzled when Bell laughed. Better to be laughed at, though, than held at arm's length. She smiled ruefully. 'You see what a hopeless bumpkin you have for a maid,' she said. Then, keeping her voice light, 'You need not keep me, if you see I do not suit – if you have changed your mind?'

'Oh, no!' Bell looked horrified. 'I am sorry. I didn't mean to hurt you.' She frowned, and then added with sudden honesty, 'I suppose I am as new a mistress as you are a maid. Do you know I felt quite nervous of you

68

coming? Is that not foolish? But we shall learn together, do you think?' She looked anxiously at Hope.

Hope drew a long breath. 'I think we may,' she said, and smiled.

'It is nearly time for dinner,' said Bell, distant again, 'and, I must make myself ready.'

'Shall I do your hair, my lady? That must be part of my maid's duties.' Hope smiled, and Bell smiled back, shyly, and sat down at her little table; two silver-backed brushes were laid out there. Hope loosed her braids, unwinding the brown threads down their length, and shook out the fine, heavy hair, crimped like silk. The skin of her hands seemed too rough to touch such splendour. She took a brush, and began to smooth it as gently as she could; but she felt the narrow shoulders tremble slightly against her hand.

'I'm sorry, do I hurt you?' She looked into the little mirror, that only showed her Isabella's face; but Bell just shook her head. Hope was at a loss.

'I have read some books, you know,' she said lightly, continuing to brush determinedly at the long fine hair. 'The ballad singer brings little stories, as well as songs.'

'Oh yes, I know them – I had them when I was small, I loved them. I've still got some, shall I show you?'

Hope brushed steadily on, to stop her springing up again.

'Not now, or you will be late for dinner. We can look at them tomorrow.'

By the end of the day Hope felt like a wrung out dish rag. She walked out into the stableyard for a few moments, to clear her head. The last half hour had been worse again. Bell had sent her down to fetch water from the kitchen. She had lugged the pitcher upstairs, trying not to think about what would happen next. Was Bell going to wash? Was that what gentle folks did, wash before bed, and make themselves cold? She knew that they had special clothes to sleep in, not just their underthings. Was she to stay while Bell washed and changed her clothes? Help her, even? She

69

grew hot and confused. But when she came back Bell was braiding her own hair, standing in the middle of the room, well away from the bed. She was wearing a straight, loose shift, snow-white and ruffled, laced up under her chin. So that is a bedgown, Hope noted wryly; I am learning things that would astonish my mother. She stopped at a respectful distance.

'Shall I braid your hair for you?' she asked.

'No, no thank you.' They looked at each other, at a loss.

Finally Hope said, 'Shall I go now, my lady?'

'Yes – you have somewhere to sleep?'

'Yes, my lady. Shall I bring more water in the morning?'

'Thank you, Hope. Yes, please.'

And she had come away. There was no moon yet; the house was quiet. A horse shifted and clinked in the stables, and a cat slipped by at the foot of the wall. It was some relief to put her head under the pump, and wash her hands and face. Now she must go in, to Dolly. She took a deep breath.

Dolly was in the kitchen, finishing some washing up.

'Whatever have you done to yourself? Here, use this.' She flung her dishclout at Hope. 'My dear, we wash indoors in this kitchen. Or was your first day so bad you had to try to drown yourself? Come on, you can get dry upstairs. I'm tired; let's go and make up our bed.' She prattled on all the way up the many twisting stairs, and scarcely stopped until they were getting into bed. Hope stretched out carefully, keeping herself to herself. But she need not have worried. As Dolly chattered on, Hope slowly realized that her cousin had completely forgotten – or chosen to forget – their old games. She was as oblivious of Hope as if she were a bolster. And it did not take long, once she began to listen to the flow of words, for Hope to work out why.

'He's very handsome and strong. He has beautiful

teeth, I turn to jelly when he smiles! And he's got money put by, and the promise of a cottage and workshop up at the Moor – don't laugh, you never thought I'd be one to go and live up there, but we're going to set up in saddlery, he knows the trade, he says, and he could do fine work for the house, Sir Walter will – Hope? Are you asleep?'

'No, no, go on. What's his name, did you say?'

'You've not listened to a word! John, John Dickson, you know, in the stable, with father. Father favours him, I know; mother's the only problem, says we should wait another year. A year! He's dying for love of me, he says. Why do you think I wanted this room?'

'Why?'

'Oh, Hope, you're such a baby! Well – don't be surprised if you find you've got the bed to yourself, some night very soon.'

Hope smiled with relief, into the apple-smelling darkness. Some people, she thought, might well feel put out at being forgotten for a Mr John Dickson, in the stable. But I have other irons in the fire.

Over the next few weeks, as a lovely May led on to an uncertain June, and the elderflowers dripped in bursts of surprisingly cold rain, Hope and Bell found a way of getting on together. As Bell became more accustomed to Hope's presence, she began actively to enjoy the companionship she had missed before; and Hope was careful not to startle her or make any sudden demand upon her feelings. It was very like winning the confidence of a wild creature: it required a great deal of patience and no sudden movements. Hope sometimes felt stifled in the house, and longed for the freedom of the forest; but she would have endured far worse for the sake of spending her days with Bell. She brushed Bell's hair, and tied and untied it; she helped to tend her clothes, and gradually also to dress and undress her, tying laces and folding neckerchiefs into place. With Mistress Johnson's help they measured Hope for new

71

gowns, befitting her new dignity, and together they sewed them, in blue cloth from the household store. Bell leaned against Hope's knees as they sat in the rose bower in the garden trimming white currants for the kitchen. They walked out together, and ran through the meadows side by side, flopped laughing in the grass, out of sight of house and village; and talked. Neither had had any sisters to share confidences, and talking endlessly and inconsequentially about themselves was a joyful discovery.

Of course they talked about politics, and the rights and wrongs of the Cause – wrangling like tavern lawyers, Hope said, since there was no part two girls could play in the struggle. Bell was on tenterhooks for the King's landing, but it seemed endlessly postponed. Wild rumours of treachery and betrayal reached them throughout the summer. In March the great minister Bolingbroke had fled to France and no-one seemed sure whether he was truly a supporter of King James or simply a government informer. Some said the King would land with a great force of French troops, others that he would come alone, to join his loyal officers in Devon. There was no news at all from Lord Ormonde. Hope found it hard to understand a cause which seemed to have no leader and to be so full of contradiction and uncertainty. Secretly she thought their hopes must be lost through such confusion, but she did not speak her mind to Bell, whose faith in the coming of her king was undiminished.

There was one topic, though, on which she had to speak out. They faced very quickly the problem of their differences in religion. On the first Sunday Aunt Cissy said no kin of hers would disgrace Sir Walter by not following him to Church, and Hope confronted her with a blank refusal. It was Mistress Johnson who rescued her again, telling her aunt to mind her own affairs, and not come between the girl and her mother. After that Hope went off each Sunday to the Meeting, or to the chapel at Carney, and had the dubious pleasure of walking back

72

to the Moor and spending an hour trying to explain herself to her relations at the forge. Sometimes her mother came there; but not often. Bell meanwhile accepted Hope's faith solemnly, like a child; but Hope felt more and more the gap between the strict and joyless creed of her mother's folk, and the faith in freedom of her great grandmother's time. She could not discuss such problems with Bell, even though they mostly talked about themselves. They talked of their lives so far, and their lives to come, now they were together.

'And now I shall always have you for a sister,' said Bell happily one day, 'and never be lonely any more.'

Hope kept her eyes on the grass stalk she was peeling, and held her voice as steady as she said, 'But you will be married before very long, and then you won't need me any more.'

'No I won't – why do you say that?' Bell looked startled. 'I don't think of it.'

'But you will have to think of it before very much longer,' Hope insisted, shredding the stalk of grass, still avoiding Bell's eyes. 'All ladies must marry.'

'I shan't,' said Bell; and then, 'at least, not for a long time. I'm too young. I have never seen anyone I could . . . think of, that way. And in any case,' she added, a little too brightly, 'you could still be with me, Hope, couldn't you, if I were married? It would still be the same. Almost,' she finished lamely.

There was a pause before Hope spoke. 'It wouldn't be the same, you know that. And I don't think . . . I don't think I should stay with you, if you were married. I don't think I could.' She looked up, and Bell met her troubled gaze with a frown of puzzled anxiety.

'Hope? What's the matter?' Then, half incredulous, 'You're not *jealous*! Are you?'

Hope thought, she does know. Her stomach knotted with fear. 'Jealous? Of what, my lady?'

'I don't know. Of me? Of my being a lady? Being married?'

Relief and despair seized Hope simultaneously. She said dully, 'Forgive me, my lady, for forgetting my place.' She dropped flat on her back, turning away her face.

'Oh, Hope!' Bell threw herself sideways in the grass, away from her, then back, and grabbed her awkwardly by the arm, scrambling up onto her knees. 'Hope, stop it. You are my good friend, and I love you.'

'Do you, Bell?' Hope lay still, looking up into her face.

'Of course I do.' Bell laughed. 'What do I have to do, to make you believe me?'

Kiss me, my lady? lie down with me now, and – Hope closed her eyes. The outline of Bell's head and shoulders against the sun burned green upon her eyelids. She shook her head, rolled aside and sat up quietly.

'I'm sorry I was foolish. Come on, let's go back to the house.' She stood up, and held out her hand.

They walked slowly back through the cowslips.

Seven

Bell tossed fretfully in the sweltering darkness. Not a breath of air stirred; the curtains of her bed stood like marble pillars. She thrust them aside, but no breeze came from her open window. From a fine early harvest time, the sunny weather had built to this blistering heat, until men and beasts alike longed for the thunder that must end it. The season's work could not be halted, whether for heat or cold, and Bell had spent the whole hot day in the still room helping Mistress Johnson. They had been at the yearly task of brewing surfeit water – a nasty, smelly concoction of some two dozen herbs, in which Sir Walter put great faith on the mornings after he had dined or drunk too well. The strong, acrid steam had stung her eyes and nose as she stood in the heat of an August afternoon, trying to take in what the housekeeper was telling her about the properties of each herb, until she felt giddy and sticky with sweat. Before she went to bed she had thought how pleasant it would be to take a bath; but when she thought what it would involve, she had changed her mind. The heavy wooden tub would have to be carried up to her room; and then all the water, jug by jug – she would not impose such a task on Hope at the end of a long hot day. She had another reservation, too, which she hardly admitted even to herself: the idea of standing naked while Hope poured the water over. Foolish, she told herself briskly; friends should have no secrets from each other. It was as good as having a sister, to have Hope to talk to all the time. Even when Alistair was at home, Bell had spent much of her time alone. And now I am not lonely any more, she said to herself. She turned over, determined to go to sleep.

Hope lay wide awake in her apple loft. Up here under the roof, the heat was unbearable. She lay as still as possible, debating whether it was worthwhile to lug the mattress off the bed and put it beside the long, low window on the floor. With the shutter back – there was no glass – it might be slightly cooler down there; on the other hand, there was no breeze, and the sweat of moving her bed was too much to contemplate. She lay still. At least she had not Dolly's hot and fidgety presence to cope with; tonight as most nights, Dolly was off and away with the lusty John. Hope thought of them, somewhere out in the meadows together. A much better place to be than this . . . but not with John Dickson. She imagined what it would be like to lie naked in the cool, damp grass . . . and wrenched her thoughts back resolutely from an involuntary picture of Bell, stretched soft and welcoming beside her. It was too hot for that. She turned her pillow again and tried to sleep.

Bell was dreaming of taking a bath. In the dream she did not mind that Hope stood beside her, pouring liquid over her body. She stretched luxuriously, reaching up her arms so that the streams of water ran down her belly. But the waves of sensation were not cool; they were hot. Liquid fire poured over her breasts and thighs, wave after wave, until she woke with a shuddering cry, staring at the hot velvet darkness.

They were both up at dawn. Bell had to make do with a wash in her little closet, from the ewer Hope brought up to her; she looked down from her window and envied Hope splashing herself and her shift recklessly at the pump. They had planned to escape for a little while from Mistress Johnson's lessons in herblore and preserving, by walking out to Carney in the cooler part of the morning to see a litter of pups Sir Walter intended to take into his pack; but as they were setting off Peter, the footboy from the clergy-house, came racing into the yard with a message for her father and a written note, addressed to Bell herself.

'It's an invitation,' she said, wondering, 'Look, she asks to me to go and dine at noon, to meet her sister Gilliam from Bath.' She turned it over, amazed. A formal invitation, to her. Peter was eager to elaborate. 'It's Missis's sister, and her nevvy – great doings!' he said, 'He's no end of a milord, in a great periwig like two black lambs fighting on his shoulders; drove up in a woundy big carriage last night, all of a lather, can't get back home to Bath City without a rest for their beasts, we've to put them up; cool as cucumbers!'

'That's enough, Peter, thank you,' said Bell, turning away. She read the note again.

'Suit yourself, miss; what shall I say? Are you for coming, then, eh?'

'Tell my aunt I shall not fail to come,' she said, with as much coolness as she could muster. He grinned and tugged his forelock, and raced off to give whatever his message was to her father. Even if it is only aunt Patten, still it is my first formal invitation, she thought. She supposed she would have to ask her father if she could go. But still, it was interesting. A cousin – in a fashionable periwig. 'Come, Hope,' she said, 'I must find something fit to wear.' Hope followed her without speaking.

The message to Sir Walter was apparently a plea for help – 'As usual,' he said to Bell. 'Patten is a shiftless fool – two unexpected guests and he's in a flat panic. Tell him I'm sending the claret by Benchley, so you'll be ahead of it, my dear, and you can take him a couple of brace of pheasant. Take a boy or your maid or someone to carry them. They'll be wanting them in the kitchen. Try to stop your aunt charring them to cinders. And Isabella –' he smiled conspiratorially – 'mind young Gilliam. He's a devil with the ladies, so they say; and he's high in my Lord Wyndham's good books. Saves M'lord a mint of money in his land and law dealings. And she – your Aunt Gilliam – she's red-hot in the Cause. You could do well to make an impression, eh? You'll be bringing me back all the latest news from France, when you return.'

They walked slowly through the village, Bell chattering excitedly as she preserved her best dress from the dust. Hope was rather silent. She carried a basket of plate, and the four pheasants on a string bumping against her leg. It was already very hot. They arrived just before noon, to find the 'woundy big carriage' that had so impressed Peter standing at the door of the clergy-house – it was far too big to go down the little passage to their stable. It was an astonishing vehicle, painted bright red and varnished all over to a glaring shine, the spokes and handles and nail-heads all picked out in gold. Bell ventured to step up onto its bright black running board, and peered in.

'Oh! Look, Hope, look at the inside! It's all fitted out like a sort of padded closet – with racks and hooks and little netted shelves, and the most sumptuous velvet cushions! Come up and look!'

Hope did not respond. She stood in the dusty path, not even looking at the carriage. Then she said, 'Here's your Aunt,' and turned away.

'Isabella, my dear, good, come a little early, will help to entertain while I – what, pheasants! Bless your good father. And he sends Hope, too, how very kind, a great help – run straight in with the birds, my dear, May does know how to pluck them if she is not too flustered, otherwise perhaps you – thank you, dear.' This last to Hope's retreating back, who after flinging an unfathomable glance at Bell had plunged down through the parched and yellow garden to the back door. Bell had no time to worry about that.

'Come now, my dear, meet my sister, I have but a moment –' In the gloomy hall, where at least today they were glad that the sun never came, Mistress Gilliam and her son sat in the two armed chairs. As he rose gracefully and bowed, Bell's eye travelled up the man's exquisite length: bright chestnut high-heeled shoes, silk stockings, tight blue breeches, a coat with military frogging and the widest skirts in the world; and the famous glossy black full-bottomed wig. His face was white and smooth, adorned with the merest fine line of hair above the lip, scarcely a moustache, a mere suggestion; and a black patch, crescent-shaped, elegantly under his right eye. This was a Man of Fashion, Bell thought. She had never seen one before. She prayed he would not immediately know how awkward and shy she was. His mother was a formidable woman, no larger than Aunt Patten, but the reverse of her – where Bell's Aunt was yielding and soft, faded and drooping, her sister was upright, substantial and energetic.

'I am glad to see you, Miss Wiston, glad to see you. We are here on the gad, so to say, a chance to see my sister, once in the way, on our route back to Bath. Come sister, here is your good man.' She seized Uncle Patten as he came in, and led the way to dinner.

Bell sat up straight, feeling all the knobs down each stick in the back of her chair. She was acutely conscious of the eyes of the man of fashion, Mr Gilliam. Whenever she raised her eyes he seemed to be looking at her, a fat, foxy smile on his smooth face.

'What can I give you, Bell, my dear?' her uncle said.

Bell looked hopelessly from the greasy mutton with blood in the dish at one end of the table to the flabby white boiled capon at the other. She wondered why her aunt's food was always so dreadful.

'A little of the fowl, please, uncle,' she said in a small voice.

When all were served – she noticed that her Aunt Gilliam seemed oblivious to the food, and simply cut and chewed her way through her mutton without looking at it, while Mr Gilliam took little and ate less – her uncle turned the conversation to politics.

'Well, then, Gilliam, so you think the King will land at Plymouth?'

Mr Gilliam willingly stopped picking at his plate, and looked up. His eyes were rather small, Bell decided, and a very non-descript colour. 'Indeed sir, the talk at Orchard Wyndham is of a landing any day now. We expect my lord Bolingbroke as well as His Majesty, of course, and who knows how many French troops to back him.'

His mother broke in. 'No need of foreign backers, Charles, as I have said before; King James's loyal subjects here are ready and willing to acclaim him, as soon as he sets foot in his rightful realm.' She put down her fork, and looked challengingly at Uncle Patten.

'Ah – yes, indeed madam, that is so,' he hurried to say, 'My kinsman Sir Walter here is a great supporter, as are both his sons.'

'Indeed? And what are they about?'

'Why, Captain James serves with the Duke of Ormonde, and his brother is at Oxford.'

'Oxford is loyal, I believe, though not likely to prove as important a centre as we have at Bath.' She sat back from an empty plate with a look of completed business. Her son took his glass, and raised it politely to Isabella.

'Health to your gallant brothers, Madam; may they be victorious, and return home safely under a glorious new reign.' She smiled, and took up her glass in return. He added, 'And may their charming sister be as victorious as they are, though in a softer battle, and for a different king – the king of her heart.'

William guffawed, then tried to change it into a cough under his father's glare.

Mrs Gilliam sailed on, oblivious to Bell's confusion. 'Bath is, as I say, likely to be the more important centre. Sir William said to me,' she turned to Bell, condescendingly, 'Sir William Wyndham, child, the Shire Member – we have been staying at his house these three weeks, about the great business – Sir William said to me, Madam, Bath is as loyal a city as any in the realm, and in Bath then is no more loyal man than you, upon my word.' She sat back, folding her hands decisively before her, and adding, 'Sister, I think we have eaten all we are likely to eat of your first course.'

Aunt Patten looked vaguely round the room, and lighting upon Peter standing at the sideboard, told him to clear the table.

'You may get Hope to help you bring in the second course,' she said. She smiled at her guests. 'Sir Walter has so kindly sent us two brace of pheasants, to eke out our humble dinner; otherwise the second course would be nought but a dish of pickled eels – I hope you will like them, they are my own putting up – and a poor whipped syllabub I made this morning.'

Peter gathered up the virtually untouched plates from Bell and Mr Gilliam; Hope was at the sideboard, attempting to stack the dishes so as to get them safely out of the room.

'Ah madam,' said Charles Gilliam, 'there is nothing I relish more than a country syllabub – good food is so hard to find in Town, and a syllabub, as sweet and fresh as my cousin here, is a truly rural pleasure!'

Hope ground the plates together regardless of the mess. She hoped the syllabub would choke him. She shouldered through the door and stomped back to the filthy, oppressive kitchen. May, who had been quite useless with excitement all day, was struggling to scrape a wizened pheasant off a dirty spit. Hope picked up a tub of table salt from the dresser. 'Give me that,' she said, 'and come and sprinkle the powdered sugar on the syllabub.'

'Look how it sparkles!' said May, pouring. 'Shall I put more?'

'Yes,' said Hope grimly, 'Put as much as you like.'

'And then Willam – you know what a hog William is, he always eats faster than anyone else – William took the first spoon of syllabub, and spat it right across the table with a whoop like a stuck pig! It spattered everywhere, all over Mr Gilliam's coat sleeve, can you imagine? He was most genteel, scarcely started at all, only whipped his napkin off and dabbed it away. Then he asked me if I was all right, most thoughtfully.'

'So he never ate any?' Hope asked.

'Oh, I don't suppose he swallowed much of it, stupid boy, it would do him no harm, it was only salt anyway, I can't imagine –'

'I didn't mean William.'

'No-one else ate it, if that's what you mean. My poor aunt was mortified, of course, but Mr Gilliam passed it off, he –'

'Oh.' Hope shifted the basket, now containing empty bottles as well as knives and forks, to her other hand. She was walking a step away from Bell, her eyes on the ground.

'Hope – is anything wrong?'

'Why, what should there be wrong?'

'I don't know. You seem very quiet.'

'I'm sorry.'

'No, I didn't mean – Hope, what is it?'

Hope stopped, and put the basket down with a clank at her feet. 'Oh no, there's nothing ails me,' she said, 'I've been shut up in a hot, stinking kitchen all day with no company but Peter Atkins and daft May Bridges and a couple of thousand flies and black beetles and six spaniels and two snivelling babies, nothing fit to eat or drink but other folk's leavings and five people's work to do, while you sat in your finery in your aunt's parlour with this pretty fellow wearing three families' yearly substance on his back and a dead sheep on his head, talking folly and treason and signifying nothing, whoring after false gods, bowing down in the temple of Mammon. What could be wrong with me?'

Bell was aghast. She ran back to Hope, who pushed her away and stamped off into the roadside dust.

'I'm sorry, Hope, I didn't think –'

'No, why should you? That's the trouble. Why should you think of me? I'm only a servant, only your maid, to fetch and carry, aren't I, as soon as you set eyes on a man.'

'What? Hope!' She was being so stupid, unreasonable. 'What's that got to do with it? I went to please my aunt, to help, you know that, I –'

'Oh yes of course; family obligation; your position, my lady – lady of the manor. I understand all that perfectly, I do assure you. I have obligations too, unfortunately. If my father did not need to keep his place, which I am sure your father would see to it he lost, then I'd go away right now, go back where I belong. I had rather be a doorkeeper in the house of my God, than to dwell in the tents of wickedness. Psalm 84.'

'Hope, what are you talking about?'

'She was right, my mother. You bear a power over us, an evil power, you play with us like toys or pets, and when you're tired of us you throw us away like husks, sucked dry. No man can serve two masters.'

Bell could not tell whether to laugh or cry. Hope was stamping about raising a choking cloud of dust; she had knocked the basket over, and the bottles were rolling under their feet. Her face and eyes were red as fire as she kicked out at the tussocks of dried grass. Bell caught her arm, and hung on, to bring her to a stand.

'Hope, stop it! Stop behaving like this. I don't know what's come over you, but come back home quietly and we'll talk about it. Please, Hope, stop it, stop it!' She fought not to cry. Hope at least was standing still now, as Bell fumbled for her handkerchief and hid her face. There was a long pause.

'I'm sorry, my lady,' Hope said in the end, in a little tight voice. 'I was mistaken.' She stooped at her mistress's feet, and began to gather the bottles back into the basket. Bell saw that they were all covered in dirt from the road, stuck to the dregs of claret that had dribbled out.

'I'm sorry about the pups,' she said, 'Perhaps we can go to Carney and see them tomorrow.'

'What?' Hope was kneeling in the road, arranging the basket. She looked up, her red eyes smouldering.

'The puppies – the litter, at Carney. We'll go tomorrow.'

In a distant, dreary voice Hope said, 'Oh, yes. I had forgotten them.' She stood up, and turning without looking at Bell, started to walk back to the Hall.

Eight

It was seven by the stableyard clock when they arrived, a tense and silent procession of two. Even at home, things were not as normal. A tired horse, obviously pushed to the point of foundering, and still hot and shivering although it had been rubbed down and blanketed, was being walked up and down the yard by John Dickson.

'It's Beauty!' Bell exclaimed, running to the horse's head. 'John, is my brother home? There, girl, never mind – has she drunk? When did he arrive? It's a shame to push her so. There girl, there.' The mare seemed to recognise Bell's hands and voice, and gave a tired whicker of welcome.

'This half hour, my lady – mare is nearly fit to rest now. I have warm mash for her.' Dickson was a good groom, Bell thought, she must put in a word for him to her father. She turned to Hope – to see her back just disappearing into the kitchen. She stroked Beauty's nose.

'Captain James is in the hall, my lady,' Dickson went on. His face was guarded.

'Is anything wrong?'

'Couldn't say, my lady.' He got the horse moving again.

James and her father sat out of the slanting evening sunshine, beneath the gallery. James was not in his regimentals, but an old stuff coat he wore for hunting; he had laid aside his wig, which made him seem older and somehow diminished. His face was darkly flushed. A half empty brandy bottle stood before him on the table. Her father greeted Bell with some relief, she thought, and asked her to sit with them for a little, and tell them about her visit. James said nothing, beyond a word of greeting; he was preoccupied, until she said that the Gilliams had been on their way from Orchard Wyndham. Then he looked up sharply.

'Have they news?' he asked.

'It did not seem so. They are confident that His Majesty could land any day now, they told my Uncle Patten.'

'Are they so? Is Wyndham at home?'

'I'm sorry, James, I am not sure. They spoke of him, but –'

'Never mind. He's not in London, that's sure. No one with any sense is left in London.' He stood up, and strode to the window. He shouted, 'John, damn you, what are you doing? Get that animal out of sight!'

'Oh, but –' Bell began, but her father put a restraining hand on her knee, slightly shaking his head. When James went striding down the room out of earshot, he said softly 'Don't anger your brother, pigeon – he has troubles enough to think of. Shush.' James left the room, without so much as a glance of leave-taking. His father frowned. 'He is unmannerly,' he said, 'but he has excuses. He is cashiered – sacked from his regiment – he and all his brother officers loyal to the Cause, all insulted, disgraced. And his debts . . .' Sir Walter's eye strayed round the room, with a look of deep apprehension. He pulled his attention back to Bell. 'And his commander is gone – gone to France, he says.'

'Lord Ormonde?' Bell was breathless.

'Yes, girl, Ormonde. Never sound, I knew that, never sound at bottom – any man's fellow, no man's friend, Ormonde; all talk; no bottom. Poor lad.' He patted her knee again. 'Still, the Cause is not lost yet, never fear for that. The right will prevail. The landing will be in our own, loyal county.' He looked old, Bell thought, though he had not drunk so much as her brother; old and worried, the creases deepened around his eyes.

When she went to her room, hours later, she half expected Hope to be there; but she was not. So she would not see her tonight. She could not go seeking her from kitchen to stable, even with the house overset as it was by James's onslaught; and she would not send for her – like a servant. She sat in her window for an hour, looking out into the gathering dusk, her nerves set on edge by the swifts that screamed by, again and again, between the buildings. Then she went lonely to her bed.

Hope woke next morning feeling that perhaps it was not all quite so desperate after all. She had cried herself into a sick headache, and then at last to sleep, the night before, convinced that Bell was set upon a husband at the first opportunity, and took no thought for her at all. Now, as she breathed in the fresh morning light, she wondered if that was perhaps a little hasty. Bell is determined and independent, she thought, she would not take easily to being traded off as a wife, to sit in some city parlour and never see the woods or run in the meadows again. And she does like me. She let her mind dwell on their good times together – the talk, the laughter; May morning in the forest. She does. But she won't think about it; how could she understand what she wants? I am ahead of her, Hope thought. I have somehow to show her. She got up, and began to dress; her dusty petticoat reminded her of the scene in the road. Silly, she thought; then, I have behaved badly. She ran down the stairs.

She woke Bell with a tray of breakfast things; new milk, a hot roll in a cloth, fresh butter, golden plums, and three late roses, perfect white. Jacobite roses, she thought, mocking herself. They were a little stiff and shy together; but it did not last long. By the time Bell was dressed, they were laughing with relief. They spoke of James coming home – 'I hope he won't bother you,' Bell said.

'Oh no, surely he will have forgotten,' Hope replied. All that seemed very long ago.

'Yes, perhaps. And he has got things on his mind. I don't expect he'll stay long.'

'I'll be all right;' Hope said, 'I will tell you if there's anything. Now, I shall tidy up while you go and make your duty to your father.'

'I'll ask if we may go about the pups,' Bell said, from

the door.

She had not been gone more than a few moments when there was a sharp tap at the door, and Captain James, in full fig, regimental coat, boots and spurs and new-brushed wig, came striding in. He checked when he saw his sister was not there.

'Where is Mistress Isabella?' he snapped.

Hope did not know whether to face him brazenly, and trust to his preoccupations to have wiped out his memory of New Year, or to attempt to hide herself. On an impulse, she hung her head as if awkwardly shy. 'If you please, zur, gone down to My Lord.'

He began to go, but then turned back. 'Who are you? I don't know you, do I?' he came across the room. Hope backed obsequiously round the side of the bed.

'Speak up girl. I asked you' – he stopped, 'why, it's Amaryllis, as I'm alive! Well, well, well. So you found your way into the family after all – and I not home to welcome you. A thousand apologies, my dear.' He stood slapping his gloves into his left palm, ridiculously pleased with his notion that Hope was in pursuit of him. All his urgency about talking to Bell was put aside. He slid towards her round the end of the bed, backing her into a corner. Hope had a sudden vivid picture of the old dog fox that came after her mother's poultry, twitching his flea-bitten brush. The hen he gets is the hen that panics. She stretched her face into a foolish smile.

'Beg pardon zur, I mun go downstairs now, I be all finished up here.'

'Good,' he responded, 'then you may come and help me unpack – my room is all tumbled, as I left it when I arrived. Come, Amaryllis.'

Trapped against the wall, Hope pushed the simpleton act a step further, and flapped her hands at him, advancing as if confidentially. 'You are a wit, zur, begging your pardon. I know Mistress Johnson would never leave no gentleman's room in a pickle, to be sure!' She wriggled past him, giggling.

This was a mistake. It was obviously to his taste to seduce half-wits. He sidled across the room ahead of her, and put his hand on the door. 'Well, you must come and judge for yourself. I've a pretty present for you, from my travels – a very pretty thing indeed –'

Hope felt her contempt giving way to fury. He must think me a child, and still he wants – anger began to get the better of her pretence.

'Will you stand aside. I –' then the latch lifted under his hand, and Bell stepped into the room between them. There was a tiny pause, and then, before James could put in his word, Bell said swiftly, 'Thank you Hope, you may go,' and opened the door she still held behind her.

'Thank you, my lady,' said Hope. She made off laughing a little. In some things at least Bell was very decisive.

Over the next two weeks, however, it became increasingly difficult to escape so easily. Before she grew wary, Hope encountered James twice about the house, once having to take to her heels when he caught her in the corridor by the family bedrooms, and nearly had her trapped. She did not speak of it to Bell, but without speaking they began to take care they were as nearly as possible always together. It was no hardship. They went out for as much of the day as they could, whenever James seemed to be likely to hang about the house. This he did with increasing regularity. After a few days visiting friends in the neighbourhood, and a trip to Frome, he seemed to be at a loose end, with far fewer visitors than he usually brought home, and nothing to do. Quite unmistakably, he was looking for something to fill his time and distract his mind, and he took to stalking Hope.

When he cornered her again, drawing water at the pump, and laid hands on her boldly in broad daylight, she dropped the simpleton arid told him plainly that she did not welcome his attentions. This seemed only to sharpen his appetite; she began to feel nowhere was safe. He had obviously won Dolly over; she nudged and pinched Hope whenever he came in sight, and could not be relied on to stay with her when he came into the kitchen.

'What's the matter with you?' she demanded, 'is he not a well-made gentleman? Most girls in this village would give their teeth for him, I can tell you. Don't be such a ninny! I thought you had got over all that Puritan nonsense. He can make your fortune, girl! Think about that!'

Hope managed to keep clear of him until the middle of September, a gusty day when all the summer dust was laid at last by the first real rain, and the grateful smell of slaked earth was spiked with less pleasant stinks wakened by the wet in all the dirty corners of the house. Sir Walter had an attack of the rheumatics, and kept his room, grumpily demanding that Bell should read to him and sit by to plump his pillows. Hope found a job in the still-room, slicing the first apples to be set to dry. Eventually they came near the end of the third basket, and Mistress Johnson said, '.Just run down to the top barn, Hope, and check that there are no more – we might as well do them all in one.'

She was on her way back, empty-handed, when she encountered James. He had been out riding, despite the rain, and was spattered from head to toe; he had a healthier flush about him than his sallow face usually carried. He stopped her. with obvious relish.

'Amaryllis! Well met! You've been avoiding me, don't deny it – but here we are in the end. Come now, don't be coy. Come here.' And he simply seized her by the wrist, and pulled her into his arms. He was cold and muddy, but all too obviously eager. She struggled to free her face, to protest, and he caught her violently by the back hair and thrust his mouth on hers, all teeth and bristles. She tried to stamp on his foot, but could not find it. 'Would you, puss!' he exclaimed, pinioning her arms. She went limp for a moment and as he shifted for a footing brought her knee up with all her force. She was lucky. It connected. He staggered back, spitting curses, and she turned and ran.

Bell was with her father; nowhere in the house was really safe from James in an angry mood. Despite what her father had said, it would not do to go to Uncle Joshua. She would not risk being sent home. Excusing herself from Mistress Johnson, Hope went down to the clergy house, and spent the rest of the morning teaching little Charlotte to say her letters, and to throw straight, since that was what she asked to learn. She came back when the family would be at dinner. She was met at the kitchen door by Dolly.

'You've done it now!' she said, pulling her in. 'Whatever did you do to him? He's spitting nails! I said I didn't know where you were – where were you? Come in, it's pouring.' Dolly would not leave her be. It was more than her usual idle fuss; Hope suddenly realised, in the stream of chatter, that she had been set on by James. She had been bribed, no doubt. And when the chatter got round to John Dickson, and the cottage, it included a new element – they were to go in this very Michaelmas Day. Hope felt a chill in her stomach. Yesterday Dolly had not had any such promise; what had she done, or agreed to do, since then? She broke into her flow of words.

'It's raining hard – you'll be home tonight, I guess?'

'Oh no-not tonight. Dolly smiled at her, a foxy smile. 'I'm going up to the Moor tonight, with John, to see the cottage. We'll be staying with friends.'

Hope escaped from the kitchen before the family came from dinner, and went to Bell's room, trusting she would be allowed to come up while the men drank. Hope looked round at the now-familiar space they shared, the old hangings they had been mending, the chairs by the window – soon they would move them to the fire – Bell's ancient carved bed with its dusty hangings and worn white cover. She sat down-lay down, across it, reaching for Bell's comforting, exciting perfume in the folds of her pillow. She felt absurdly near to tears; she got up quickly, and lit a candle. It was nearly dark already; summer was over. The door opened and Bell came in.

'Are you all right? I wondered where you had hidden. Don't worry, I know about this morning.' She grimaced in distaste. 'Will you be safe tonight, Hope? Dolly will be with you?'

'Yes – but –'

'But what?'

'She's often out at night.'

'Can't you ask her specially?'

'No. She – he – she told me she won't he in.'

'James?'

'Yes. The promise of a cottage, so she can marry.' Hope tried to laugh. 'Real patronage, no mere ribbon for caps. He must be desperate.'

'He wants you – and he doesn't like you, any more.' Hope was surprised at her gravity. Bell went on, 'But he shan't get you. From now on you shall sleep here.' She ran across and pulled the curtains on the darkness and the wet. 'The cold nights are coming, Dolly is going off to her wedding – and you shall sleep with me.'

Bell woke in the early light. She felt warm and comfortable. As she surfaced she knew why: Hope's body lay all the length of hers, in her bed. Hope was still asleep, breathing evenly. With great care, Bell moved so that she could raise herself and look at Hope's face, peaceful and open, her plait loosening on the fringed pillow.

When she had thought of it last night, had asked Hope to sleep with her, she had felt a kind of relief, as if something inevitable had finally happened. It was almost as if James had done something for her that she could not do for herself. Hope had said nothing at first, just looked at her with a questioning intensity that made Bell suddenly nervous. She occasionally had this feeling when she was with Hope – a kind of fluttering tension; foolish, for there was nothing to be afraid of. To cover it, she said, 'Poor James! Climbing up to the dusty attic in his best wig!' and they both laughed.

They had whispered and giggled together as they undressed, exulting in his defeat. It had been fun, conspiratorial, climbing into bed and pulling the curtains, lying quiet to see if James would leave his room – she thought she had heard him, but they could not be sure. She would find out this morning, if he was angry: he would be bound to have worked out where Hope had gone. And they could do it every night: lie together and talk in whispers and laugh, and then curl up warmly to sleep. She thought, I never want to sleep on my own again. Hope opened her eyes and saw her looking, and they both smiled.

Hope was still tidying the room when Bell came back with the news.

'James has gone! A messenger came, in the night – it's Alistair, he's hurt in fighting in Oxford. Not badly, father said – he's at an inn on the London road – Norton – and James has gone with a horse for him, to fetch him home.'

Her father had been up and dressed when she had come down into the hall, stamping about in a high state of excitement and cursing the Hanoverian usurper and his brutal soldiery. A potboy on a coaching horse had arrived, well before it was light; now James was on his way to the Rose at Norton and would be back before night if Alistair was fit enough to ride. He seemed to think he was, since he had sent for a horse as well as for money to pay his lodging; how he had been hurt, and how badly, or how he came to be so near home, none of them knew.

They spent a miserable day indoors. By nightfall there was still no sign: Bell tried to stay up with her father, but eventually he sent her to her room, where Hope was waiting. When they were almost ready for bed, there was a clatter of hooves in the yard.

'He's here!' Bell rushed to the door, hair streaming, and downstairs in her nightgown, heedless of Hope's attempts to throw a shawl round her.

In the hall the fire was still burning brightly, and all the candles still alight. There was shouting in the yard, then James stamped in, bringing the cold and wet with him. Ignoring her, he peeled off his sodden coat and dropped it behind him, making straight for the fire. Behind came her father, holding Alistair up beside him. Bell was horrified; Alistair's face was a ghastly colour and he sagged sideways in his father's grasp, protecting his left arm. He had no cloak, and his wet clothes were filthy.

'Isabella, my dear, help me to get your brother's coat off.'

Alistair smiled at Bell, with what seemed an enormous effort. 'It's all right, don't look so grim. I'm just tired – too much excitement, eh? I expect if I'm not careful I'll be sick.'

The childhood reference did not comfort her. She took him from their father, helping him to the fire and lowering him tenderly into a chair. James made no move to help her.

'What is the injury?' she asked, tentatively taking his hand.

'It's all right now. It was my shoulder – put out of joint – but it was left for a day or two before I could get it seen to. God, Bell, it pained then! But it's better now; just needs nursing up.' The colour was completely drained from his face; he had dark, bruised marks around his eyes. All the time he was speaking he had been holding his hand to his left shoulder as if he feared his arm might drop off.

James snorted. 'You'll never make a soldier, Alistair. What a commotion! Get a pint of brandy inside you, man, shift into some dry clothes and let's be off.' He turned to their father and spoke urgently. 'There was news at the Rose: the landing is planned for three days' time. I must be there; and Alistair would do well to make the loyal welcome with me. God knows we need to stand well with the new king if Wiston is to he saved.'

Bell looked up sharply, aware of something that she did not understand. But her first concern was for her beloved brother. 'Alistair can go nowhere tonight, or for some time,' she announced firmly. 'I shall look after him. Help me take him upstairs, James.'

Alistair struggled to his feet. 'I'll ask no further help of you, brother,' he said coolly. 'I thank you for your assistance. Our sister is right, I fear: I shall go no further tonight, at any rate.' With an effort of will that hurt Bell to watch, he walked stiffly down the hall and, with painful slowness, mounted the gallery stairs. Bell picked up a candlestick and followed him.

By next morning, with James gone again, Alistair looked more normal. Washed and trimmed, wearing his familiar old blue suit, he seemed her dear Alistair again. All but the useless arm slung across his chest.

'It will mend, never fear. I need to exercise it, as soon as it's less tender. I can ride quite well without it; I must go soon, to Bath.' They were sitting in the hall alone; father had gone off to take his young hounds cubbing. He felt better doing his usual things, Bell thought. She was not sure what the matter was, but it seemed very serious. Alistair patted her knee.

'Don't look so glum. We are on the brink – very soon it will be resolved, one way or the other.'

'One way or the other? Are you not confident, then?'

'Oh yes, fairly confident. But power is in their hands, George is on the throne; possession is nine points of the law – we saw that at Oxford. Oxford is a whole city loyal to King James, right through – town and gown, everyone – but we were all overset by a battalion of horse soldiers. It was a lesson.' He looked away, out of the window, where the first handsful of yellow leaves were blowing in the yard. 'I got out by the skin of my teeth; many are in jail – and the Jacobite flag does not fly there any more.'

'How were you injured, Alistair? Was it in a great fight?'

He laughed, a little bitterly. 'No. I fell off a wall,' he said. 'I was fixing a garland that had been torn down by the soldiers, on the tower at Magdalen. There was a sudden shout that they were coming, I turned sharply – and fell off the college wall onto my shoulder. Lucky I did not break my foolish head. So then I was arrested, but there were dozens of us being herded, and I leapt out of the cart and hid in a ditch. Then I simply walked away, homewards, getting lifts from friendly carriers or farmers – once in a night-soil cart. By the time I got to the Rose I was done for. So I called for brother James.'

She took his hand, to show she did not despise him, and cast around to change the subject. 'Why do you go to Bath? James has gone to Plymouth.'

'There is a great muster at Bath, all the English volunteers and weaponry are gathering there, under Lord Lansdowne. It will be it brave sight'

'And James?'

'James thinks he will do best by bending the knee as the king steps ashore. Mayhap he is right. But I fear the king may not now come there at all. The government troops are so close upon us that it might be judged better for him to land in Scotland, where my lord the Earl of Mar has raised his standard in the Highlands. If so, then James may lose all on this last throw.' He grimaced, and gave a short, strangled laugh. As if to hide his face from her, he got up and went to stare out of the window. She went to stand beside him, careful to avoid his shoulder.

'What is it, Alistair? I have a right to know, do I not?'

He looked at her aside. 'Yes, sister, I think you do. Well, then. James is not only cashiered from his regiment, he has come home with disastrous debts: debts of honour, that he must pay, and that will cost us all we have, house and all, if we cannot find another way to pay them off. If he could have stayed with his regiment, he says, he could have set all right. But it seems to me that it was trying to right himself that way that led to most of the losses.'

'Losses? They are *gambling* debts?'

'Never look so amazed, poppet – all the officers game; many college men game. I am averse to it myself – there are better ways to employ the mind – but not for James. James is a gentleman to the core, and the eldest son. And so he has lost Wiston, unless he can get thousands of guineas, somehow, out of King James.'

She read the many layers of disappointment in his face and words. The loss of faith in his half-brother was not much – that had gone long ago – but the sense of his own helplessness, as a younger son, could still twist and gall him, when he thought now of the loss of their beloved Wiston. And the sullying of the Cause hurts him, she thought, the brave, chivalric fight for the rightful king turned into a mercenary gamble for favours and preferment. 'There's always Coldbatch,' she said, to comfort him.

'Yes, Castle Coldbatch! I had forgotten! We can go and roost like ravens in the northern hills! We could turn bandit – I always thought Castle Coldbatch sounded like a hold of pirates and desperadoes, up a mountain, preying on passers-by – your money or your life!' He poked her in the ribs with his good hand, laughing; then he took her hand, and led her to sit at the great table. September sun fell yellow across the notched and seamed oak, fissuring its dark golden shine with lines of shadow.

'Listen, Isabella. I said you should know, and so you should; you must be prepared. This is a part of it I had not thought of, but for you it is important. If the worst happens – any one of the various things that might be the worst – then remember Wiston is his, after father – the park, the farm, the woods, the house – all here is his; but Castle Coldbatch is yours. Not he nor his creditors can touch it, and nor can any attainder nor persecution for treason to the Hanoverian power. The house in Shropshire was left you in a legal settlement by your mother, from her mother, to be yours in perpetuity. You cannot be deprived of it. Let no one tell you otherwise, you understand?'

She nodded. He rapped the table, as if he had settled something, and sprang up as strongly as he could. 'But all will be well, you'll see. All will go swimmingly, once the king is come into his own again.'

Hope told herself she must put up with Bell's sudden and complete defection from her company to Alistair's. She knew Bell loved him – she had talked about him often enough – and here he was, looking like a ghost, his shoulder smashed and his high hopes of following their wonderful new king smashed with it, seemingly. Hope was struck by the likeness between him and Bell. Alistair's hair was a lighter brown and his complexion fairer than his sister's, but otherwise they were almost as alike as twins. They both had the same smiling brown eyes, so different from James' cold grey stare. Hope could not really resent the presence of someone who reminded her so strongly of Bell; she made herself as content as she could; after all, she had Bell to herself every night now. Sleeping together, she had to admit, was both pleasure and pain. Bell was innocently affectionate; but there were times when her closeness, the warmth of her body so near and yet so far, were almost beyond bearing, so that Hope must hold herself rigid, fists clenched, or pretend to fall asleep on the far edge of the bed. But she told herself that it was worth it; and one day, maybe there would be something more.

She spent the days helping Mistress Johnson to put up the last of the harvest of garden and orchard. Hope liked the housekeeper; a sensible woman. She told Hope confidentially that she thought there was something very much amiss.

'To do with Captain James,' she said, mysteriously. She plopped another pear into the pickle. 'A bad business. Money. Mark my words.'

Days passed, and Alistair began to mend. To Hope's experienced eye, the shoulder did not look badly hurt. She watched as he and his sister rode out in the bright autumn sun, and came back galloping and laughing like children. But within doors things were not so cheerful. Sir Walter seemed at first simply sunk in gloom, sitting alone in the hall drinking brandy most of the day; but after three days he grew restless, and rode out himself on a round of visits, and came home disgruntled to shout at Uncle Joshua and John Dickson. For though Michaelmas Day was come and gone, John was still about the stables, and Dolly in the kitchen. It seemed James had not come up to scratch with his promise about the cottage. Dolly was by turns truculent and spiteful.

'That Captain James! No gentleman, if you ask me! Poor Hope,' she said, spitting juicily on her smoothing iron. 'Poor you, led on by him. I warned you about his filthy promises.' Hope raised an eyebrow, but said nothing. Sir Walter raged round the house, eventually alighting on Benchley, dozing as usual in the kitchen, and demanded to know where were the family pikes.

'Pikes, Sir Walter?'

'Pikes, man, halberds – weapons, weapons. Used to be a great pile of them, from old Sir Wolfbane's time. Good strong stuff. Seek 'em out. But first bring me my pistols in the hall, and rags and sand and oil; get on man, what are you waiting for?'

Up in the hall, Bell watched her father repeatedly dismantle, clean and polish his ancient pistols, half as big as muskets, and get sand and oil all over the table and up his sleeves. She dared not say anything. Alistair, who would not sit with his father any more than he had to, went to his room pleading tiredness and his sore arm. In private he asked Bell to be dutiful to the old man.

'He sets my teeth on edge,' he confessed. 'Half the time he curses James to me, up hill and down dale, and in the next breath he is cursing me for criticising my brother. So I steer clear. But he's worried about the landing; so are we all. Over a week now, and no news.'

Alistair took his turn of duty after dinner, trying to moderate the black tempers induced in his father by an evening's port on top of a day's brandy. Bell fled to her chamber.

Hope saw that the day had left her tight-strung as a bow: she sprang into the room like a bent branch suddenly released, chattering like a starling about the Cause, and James, and the landing, and Alistair's everlasting shoulder. Hope made her slow down eventually, and sit to have her hair done. Then she fetched her a bowl of bread and milk – Bell did not seem to have eaten anything at the dinner table. Eventually they climbed into bed. Bell said, 'You are kind – thank you. I know I am being difficult.' She tossed restlessly, too tired for sleep. 'I feel all wrought up; I'm sorry.'

'Lie on your face,' Hope instructed, and began to rub her down like a horse, gently smoothing the muscles from her shoulders all down her back, again and again. She rarely allowed herself to touch Bell; and now she felt that she could not stop. It was like a miracle, the curve at the base of Bell's spine; even through her shift it had the most delicious beauty. Hope rubbed and smoothed, until she felt the tension begin to go out of Bell. Time to stop, for another kind of tension was rising in her own belly. Bell sighed and turned over in her arms. 'Thank you,' she said, 'lie down now.' And she reached up and pulled Hope down. For a second Hope was nearly lost; then, with an effort of will she pulled herself away and turned over as if to sleep, chiding herself for a fool.

When there had been no word for ten days, Bell came upstairs one night more than usually distraught, and said Alistair had promised father that he would ride to the Rose at Norton to seek for news. The traffic up and down the London road must surely include some Jacobite intelligencers. He was to go in the morning.

The next day was soft and clear, a morning like early summer, except for the yellow leaves drifting thickly now, and the slanting of the light. They sat in the window, attempting to sew the seams of a second gown for Hope. Even straight seams needed more concentration than Bell could command, Hope thought, as she watched her putting in stitches at random and stopping every few moments to gaze out of the window.

Suddenly Bell said, 'What's happening? Look – where's Joshua going?' Hope sprang to look down, as her uncle slammed in through the gate. They struggled to unlatch the window, but it was swollen and stuck, and before they could call out Uncle Joshua, moving faster than had ever been known, was down the yard and into the great door of the hall. They looked at each other in consternation.

'Could it be Alistair? An accident?' Bell said.

Hope reassured her, 'No, surely not, he must be at Norton by now, or nearly so.'

'What then?'

They were not left doubting long. Feet pounded up the back stair, and Dolly burst in, her eyes wild with relish of

101

the excitement.

'It's the dragoons! Pa says they've come for us! Upalong the Frome road, only a step. Sammy Hitchcock left his team standing in the furrow, came racing down. They're coming! Lord save us!' And before they could reply, there was the crash of the stableyard gate flung open again, and the clatter and trample of horses. They rushed to the window. At least ten men, all in scarlet and blue, two of them with the cocked hats and feathers of officers, were dismounting in the yard. At a word of command, half a dozen of them gathered behind one of the two officers, who advanced on the hall door. As he raised his fist to knock, it flew back, and there stood Sir Walter, a pistol in each hand.

Ten

'Sir Walter Wiston?' The officer's voice rang strongly round the yard.

'That is my name, Sir. Who are you?'

'Captain Wellow, Egerton's Dragoons, at your service. I have orders, Sir, to arrest you for high treason, in the name of King George.' He moved a step, but halted as Sir Walter jerked his pistols menacingly.

'King George be damned! No German pigfarmer is king in this country, and his hirelings do not command in this house. Get your filthy toad-eating mercenaries off my land, sir. Go!'

Captain Wellow did not seem to Bell to move; but one of his troopers, a small man with a long pitched pigtail down his back, brought his musket to the ready. There was a deafening explosion in the courtyard. The trooper fell. Smoke rose towards them from the pistol in Sir Walter's right hand. There was a second report. the other officer, a tall, blond man standing back with the soldiers who were holding the horses, had shot the second pistol out of her father's hand. He fell to his knees with a cry, and sank sideways on the cobbles. Chaos broke out.

'Father!' Bell exclaimed, and ran out of the room and down the stairs.

Hope stayed at the window to see Sir Walter sit up, putting his good hand to his head, and Bell fling herself out of the hall and fall on her knees beside him. The soldiers had gathered round their fallen comrade, except for two who flanked their officer, training their guns on Sir Walter – and now, on Bell. The blond officer, the one who had shot at Bell's father, shouted, 'How is he?' and a trooper looking up said, 'Gone, sir, I'm afraid.' Cursing, the officer turned on Sir Walter, but Captain Wellow put out a restraining hand, and he fell silent.

'Now then, Sir Walter Wiston,' Wellow said, 'do you

hear? You have killed this man. You cannot resist – it is foolish and wrong. Stand up, sir, and give me your weapon.'

Sir Walter growled, and shook his head, but whether in dissent or simply to clear it was not apparent. It was Bell's voice that replied, shaking only a little, a clear high note.

'My father cannot stand – your friend has disabled him. He is an old man, shot down on his own threshold. He is a Justice of the Peace. You will regret this. I must get help for him at once.'

'I'm sorry, madam,' said Wellow. He did not remove his hat, or change his stance when he spoke to her. 'I have orders. Your father is resisting arrest. He is in grave trouble.'

'Where are the sons?' The other officer's voice broke in, rougher and less restrained than Wellow's 'You, bitch, where are your brothers?'

'Ashburton! be quiet!' Wellow apologised again. 'We are in haste, madam. We have warrants for your father and for both your brothers, Captain James and Alistair Wiston, Esquire. Tell us where they are.'

'I will not,' said Bell, 'but this I will tell you – you will not find them here.'

'That is your last word? We shall find them, Miss Wiston. Come, be sensible. We will not leave without them, I assure you.'

'My father is in pain! Let me get help for him!' Bell bent and put her cheek to Sir Walter's, whispering comfort, Hope assumed. Ashburton spoke to Wellow, and started to order the troopers; two went out of the gates, and three entered the hall. Hope thought quickly. They would find no one; but they would wait, Wellow had said. Alistair would be back, all unaware, by nightfall. She picked up her shawl, and slipped away by the back stairs.

She went straight to the clergy-house, and by fortune found William just dismounting from his father's old mare. He took very little persuading that he could be a great hero at small risk.

'Ride!' Hope said, 'Remember – Norton, the Rose. Good luck!'

She slapped the horse, which whinnied and set off at a jerking canter up the lane. Hope shook her head. She would not give much for his chances of getting there; but she had done what she could. Now she could go back to Bell; at least, after she had told the Pattens what was happening. It took her longer almost than she could bear to get away from Mistress Patten's tirade of alarm and concern, but at last she was free and running back, clutching a remedy against shock that Mistress Patten had thrust upon her.

This was lucky. She rounded the corner to the gates, and ran into the arms of two troopers standing guard

'Now then – why, this is the girl that ran off! It was you, wasn't it? I saw you. You went to warn the young Wiston gents, didn't you? Where are they, eh? Speak up!' He twisted her arm.

Hope tried the simpleton again. 'Lord now, zur – Let go on me, do! I went for to go for to fetch this here!' She held up the green, corked bottle. He peered at it.

'What's this, then? Quickly!'

''Tis a sovereign remedy, zur – they keep it at the clergy-house, 'tis for all wounds and shocks, 'twill cure the poor young man, most like, and master too.'

'If you can cure Zeb, love, you'll be a famous witch and no mistake – he's dead meat, that one.' But he slacked his grip. 'Show us this stuff. Go on, Samuel, take the top off it.'

His mate uncorked the bottle, and sniffed gingerly. 'I dunno,' he said in the end, 'smells like rotted leaves, on a background of spirits.' He put it to his lips, then thought better of it, and put the cork in again, spitting.

'Right then – 'tis a country remedy,' the man who held Hope said, 'that's just what they do smell of. Waste of good spirits, it is.' He pushed Hope away. 'Go on, girl, take it to your master then. See if you can put some good sense into him.'

She slipped into the kitchen, avoiding the trooper at the hall door. Their fallen colleague had gone. There was blood on the cobbles. Aunt Cissy greeted her with slaps and scolding.

'Where ever have you been, hussy! We are all overset and put upon, here's twenty men ordering food and drink like they owned the place, beefsteaks and ale, if you please. You'll get no ale in this house, I told them, cider you might see, and now Benchley's broached the squire's best ten-gallon for them – such goings-on! – and Miss Bell that worried about you on top of her poor father –'

'She was worried about me? I must go up.'

'You'll stay and help us here, my girl, now you've come.' She thrust a half-peeled turnip into Bell's hands. Mistress Johnson intervened.

'She had better go and speak to my lord and Miss Wiston. They were concerned. I don't ask where you've been, lass,' she said to Hope, 'but I trust you can find means to tell them. They are eating a bite in my lord's chamber. The officer, Wellow, is with them. The other is in the hall, with all his men, all that are not stood round to guard us from the Lord knows what. Go now, quickly, and keep your wits about you.'

But Hope did not reach Sir Walter's room. As she turned into the bedroom corridor, his door – it was the one opposite the head of the hall stairs – opened, and two troopers came out, followed by Sir Walter, pale but upright and wearing his hat, and the officer Wellow. Bell followed them, down the stairs towards the hall. Hope inched forward to look down over the gallery.

In the hall the soldiers looked up from their dinner, but they did not rise. Sir Walter stopped on the second stair, looking bitterly at the scene of his dispossession. Bell crept to his side, and he put his arm round her. Hope saw that his hand was heavily bound up. His voice was shaky; she could scarcely hear him as he bade Bell

106

goodbye, and said, 'Wait here, my dear; I trust you to the honour of this gentleman.' He looked down the length of his own table to where Ashburton was sitting in his chair, already red-faced, a cider mug in hand. 'The honour of this gentleman,' he repeated in a louder tone, 'and to the protection of the laws.'

'Ensign Ashburton will look after Miss Wiston, Sir Walter. He will wait here until one or other of her brothers returns; after that, the authorities will decide what should be done here. Come now. We are saddled up. Let us go.'

Sir Walter kissed Bell, and walked away down the length of the hall, past the soldiery, never looking back. As the door closed on him, Bell turned and fled up the stairs, into Hope's arms. Hope hurried her away to her room.

For what seemed like hours, there was no comforting her. She had defied the soldiers, stood up for her father and fended off questions and accusations, denied that they knew anything about her brothers' whereabouts, for three solid hours; and now she wept and wept. But she eventually took comfort from Hope's message to Alistair.

'Maybe William will find him,' she said, 'There's a good chance, there's nowhere he can miss him on the Norton road. What will he do when he hears? Perhaps turn round and go straight to Bath. You were wonderful, to think of it so quickly and get away.'

They sat in the deepening gloom of the autumn evening. The singing of the troopers began to drift up the stairs to them; they were well into the ten-gallon cask, it seemed. At about eight, when they thought Alistair must surely be safe, there was the sound of boots in the corridor, and a loud knocking. Hope squeezed Bell's hand, and went to the door. A trooper stood there, leering, his coat open and his shirt spattered with food.

'She's wanted,' he said.

'What?' Hope tried to lessen the gap in the door, but

he stuck his foot into it.

'The little mistress. Ensign Ashburton wants her. Now.' When Hope did not move, he shouted past her, 'Shall I come and get you, missis?'

Bell was behind her. 'Come with me, Hope,' she said.

'No. You. On your own. My Lady. Ensign's orders, particular.'

Hope never knew how she got through the next hour. The trooper shut the door in her face and threatened to show her something she'd not forget if she poked her nose out; when she tried, five minutes later, he was still there. It seemed a lifetime before she heard running steps, and the door flew open, and Bell, her head up, her face the livid white of a corpse, plunged straight across the room. She sat down on the bed. The trooper thrust his head in after her and shouted, 'And count yourself very lucky, sweetheart, very lucky indeed,' before he slammed the door.

'Bell! What is it? Bell!' Hope put her arm round her mistress. She was as rigid as a board. 'Come now, tell me. Bell?'

Bell turned and buried her face in Hope's shoulder, and hugged her fiercely. They sat unmoving, not crying.

'I'm all right,' Bell said, 'all right.'

'Did they hurt you? What happened?'

'Questions. They are all drunk, the officer drunkest, or most cruel, I don't know. It was horrible. They – had hold of me . . . but they did not hurt me much.' She shifted herself uneasily against Hope's side.

Hope held her. She felt a sort of black wave of fury. She wished she were a man. She would go and . . . what? Killing, cruelty, their stupid Causes and convictions, drunken self-importance. She stroked Bell's hair. Bell put up her head, and smiled a little. 'I defied them. I told them nothing. And Alistair has not come – he will get away, to the king.'

Hope sighed. There was nothing she could say.

108

'Have they let you go, do you think?'

'I don't know. He just said I could go, in a fury. One of the men said – said they would all teach me to know my place. As a woman. He – the officer Ashburton – laughed, and said it would be his turn first, when the time came. But then he told me to go and think about it, till morning.' She looked apprehensively at the door. 'One of them might come, though. Or more than one. He is not a very good officer.' Her voice cleared a little at this observation.

Hope said, 'We must try to sleep, eventually. Shall we block the door with something? There's the table.'

'Oh, I have a key – in the drawer.' Bell got up and pulled out the deep drawer under her chest of winter clothes, and brought out a large key. It fitted the door, and could even be persuaded to turn. They held their breaths at its creaking, but there was no challenge from outside.

'I have never felt I needed it, and once when I was small it poked me in the eye, sticking out of the door, so I put it away.'

Hope smiled and took her hand, and they made themselves comfortable inside the safe tent of the bedcurtains, without actually undressing and getting into bed. After they had put out the candle, they lay listening. Hope stroked Bell's hair. At last all seemed quiet, and they drifted into sleep, exhausted.

They both woke abruptly. Bell clutched Hope. They were lying together, Bell's head on Hope's shoulder, her arm across her.

'Be quiet,' Hope breathed in her ear. Then it came again – a sharp, deliberate tapping at the window. And then in a low voice, 'Bell!'

She was on her feet and across the room. 'It's Alistair!'

He climbed over the sill, rustling the old ivy. 'At last. I thought I would never wake you.' He close the window and leant against the shutters, rubbing his shoulder. 'Tell me what's happened. I came back to the clergy-house when it was well dark, and they say they took father away. The place is crawling with damned dragoons – mostly dead drunk, fortunately. Hey, no crying – come now, little one.' He took his sister in his arms.

'I'm not crying, Alistair,' she said as composedly as she could. 'There is not much to tell besides what the Pattens will have said, I think – they have warrants for you and James, as well as father. They are waiting for one of you to come back. I have not told them anything at all. I'm so glad you've come!'

'What happened when they arrived?'

Bell flinched at the memory, and moved apart from him. 'Father – you know he had his pistols ready – he shot a soldier. Dead. It was terrible. And one of the officers – the one that is still here – shot him. Only his hand, but he is very shaken.'

Alistair pulled a face. 'That's bad. Very. I must go straight to Bath – I only came to show you I am safe, so you won't worry.'

'You are not going to leave us? Leave us here?' Bell could not stop herself from catching hold of him.

'You are safe, surely. They will go soon, when they find we are not returning, and you can manage with Mistress Johnson.'

'Oh please, Alistair, no – no I can't. We are not safe with them.'

'What?'

She turned away, unable to tell him. Hope's voice broke in from the darkness of the bed-curtains. 'The officer – Ensign Ashburton is his name – insulted my lady. They are drunken and rude, sir, as you truly said; on my honour, she is not safe here.'

'Hope?' Alistair peered across the room, and turned back to Bell. 'Bell, what did he – no! never mind.' He bared his teeth, and walked to and fro, returning to the window. 'Well then, we must both go.' He looked into the yard. Bell went to him, and he put his arm round her again. 'Look, there is no one at the stable door. Maybe some are asleep inside, but we won't know that until we go down. We must risk it, to get a horse for you. Put your things together, whatever you must have – must have, mind – and a change of linen. We will go to the Gilliams; they can provide what you will need for a few weeks.'

Bell said, 'Yes, straight away. And Hope must come, too.'

'Hope? Why?'

'What will happen to her when I am gone, Alistair? And I cannot go to Mistress Gilliam's fine house in Bath without a maid. I won't go without her.'

He looked at her in annoyance at what must have seemed to him a fit of the vapours; his look changed to a slight puzzlement as she faced him. He looked across at Hope, who was standing still, in the middle of the room. 'Very well, if you say so, pigeon,' he said gently, and Bell had to swallow hard, not to cry.

The soldier in the stable was so deeply and drunkenly asleep that he did not even wake when Bell's gelding called out to greet her. Before dawn, they were clear of the house, and on the road to Bath.

111

It was dusk of the next day before they crested the final hill, and looked down on the city. They came to a creaking stop; Hope raised her head with an effort and stared. The city filled a long hollow in the hills, from brink to brink of a great pewter-coloured river that curled in a three-quarter circle round its walls. Only a few buildings straggled up the hill to meet them on the nearest bank. In the midst of the circle was a great church, its tower etched black on the slate grey sky. Around it, like a monstrous barnyard for a farm the size of the whole county, a multitude of thatches were piled. They stood at every angle and at many different heights and slopes, in rows, off at odd corners, and tumbled or stacked one upon another; right up to the walls of the church itself they crouched and shouldered for space. Here and there a large slate roof floated amongst them, smooth as a pond. The evening mist was thickening in the valley, pricked in a thousand places by the city's lights.

'Bath. And safety,' said Alistair, with satisfaction. He shook his reins, and the old bay stirred again into the jolting, patient, agonizing rhythm that had tortured Hope for nineteen of the twenty hours they had spent on horseback. It had never occurred to her that riding would be painful; she felt as if she had been beaten all over, and only will-power was holding her upright. She looked back, and Bell smiled encouragingly for the thousandth time that day; but even she was drooping in her saddle, and her little gelding's head was low as he followed obediently down the steep and darkening road.

They passed unremarked across a beaten road of stone – the Bristol turnpike, Alistair said – and over the river by a stone bridge. Passing through a great gateway they came into a narrow, closebuilt street, awash with a stinking slurry more like the slime of a pigsty than the ordinary mud of a road. In spite of the lateness of the day, and the gathering dark, it was filled with dozens of people. Women in shawls hurried through the mud extraordinarily fast on high pattens, avoiding the groups of fashionable gentlemen who stalked along the clearest pathways, by the shopfronts and house doors, talking and laughing loudly. Pairs of men in matching coats trotted by, carrying tall upright boxes slung on poles. Hope stared down on their greasy hats. She was too tired and miserable to wonder what was in the boxes. The strange, unpleasant smell brought a sharp slime into her throat. Housefronts swayed by; the buildings seemed to close in until she was staring point-blank at the carved and painted symbols over their doors – she could have reached out and touched a golden loaf, or carried away the pestle from a silver mortar. Through a haze of pain and tiredness she stared up into lighted rooms where ladies sat only a few feet away, and drank tea, oblivious of their passing. The street opened out, and they passed in front of a huge building, as big as a church, or as the house at Wiston, but unlike either of them: it was barricaded behind tall white pillars, and scores of people in silk and powder were crowding up the steps towards the doors.

Their horses splashed through a running ditch, turned yet another corner, and came at last to a stop. It seemed to be the end of the city, if not the end of the world. Hope could make out nothing but shapeless piles of wood and masonry, scattered about in a sea of mud. In front of them was a row of three houses – at least, she could see three doors, with strange half round canopies hanging over them, and huge glass windows on either side. They were built of a white stone that glared unnaturally in the light flooding from the windows of the central house; the rooms within seemed to be crammed with people.

Alistair lifted her down. Servants tumbled out to meet them, taking the horses, ushering Alistair and Bell away; and in only a few minutes Hope was sitting in the

114

Gilliams' kitchen. Where there was a great deal going on: servants – as many as at Wiston, in a room only the size of their second scullery – were whisking out and in with tinkling trays of food and glasses and great open serving dishes, running like goats up and down a steep flight of stairs. No-one took any notice of Hope, until the footman who had led her in came back. He was a man of about Eli's age, but slighter, and with a perpetual grin and a cast in his left eye. He wore a plum-coloured coat which still smelled of its dye, and a wig as big as any gentleman's – almost as big as Mr Gilliam's own, thought Hope with a spurt of amusement, recalling that day at the clergy house.

'Your lady wants you,' he said. 'Bring a chamber jug – over there.' He watched, making no move to help, as she dipped the painted ewer into a bucket, and looked for a clean place on her skirt to wipe it. She was suddenly aware of what she must look like: she was covered in mud, and still wearing her cloak. The serving-man was watching her curiously; she set her jaw and headed for the stairs. He left her at a little door, white-painted like the rest of this extraordinary house of whipped eggs and sugar. They had climbed at least six flights of steep stairs, or so it seemed to Hope's aching legs and back.

Bell was sitting on a little bed, in the centre of a pretty little room, looking tired and lost. She sprang up and rushed to hold Hope, hugging her as if she would never let go.

'Are you all right?' she said, 'I missed you so – all that way, and then they sent you off into the kitchen! I thought I should die! Alistair doesn't understand how much I need you, and I don't think Mrs Gilliam does either; she looked quite surprised when I asked where you were. But you are to sleep here, at any rate. They're short of beds, with all these people and their servants in the house, so I think it was quite convenient, even though she did expect you to sleep in the attic with the other maids. I tried to explain to her that you are more like a friend than a servant to me,' she frowned, 'but I could see she thought me odd.'

Hope's heart sank. Living in a strange house was going to be difficult. She felt too exhausted from the journey to think clearly about what Bell was saying. She said carefully, 'What else can I be but your servant, Bell? While we are here I think we must try to do as others do.' Seeing the look of panic on Bell's face, she added reassuringly, 'Except when we are alone, of course. Then we can be friends, as we always are.'

Bell's face cleared. 'And we will look after each other,' she said, taking Hope's hand. 'Look at you! Staggering on your feet! Poor Hope, I must be your maid servant and help you to bed. Come on and get that cloak and dress off – you're wet through.'

Too tired to protest, Hope let herself be treated like a child, scolded, taken care of.

'I kept looking at you bouncing up and down on that horrible pad-saddle – it's the one with the broken rib that sticks up, isn't it? I told father to throw it away ages ago, I didn't even know it was still in the tack-room until Alistair brought it out as we were saddling up, and there was no time to go back. I can't imagine where he found it.' She dropped the muddy cloak in a corner by the door. 'Did you ever ride at all, before?' She ran back to Hope. 'Come on, undo your laces, I want to take this bodice off you. It's stuck all down your back with mud. Come over here, by the fire. Isn't this fireplace tiny? It's like a toy house, don't you think? At least it's not very cold tonight. You can wrap up in one of the blankets.' She dumped Hope's bodice and petticoats on top of the cloak. Feeling ridiculous in her crumpled shift, Hope went to sit down on the tiny stool by the little fire. She winced at the effort of letting herself down so low, and then stood up smartly: her backside was too sore for a wooden stool. Bell came back to her.

'You're bruised, aren't you? Come on, let me see – did you bring warm water? Come on, Hope, show me. Lie down on the bed.' She dragged Hope to the little bedstead, pearly white, like everything else, with little flimsy curtains painted in a little pattern all over. Hope fell on the counterpane in confusion, and buried her face; she fought with herself not to resist as Bell stripped up her shift, and the air hit her thighs and buttocks.

Bell gasped. 'Oh, you poor thing – the bruises are dreadful, and blackening already – and you've got broken skin, here, and here.' Her fingers brushed Hope's inner thighs. Hope gritted her teeth to stop herself crying out. Bell pulled down the shift and bustled away.

'I think I've got arnica paste, it was on my table, for my sprained thumb, do you remember? Mistress Johnson gave it to me weeks ago. Here it is.' She dropped her dressing bag on the floor, and came back to the bed. She lifted the shift again, and began to smooth in the paste.

Conflicting sensations raged through Hope: the bliss of Bell touching her; the miserable certainty that she would not do it if she shared any of Hope's feelings at all; and the sheer agony in her backside. It was too much; she bit into the counterpane to stop herself from crying, and prayed to be released.

Twelve

Bell quickly grew used to conversing with flirtatious Irish officers and fending off the drunken self-importance of her brother James's regimental friends – there were politenesses her father had never dreamed of. She realised that Charles Gilliam, whose attentions had so oppressed her when they first met, was equally gallant to all ladies; she learned to enjoy his outrageous compliments without taking them seriously.

The company was mixed: several Scots, dressed in strange chequered trousers, came regularly, and sometimes a quiet, intense Frenchman whom her cousin Gilliam whispered to her was a Jesuit priest. Soon after they arrived Mrs Gilliam gave a party to which the priest and several other Frenchmen came, especially to entertain Mr Pope, who was a poet. Her aunt gave Bell his latest poem to read beforehand; it was very amusing in a cruel kind of way, all about a fashionable girl whose lover stole a lock of her hair. She expected the poet to be a great wit, and very handsome. But he was a disappointment. Tiny and bent, all dressed in black, he looked like a rumpled starling, talking incessantly about himself and darting his eyes about the room to see who was looking at him. He did not speak to her at all. Hearing Alistair was at Oxford, he asked him a question in Latin, and curled his lip and turned away when Alistair answered in plain English. He refused to play cards, and seemed to grow more and more ill at ease; when Aunt Gilliam tried to talk to him about the Cause he affected a wish to listen to the music. He left early. But Mrs Gilliam was undeterred; the next night more relays of Jacobites and potential recruits crowded her rooms, eager to listen to the exciting story of the Wistons' escape and to drink to the success of the Cause.

Far from finding that she and Bell shared a special secret life together, Hope felt that they were being pulled inevitably apart. She sat for hours in their little room, waiting for Bell's return from one expedition or another. Bell was always eager to describe her new experiences, whether of shops or coffee houses, walks or visits; far from comforting Hope, these excited descriptions simply made her more aware of all that she could not share.

Their only real time together was when they were in bed, and for a precious hour of quiet in the early morning, before the town household was awake. Hope would creep down to the kitchen at first light, collect a handful of fresh rolls from the delivery basket that stood outside the back door, and draw a jug of cider. But on the tenth morning of their stay she returned to find Mrs Gilliam stationed at Bell's bedside, wrapped in a scarlet bedgown and looking very pasty in the face.

'Here's your maid come back. Good heavens, girl, what have you brought?' She peered into the jug and sniffed. 'Cider? I didn't know there was any in the house.' She smiled indulgently at them both and patted Bell's cheek. 'Bless its innocence! what country ways! Is that what gives you that fresh complexion, child? Perhaps I should try the cider cure myself! But come, you must not breakfast yet – your girl can drink the cider – you must go with me to the Bath.'

'The bath, madam?' Bell looked perplexed.

'The Cross Bath – I go regularly for my rheumatism, and it will help to recover you from the dreadful shocks you have suffered, and that desperate ride. I am Pumped most days; but you may just sit a little in the water and look around you.' She rose to her feet and smiled down at Bell. 'At least in the Bath you need not feel conscious of your clothes! Really, I did not know where to look when Lady Cecilia was quizzing your gown last night. My dressmaker will be here later today, to make over some of my old gowns for you – just for the time being. They are not of the latest fashion, but they are at least of this century!' Pausing at the door, she continued briskly, 'Up now, my dear, and change your shift. I'll fetch you a cloak, and you'll get a bathing dress when we arrive. The chairs are waiting, so bustle!' She swept out.

Bell looked desperately at Hope, but Hope only said, 'Bustle!' and snorted with laughter.

A little over two hours later Bell, dishevelled and more than a little damp, climbed out of the chair which had brought her home and hurried into the hall. She stood sniffing – the pungent fumes of the hot baths had made her nose run – and shivering in her damp clothes. Mrs Gilliam, a sulphurous-smelling mound of sodden linen, bore down on her.

'Do not stand still, my dear, you will be chilled. Susan will give you dry towels' – pushing Bell ahead of her up the first flight of stairs – 'and then you must go straight to bed. Cover yourself up and stay there until you have sweated. You may sleep – I often do after the Bath – and then send your girl for your chocolate.'

Bell seized the towels offered by Mrs Gilliam's maid and escaped up the next flight to her room. She hesitated for a moment outside the door, wishing, for the first time since Hope had come to live with her, that she could be alone – that she did not, just this once, have to tell Hope the adventures of the morning – at least until she had had time to order her own thoughts about what had happened. But almost immediately the door was opened and Hope, no doubt primed in her role by the household, appeared to take her in, like a bundle of wet washing.

Bell spoke with an effort. 'Mrs Gilliam says I'm to get into bed again.'

'Why? are you ill?' Hope reached out a concerned hand.

'No, but I'm still wet.' Avoiding Hope's touch, Bell hurried across the room and slipped between the sheets. There she struggled out of her wet shift, dropping it on the floor and pulling the covers up to her chin. Without looking at Hope she said brightly, 'Would you like to

121

hear about the Bath? It is quite unlike anything. Had you ever heard of it before?'

Hope shook her head. 'Tell me.' She came to sit on the side of the bed.

Bell moved her legs very slightly, so that Hope was not touching her, and plunged on. 'I felt so stupid! I knew there were baths here, of course, for the sick, to cure diseases, you know? But I didn't realise they were – well – fashionable places. The bath was full of ladies and gentlemen, all swimming about and talking to each other as if they were at a – a ball or an assembly; but with hardly any clothes! It was so strange . . .'

Hope burst out, 'You took your clothes off? Bell, you did not do such a thing!'

Bell giggled, freed from her own restraint by the comical expression of outrage on her friend's face. 'No, of course not. But you know I only went out in my shift, and Aunt Gilliam's cloak. The bathwoman takes the cloak and puts you into a big stiff linen dress, like a great bag, to hide you, and so you go into the water.' She did not add that as the bathing dress soaked up the warm water it clung to the bodies of the bathers in a way that made her blush and look away, so that she had gone all the time with her legs bent and only her head protruding from the steamy surface. 'The steam is quite thick, especially on a cold day like this, and it smells like . . . well, rather like a bad egg. And the steam is yellow. You need a handkerchief – I had to borrow one from Aunt Gilliam, but most of the ladies had the things they needed on the prettiest little trays floating along in front of them. And they had the most elaborate caps and hats on, as if they were in the street!'

Hope's face was a picture: curiosity at war with disapproval. Curiosity won. 'What did it feel like? Were you frightened?'

Bell thought of their arrival in the stone courtyard, of the greasy familiarity of the bathing woman, and of her first sight of the enormous Cross Bath, surrounded by curtained arches and full of heads. She had been so frightened that Mrs Gilliam had had to pull her down the steps into the water. But now she said, 'A little, at first; but one soon becomes accustomed, you know.'

'Well, I think it sounds like the Infernal Pit of Hell,' said Hope. 'All smoke and lewdness. What did you do?'

For a minute Bell felt a dreadful urge to invent all manner of witty conversations and handsome gentlemen, but she said honestly, 'I sat in one of the little alcoves and watched, and hung on.'

'Hung on? Was it deep?'

'No, but there were springs – if you walk about, they can hit you and knock you over. And they're hot – I stood on one and it was really hot – scalding. The ladies and gentlemen laughed at each other, when the springs caught them, and the gentlemen swam about. The ladies all had bathing dresses on, like mine, but the gentlemen didn't ...' She could feel Hope's frozen expression without looking at her, but she couldn't stop. 'They dived down under the water and they were ...' picking at the bedspread '... rude,' she finished lamely. Then hurriedly, 'But not to me; no-one took any notice of me, even when Mrs Gilliam went to have her legs pumped.'

'Pumped?'

'Yes. They pump the hot water over the parts that hurt. One old man had his head pumped – he looked like a dog in a stream.'

'And no-one talked to you at all?' insisted Hope jealously, 'and you didn't talk to them?'

'No,' said Bell, 'I just ... listened.' She shivered suddenly, and pulled the covers more tightly round her. Then, abruptly, 'I think I want to go to sleep, now. I'll ring when I need you.' She did not have to look at Hope to see the hurt bewilderment in her face, but she was desperate suddenly to be alone. She wriggled down in the bed and turned her face to the wall. After a while she heard Hope go out.

Why had she not told Hope the whole story? She tried to push the picture away, but it would not go. From her little alcove at the side of the great pool she had watched faces and bodies appear and disappear in the clouds of steam. A pretty young woman, not very much older than herself, with fair curls escaping from an exquisite lace cap, waded towards her. She seemed oblivious to the way in which her wet dress clung to her breasts; she waved merrily to her acquaintances and seemed known to everyone in the baths. Bell wondered what it must be like to be so fashionable and so confident. Was she a married lady? If so, what did her husband think about her being seen by everyone like this? Another woman approached; taller than the first, with a striking face and dark, mischievous eyes; she was a friend, for she embraced the fair one, kissing her on the lips, and taking her arm led her away from the crowd towards Bell's retreat. They came nearer, the second woman talking animatedly.

'. . . the most dreadful scandal, my dear – she will be denied all respectable society. You cannot imagine what she said to Lady Mary! She said, if her husband can go to bed with the maidservants and be thought a fine fellow by all society, why should she not do the same with her own maid! By all accounts it had been going on under his nose for months, and would have gone on who knows how long, had he not found them together –'

Her friend gasped incredulously. 'Not –'

'I assure you! in the act of pleasure, no less! and she sat up in the bed and told him the wench had given her more pleasure in an hour than he had in seven years.'

The fair-haired girl put her hands over her mouth, half laughing, half scandalised. 'How could she? Oh, my dear, whatever next? She has done all her sex a disservice as well as herself. All virtuous friendship between women' – she twinkled up at her friend – 'is cast under the most vile suspicion by such a scandal.'

The dark eyes twinkled back. 'It is indeed,' she said solemnly. 'And it behoves us ladies of reputation to

124

behave with the utmost discretion.' As she spoke, she drew her fingers lightly down her friend's throat, and – just as lightly – traced the outline of her breast. Bell, fascinated, could not look away. She could still see those laughing eyes, that caressing hand . . . She tossed feverishly in the bed, trying to shake off the woman's mocking gaze. As Mrs Gilliam had promised, she had begun to sweat; she felt as if she were suffocating.

She turned on her back and tried to lie quietly. Think of something else – something cool, and pleasant – she made a picture of the woods at Wiston; green grass, young leaves against a blue March sky . . . and suddenly there was Hope, as Bell had seen her on the day she killed the rabbit: strong, and beautiful, her face flushed, legs bare and strong . . . and then, unbidden, the memory of her own hands on those legs, the night they arrived, as she tended Hope's bruises . . . No, she would not think of that, either. The mocking dark eyes were laughing at her again. 'Denied all respectable society,' Bell heard her say, '. . . with her own maid . . .' Bell struggled to get back to the wood, the the cool green glade, and suddenly she was stumbling again over the threshing bodies of the couple in the grass on May morning; seeing again the white legs and heaving buttocks, hearing the grunts and cries . . . 'The very act of pleasure, I assure you,' said the woman at the baths, laughing gently . . . 'all virtuous friendship between women is cast under the most vile suspicion . . .'

'No, no!' Bell cried out loud. And suddenly was wide awake, staring at the white plaster ceiling.

Thirteen

Hope had told herself that Bell was tired, and still upset about her father; that everything would be better again when they were rested. But as the days went past things grew worse, not better, and a cold fear settled on Hope as she felt Bell being drawn further and further from her. Mrs Gilliam's dressmaker came, and the next day Bell was able to walk out on her brother's arm to take the air and visit the assembly-rooms dressed in ridiculously sumptuous clothes. Hope thought wryly of her own mother's objections to second-hand finery. In her new loneliness, amidst people she had not known two weeks before, it was painful to remember home and those she had left behind. When Alistair sent a messenger to Wiston Bassett about some secret or other, she got the man to take her parents a note from her, saying she was safe. After that she tried not to think about them; but Bell, for whom she had given up her family and her home, seemed suddenly a hundred miles away: shy of being alone with her, frightened of her touch. She lay in their bed rigid as a board; she talked brightly all the time about the wonders of the chocolate houses – chocolate was a dreadful brown sludge that tasted of burnt sugar, in Hope's opinion – and was trying out a strange new way of speaking, that she had picked up all in the first few days.

'La, my dear,' she said to Hope one morning, 'it is *so ennuyant* to sit moping, when one might be so vastly entertained abroad!' And she tripped off, in another of the reach-me-down dresses, all crimson velvet and fine lace, to walk in Harrison's Gardens. She would come back with reports of the civilities of Mr Gilliam's fine friends, and the splendours of the Jacobite officers, all of whom Hope would cheerfully have murdered.

The Jacobites were everywhere in the town, as Hope soon learned from kitchen talk. Their men were quartered in every inn, and the officers were entertained by all the sympathising houses; two hundred horses, for cavalry as well as draft, were grazing in quiet spots in the surrounding countryside. Mrs Gilliam's house was a centre of their operations and planning – though what planning could be done at two in the morning over the whist table was more than they could tell her. Evans, the squinting footman, was inclined to try to impress her with his knowingness about Sir William, and the King, but when she said to him 'So what is Mrs Gilliam doing, then, Mr Evans? She cannot be going to lead a platoon into battle?' he would only tap the side of his nose and hiss through his teeth as if he were grooming a horse.

Eventually Hope worked out for herself what Mrs Gilliam had to offer to the King and his Cause. It was her money. Day after day she entertained the cashiered and clandestine officers royally, and, as Hope discovered one day when a dray appeared in the back lane laden with mysterious boxes, she had filled the cellar of the Trim Street house with weaponry. Some of the household were troubled about this. Two Frenchmen came with the dray-load of guns, to supervise the unloading and storage, and Mr Evans had sharp words with them. Hope learned that Mr Gilliam had said he would not have the foreign weapons in the house; but, as usual, his mother had won.

At least, thought Hope, the guns were hidden. Anyone watching the house would have found more to suspect in the constant procession of strangers who called at all hours of the day and night, some for no more than a hot meal and a warm at the kitchen fire, others to stay for days and leave in a hurry at the arrival of some hastily-passed message. Evans purported to distrust them all, though Hope thought it more likely that he was afraid for his own safety. 'Papists and French spies is bad enough,' he hissed at her one morning as they passed on the narrow stairs, 'without Scottish ruffians filling the place with their filthy tobacco smoke! I'm surprised Mr Gilliam hasn't given orders to lock up the cutlery and plate.'

She found the cause of his outrage smoking peacefully by the kitchen fire. He was one of the biggest men she had ever seen, taller than Jack the smith at home and at least as heavy. The stem of his short black pipe was buried in a bushy fox-coloured beard. Hope wished him good morning, and asked if she could bring him anything to eat or drink. He took the pipe out of his mouth and smiled at her.

'That's a bonny greeting for a tired traveller,' he said. 'and a bonny lass that gives it. There's little enough hospitality in this flat green country, and none at all on the roads I mun take.'

She brought the bread and cider and watched him demolish it with enthusiastic appetite. 'Have you journeyed all the way from Scotland?' she asked.

He looked at her sharply, but seemingly decided there was no ulterior motive to her question. 'Nay, lassie, but it's where I'm bound, God willing, with a message for milord the Earl of Mar, from his friends across the water.'

'You've been to France?'

He winked, but gave no other answer. Even Hope knew that Bath did not lie on any reasonable road from France to Scotland; the highlander's mission was one more half-guessed mystery in the chaotic web of Jacobite affairs.

It was another week before they had news of Sir Walter. Every day Alistair would come home full of rumours and conflicting stories: about the arrests that had been taking place up and down the county, the news that their M.P. Sir William was fled to France, or raising an army in the south of the country, or arrested and put in the Tower; Ormonde was returned, or he was drowned in the Channel, or even, once, that his loyal officers, including Captain James, had gone to join him in France. There were more certain reports of dragoons quartered in half the great houses west of Shaftesbury. Then Bell came upstairs to their room one day after

Alistair had left, suddenly solemn, her new cap of that morning forgotten, to say that her father was reported to be locked up in Dover castle with other Jacobite gentlemen, awaiting trial.

'But he will be tried for killing the soldier,' she said, 'as well as for sedition, like them; Alistair says he is in great peril.' She sat on their bed, and looked to Hope. Hope put out her hands, and Bell took them; and when Hope moved to sit beside her and held her, for once she did not move away.

'He will be brave, and so must you,' Hope said. It sounded very lame, but she could not think about the old man; the chance of really holding Bell, after a week in which she had been kept at arm's length from her even in their little bed at night, took up all her attention.

'Alistair says that the king may not land in the west country after all, now – now so many people have been arrested,' Bell said, and she moved into Hope's side, under her sheltering arm. 'The northern counties, and Scotland, are full of loyal gentlemen – he is already proclaimed at Braemar. So he will probably land in the North. But there is still Bath, and Bristol too; we are safe here, and when he is king, he will quickly free all the prisoners, Alistair says.'

'Good,' said Hope, reaching up to stroke her hair. But Bell got up suddenly, and went to sit at the little toilette table by the window.

It was as if an invisible curtain separated them. Bell was out almost all the day, and even when Hope was taken along too, she found herself walking a step behind, watching Bell dance chattering and laughing beside Mrs Gilliam from shop to shop, admiring stuffs and silk ribbons and buying silly bits and pieces, for ever curtseying and smiling at one of Alistair's grand new friends, or taking the proffered arm of 'cousin Gilliam,' met all-too-casually walking abroad, at leisure in the middle of the day.

'I am not making eyes at him!' Bell's eyes flashed as she said it, and she turned away to take off her cloak and look at herself in the glass that now stood in their room. 'Don't be so vulgar, Hope! Try to grow up, please! I have to be polite to my aunt's acquaintances, don't I? And Mr Gilliam is betrothed, as good as, to Lady Mary Chandler. Ask your friend in the kitchen, who tells you everything. I'm sure he knows all about it. Aunt Gilliam says all servants gossip shamefully about their betters!'

Before Hope could react, Bell swung round, her hands up to cover her mouth. 'Oh Hope, I'm sorry! Forgive me! I wasn't thinking what I was saying.'

Hope felt as if Bell had struck her. She stared, speechless, as Bell stumbled on. 'It makes me so angry when you suspect me of flirting all the time. I don't mean to flirt, I really don't – I just try to behave as everyone expects; normally. I know it's harder for you, not knowing anyone. I'm sorry. Please? Come and sit down with me, and let's talk, like we used to. Don't be cross, Hope; we must both learn the ways of the world!'

Hope followed her wordlessly. They sat on the windowseat, their backs against the shutters on either side, and looked down into the deeply-rutted road. There were no houses across the way; this was the edge of the city, even beyond the old walls, and their view was of a forlorn, muddy field, and brown-leaved trees on the hills beyond, beginning to be combed bare by the winter winds. The only building in sight was a delapidated barn, in which, Evans said, Mrs Gilliam's wondrous travelling coach was kept. Hope watched Bell's soft curls move against the film of white lace over her shoulders, and tried to hold back the bitter words that threatened to choke her; Bell's eyes were on the hills and it was impossible to know what she was thinking. At last she looked at Hope.

'I am truly sorry. Forgive me?' and she held out her hand. Before Hope could take it, the door opened and Mrs Gilliam came in. Bell leapt from the window seat and ran towards her.

'Ah, there you are, child. Not walking with your brother this morning? I have been busy – I am sorry to leave you without diversion. But my business should please you. I have been planning a ball! We shall hold a great celebration ball. It will be a brilliant affair, all the loyal ladies and gentlemen will be there – you may meet some eligible company at last. You must have a new dress, of course; it's a pity your family jewels are at Wiston, but we must see what your credit will do with the trumpery-merchants here.' Once again she caught Bell up in the whirlwind of her busy energy, and whisked her out of Hope's reach.

This great event was to take place within a week; it seemed to Hope, when the servants discussed it, that the Jacobites were desperate to show how unconcerned and confident they were, despite the net that was tightening around them. Perhaps it was all intended simply to confuse their enemies, and give the impression that the brilliant crowds who were lingering so late in the season in the streets of Bath, instead of dispersing to their own country houses, were merely enjoying the social pleasures of the place. If that was so, though, surely they should have invited others besides their own party to their ball?

Bell disappeared into a frenzy of shopping. Her ball-dress, in yellow damask over an embroidered petticoat, was made up at home, the dressmaker sitting in the housekeeper's room day after day, and Bell required for fittings almost hourly; other tradespeople, with shoes and stockings and trims and laces, came to visit and parade their wares before her. The lace merchants especially seemed to come in secret, and to have no ordinary servants or craftspeople with them. 'That stuff's seen a lot of places you never looked at, my girl,' said Evans to Hope, tapping his nose. 'French lace, that is. Least said . . . .' So Mrs Gilliam bought from smugglers, as well as being a Jacobite herself. Bell seemed perfectly unconcerned, and would not discuss it; Hope saw less and less of her. Mrs Gilliam's maid had discovered the depths of Hope's ignorance, and now she rapidly edged her aside. Unlike Mistress Johnson, she was not prepared to teach the mysteries of her trade. 'I can't think why Miss Wiston keeps you about her,' she said briskly, 'I could find her a pretty, alert, well-trained, discreet girl, who would be twice the use you are, in every street in this town. Fresh country ways! Slatternliness, I call it; clumsy and slow. Get out of the way, girl. Go and talk to Evans – I expect you're fit to amuse a man, if nothing else, and he's in a fine fury this morning.'

Evans was put out, Hope found. He had been collecting intelligence for Mr Gilliam, and discovered that the cities of Bath and Bristol were now completely isolated in a countryside pacified by Hanoverian forces.

'It's only a matter of time,' he said gloomily. 'They'll be here, mark my words. Any day. And our Mr Gilliam knows it. He told me to get them guns moved out – but Mistress won't have it. We sent half of them off to the other end of town, yesterday night; but the rest's still here. The French ones, they are, too. Very dangerous, if you want my opinion. Very dangerous indeed.'

In the room that Hope shared with Bell, the ball intruded itself everywhere: new yellow dancing shoes, silk stockings with silver clocks, a lace fan, and the wonderful dress itself, hanging like a pale fat ghost in its protective muslin wrapper. By the day of the ball, Hope felt stifled by it all, and tried to lose herself in work, tidying the room and making the bed with unnecessary vigour, punishing the furniture for Bell's faithlessness. 'Vanity of vanities,' muttered Hope in her mother's voice, pulling up the coverlet with violence. 'All is vanity,' she added, punching the pillows. 'And the Ungodly flourish' – she aimed a vicious kick at the small embroidered footstool which Bell had recently acquired – 'like the green bay tree!'

She supposed that Bell would come in soon to have her hair done and to be dressed for the ball. Grief and rage washed over her. What in the name of all that was good was she doing in this hateful place, which had taken Bell away from her and given her nothing in return? She thought of Ruth, in the Bible, who had left her home and all she knew, and followed Naomi into the loneliness of a foreign land. Hope had loved the story from the first day that Anticipation Liddell had told it to her, before Hope could read. Had Ruth felt this lonely and cut off from joy, as she gleaned in the rich man's field? Probably it had all been worth while for her, thought Hope bitterly, because Naomi loved her. And I thought Bell would love me, but now I see she can't. Hope sank down, defeated, on the window seat, and gazed without seeing at the wintry afternoon. It wasn't as if she wanted Ruth's happy ending, ridiculous rich Boaz to come and marry her. All she wanted was Bell. She could have made herself content with so little: a smile, a touch, a sudden hug when Bell was happy . . .

Suddenly Bell was at the door. 'Oh, Hope, Mrs Gilliam says Susan must do my hair for the ball; she can dress it *a la mode*, you know, like a French lady's. Wait for me,' and she was gone again.

It was the last straw. Doing Bell's hair was Hope's private joy, the one intimate contact which had not been taken from her in this horrible house – until now. She shook with jealous fury – against Mrs Gilliam, against Susan, against the whole city of Bath. How could Bell do it? How could she let that vulgar, conceited Susan touch her? Hope picked up the footstool and hurled it across the room. Then she threw herself down on the bed in a rage of tears.

'Hope? Are you asleep? See what they have done to me!' It was Bell's voice, half excited, half apprehensive. Hope pulled herself up. For a second she did not recognise the person in the dressing gown leaning over her. Her hair was pulled tightly back from her face, and swept up behind, with extraordinary little sausage curls at the sides of her head. And they had powdered her – all Bell's beautiful brown hair was powdered to a ghostly silver. Hope stared at her with horror.

'Mrs Gilliam says I look vastly well,' said Bell, a little uncertainly, 'but it does feel strange. What do you think?' She twirled round to show Hope the back view.

'You look,' said Hope with an effort, 'like . . . a lady of fashion.'

'But do you like it?' Bell persisted hopefully.

Hope's control broke. 'What does it matter if I like it? Why ask me? What do I know about fashion? Nothing! not even enough to do your hair!' She heard her voice rising, but she could not stop. 'Ask someone who knows! Ask Mr Gilliam – or one of the Jacobite officers who look at you as if they want to eat you up! Let them turn you into a puppet with white hair if you want' – she was shouting now – 'but don't ask me to like it, because I can't!'

There was silence. They did not look at each other. Bell moved away and picked up the silk stockings. She drew them on, one after the other. Then she fitted on the yellow shoes. Eventually she said in a small voice, 'Will you help me to dress now, please?'

She already had on her stays and under-petticoats; in silence, Hope helped her put on the primrose silk dress, lacing the tight bodice and arranging the silvery lace at the neck and sleeves. Bell surveyed herself solemnly in the glass, and then turned round to be judged. She did not say anything, but her eyes pleaded.

Hope stared. Bell looked beautiful. All silver and gold, like the princess in a fairy tale. Hope wanted to reach out and touch, but a spell held her back. It was as if the real Bell, the girl she had held in her arms on May morning, had been spirited away, and a beautiful doll put in her place. The silence was unbearable.

Finally Hope shrugged, and said roughly, 'I'm sure you'll be the toast of the evening. For myself, I preferred you in green. But I suppose you would rather forget those days.'

She turned away to hide her face.

Bell followed her. 'Hope? Please? What is it? Why are

you being so unkind? Have I hurt you? What have I done? I didn't know that you –'

Hope turned on her, blazing, 'Oh yes. That's it exactly, You didn't know! Of course not. Why should you? You're far too busy to know how I feel. You've been behaving like someone I don't know. Now you look like someone I don't know. You hardly speak to me, except to say nonsense. You haven't touched me for a week,' her voice shook, 'and you ask me why I'm unhappy?'

She was crying now, tears running freely down her face, but she couldn't stop. 'I'm unhappy because I love you, Bell, and I want you; and if you don't love me, I think I want to die.'

Bell reached out, wordlessly, to take her hand, and Hope snatched it away. 'Don't touch me!' she shouted, 'I can't bear it. Go away! Go to the stupid ball and dance, and – do whatever people do at balls, and leave me alone. I'll go back to Wiston and get out of your way and you need not think about me any more!' She sat down suddenly on the bed, exhausted.

When Bell spoke, she sounded puzzled and frightened. She said slowly, 'Hope, 1 don't know why this is happening. Of course I love you, you know that. But you can't expect me not to – to see people, or talk to them. It's very unkind – hurtful – of you to say I don't care for you, because I do; but I have to live in the world, and so do you. I don't understand what you want –'

Hope looked up at her. 'Oh, yes, you do,' she said deliberately. Her voice was quite calm. She had gone too far now to go back. 'You know very well that I love you more than anything else in the whole world. And you know how much I want you, but you pretend you don't, because it is more than you can give. And I don't think,' she said simply, 'that I can bear it any more.'

Time stopped. Bell stood like a statue in the pale gold dress, her eyes wide with shock. Neither of them spoke Then Bell bit her lip, took her silk skirts in shaking hands, and left the room.

Fourteen

Hope sat in the corner of the kitchen, almost in the dark. The room was warm and full of rich smells, griddle-cakes and toasted cheese, and the round red smell of malmsey wine. She felt sick. Ball nights were party nights in the city house; they had told her: the family expected the household to be awake and ready to serve when they came home in the small hours, but the rest of the night was your own. Hope would not go to the chilly little bedroom and sit alone. Better to look on, at least, at ordinary life and laughter, the sly kisses and the cheerful insults of people at ease with each other, at home in their world. She swallowed the rest of her third glass of the warm, sweet wine.

Stiff with misery, Bell climbed out of the camphorated stuffiness of the chair amidst a silky throng on the steps of the Town Hall. She was propelled along in the crush, hanging on to Mrs Gilliam's arm, into a huge, low room lit up with a thousand flaring candles. Music struck up as they entered – for them, she realised with horror, in honour of Mrs Gilliam as patroness of the ball. The squirming wall of human backs and shoulders parted before them, and they walked the length of the room to the accompaniment of genteel applause from white-gloved hands, flickering before her downcast eyes like huge angry moths. Dazed with the assault on her senses, Bell found herself taken in hand by a wizened old man in a monstrous flaxen wig and led out into line for the first of the formal dances of the ball. As she curtsied to him, wobbling at the knees, she had a sudden vivid memory of her dream of dancing – dancing in a ballroom like this one, with a mysterious figure in green. Warmth, closeness . . . how long ago that was, and very far away. As the vision shut off in her head, she saw quite clearly that the figure in green was Hope. Stunned, she began to pace the pattern, to and fro like a mechanical doll, in the tiny space between the two next ladies.

Hope was almost asleep, her private tears unnoticed. No one had hauled her out into the firelight, laughing and mocking; someone had refilled her glass, more than once, and she had watched the fire, or the faces, or the dark depths of her wine, while they laughed and ate, and eventually settled down comfortably and began to take turns to sing. Evans was singing now, a high, pure tenor like a trickle of clear water; even when Hope listened, she could make nothing of the words, but the thin line of melody filled her eyes with self-pitying emotion.

There was a sudden, short knock at the kitchen door. Evans broke off. Before they could move, the door opened enough to admit a man, muffled in a cloak, followed by a second and a third, who shut it quickly but quietly behind them. The leader stepped into the firelight and spoke.

'We are friends – this is Mrs Gilliam's house? We have come for muskets. There will be others behind us. Quickly!' He reached out an arm urgently as if to take what he wanted. 'They are coming – there is a regiment of dragoons only two miles off on the London turnpike. If we do not resist them now, the Cause is lost.'

Bell had so looked forward to the ball, and now it was like ashes in her mouth. A dizzying procession of gallants swept up to her or passed her by, their shrieking voices dinning nonsense in her ears, their ruffled hands pawing her, their trussed-up bodies pushing mercilessly close. She felt bruised all over. She could not breathe: powdered hair and wigs and faces sent up a fine choking dust that hung in the heat under the close ceiling like a cloud; below it the air was tainted with scents and musks, starch and sweat. The interminable formal dances finally ended in a brief battle for ices, during which Bell's yellow silk had been splashed with some unnameable brown stain. Alistair, over-excited and pleased with himself in his new pink satin coat, sporting the Jacobite favour made in white ribbon, promised her that the second half would be more fun:

'Country dances – and you may choose your own partners. Who shall I bring to you? Or have you already made up your list, eh? You look lovely, sister. Quite the lady of fashion, on my word; I feel quite proud.' And he had kissed her hand and whisked away again, called to talk to a group of young men all in huge white favours, standing by the door. Looking after him, she saw the set of his shoulders change as the men greeted and spoke to him; and as she turned to her partner, the whole group left the room.

It was some time later, as she danced a second time with Mr Shrubsole, Cousin Gilliam's rather plump, dull friend, that she realised with some relief that the noise had dropped, and the crush was lessening. Taking hands to cross the set she looked past the dancers, and saw that there were indeed fewer people – at least, there were far fewer men. The walls were lined with ladies alone or talking in groups – there was a large party by the door – with only one or two gentlemen among them. The dancing set contained almost all the remaining couples in the room. She skipped obediently under her partner's arm, and saw that the other side of the room was the same. And there was not a single white favour on any coat. There was only one person she knew in the room – Cousin Gilliam, standing shifting from foot to foot. He looked very grim; and his immaculate and discreet burgundy satin, with the pale blue facing and matched brocade waistcoat, was innocent of any white ribbon. Yet earlier on, she was sure, he had been wearing a small and elegant favour. As the set ended, he came over and took her hand, brushing Shrubsole aside with hardly a word.

'Come my dear, I must take you home now,' he said.

'Where are Mrs Gilliam and Alistair?' Bell said to him,

startled and frightened; but he only smiled and took her by the elbow, leading her to the door through a room that was suddenly very quiet.

Hope swept up the shavings from the fourth box of guns and put them on the back of the fire. The stream of men, increasingly frightened and aggressive, had lasted a couple of hours, and then stopped quite suddenly; she had thought she heard firing, some way off, but she could not be sure. There were five muskets cleaned and waiting on the table, where the remains of the kitchen party had been hurriedly swept aside. Most of the household, in various states of nerves, had gone off upstairs, though not to sleep, judging by the occasional thumps and slamming of doors that drifted down. The huge Highlander – Hamish, he was called – had been inclined at first to rush off to the fight, but had decided to guard the arsenal. He stood like a tree outside the back door, musket primed and charged and at the ready. Two of the three footmen were very drunk, and Evans was in an uncertain state which Hope suspected was not so much drink as funk. As she sat down, he staggered into the room, shouldering the door aside, with another ammunition box in his arms.

'This is the last of the bullets,' he said, crashing it down next to the guns, 'Typical French. Plenty of pretty muskets – oh yes, very helpful – and no bullets. So who needs bullets? Bloody shambles. I don't mind betting –'

Theres was a thunderous knocking; not the kitchen door, but at the front. The doorbell rang.

'They're here!' Evans clutched a musket, then dropped it, and took a step towards the back door; but the knocking stopped, and they both heard in the distance Mrs Gilliam's voice, shouting to be let in. Evans pulled down his waistcoat and straightened his wig, and went plunging up the stairs.

As her lurching chair splashed through the ditch and rounded the corner into Trim Street, Bell saw to her astonishment that their quietly muddy backwater was full of swinging lights and running men; a coach – Mrs Gilliam's travelling coach – stood at their front door, its floorboards heaped against the back wheel. On the front steps stood Mrs Gilliam herself, her blazing ball gown extinguished by a brown holland apron, her piled-up hair collapsed on her shoulders and thrust behind her ears. She was supervising the loading of the coach. She called out as soon as she saw Bell, 'Well done, my dear – came off safe, eh? What an end to your first ball! No you, that man – Solomon – butts to the back, this layer, butts to the back. Where is Charles? On his way? I told him to get you away quietly when there was a chance. With luck there'll be the tail end of an innocent dance in progress at the Town Hall by the time Major General Wade gets there, and no-one of consequence left for him to try his teeth on.' She was helping Bell out of the chair; the chairmen smiled at what she said, and at her evident high humour – one even gestured with a jerk of his head and a raised eyebrow to ask if his help was needed. She sent them away with ready money, and a kind word. Bell marvelled at her. She had never seen her aunt so composed and cheerful – she made more fuss over ordering four dishes of chocolate or buying a yard of ribbon.

'Major-General Wade, Madam?' Bell asked, lifting her skirts and avoiding the human chain that came and went through the front door.

'The troops, my dear, the Hanoverian hounds. They are on their way, indeed, they are upon us. I have firm reports that they have taken all the eastward side of the city, and are working their way from house to house. The cache of arms Charles insisted should go over to Mr Arrowsmith's is no doubt in their hands already. We must give up Bath, and avoid further bloodshed. The better part of valour, my dear – live to fight another day. The king will be here in person within the month. We have but to wait.' She seemed serenely sure of King James still; Bell, shivering in the night air – what time

141

was it that she had left the ball? – wondered whether her aunt was right, or whether she might not be a little mad. As if to answer her thought, Mrs Gilliam said, 'There is no call, however, to hand over these good French guns, that cost me a mint of money, as my son delights to point out. They shall go to the North, and help with the decisive landing there.'

As if on the mention of his name Charles Gilliam appeared, stepping into the circle of flickering torchlight. His pale blue breeches and white stockings were covered in muddy splashes; his face was livid. He ran up the steps, and seized his mother's arm.

'What in the name of God is happening here? Mother?'

'Hush, Charles. Come inside. Come, Isabella.' Mrs Gilliam led them away indoors, where all the lamps were already burning in both front parlours. 'As you see, I am loading the guns. I assume you do not want them to be found in your cellars?' Mrs Gilliam confronted her son with a look of self-confidence and, Bell thought, not a little contempt. He scowled, and started to speak, and then, stopping, began to pace about and brush distractedly at his spattered clothes with his handkerchief. His mother went on, 'I shall take them to the North. The muster is in Lancashire.'

His hands dropped to his sides in astonishment, and he gaped at her, finally gulping out, 'Take them? Take them? You? Oh no. No, mother, this is too much. I positively decline to explain to the king's officers that my mother, a notorious Jacobite, has happened to take a trip to Lancashire on this beautiful November night. You shall not go. You would be caught. It would be the ruin of me – of us both.' There was a moment's pause. 'We would lose everything.' He stepped forward, and took her arm, cutting off Bell with his shoulder. He continued in an intense, creaking voice, in which the fashionable drawl and the tortured vowels had completely melted away. 'You understand me, mother. All we have is from my father's business, and my

142

profession. We are not aristocrats, not Wistons – forgive me, Miss Wiston – we are not born to the station we hold. If cash and credit, business credit, are gone, then we are nothing. Come, mother, think.'

He smiled a craven, desperate little smile; Bell looked from his face to Mrs Gilliam's, frozen into dark gullies, it seemed, behind the smudged mask of her paint and powder.

'What would you have left to offer to the Cause, mother?' Bell thought Mrs Gilliam might strike him; but she only turned to look out of the window. Bell followed her eyes; the men, obviously well instructed, had replaced the floor, and were beginning to load quilts and cushions and baskets of provisions into the passenger part of the coach.

'Very well,' said Mrs Gilliam, in a voice of deadly calm, 'very well. I will stay and help you talk to the king's officers. But you agree that the guns should go?'

'Yes of course. As soon as possible.'

'And what about our guests?' She swung back, taking Bell's arm, and fixing her son with a cold stare. 'What would you have me do with these same Wistons, whose nobility is not impaired by their lack of credit, political skill or financial good fortune? Turn them out in the street? I see the second embarrassing personage on his way here now – no doubt having redoubled the reasons why the king's officers would like to arrest him.'

Bell looked out. It was true – Alistair was bounding up the steps. He burst through the front door, and into the room. His face was ashen; wordlessly, he ran across and took Bell in his arms. He was shaking; she thought, perhaps, with tears.

Mrs Gilliam moved decisively. 'Come, Alistair Wiston, come – are you unhurt? Then all is by no means lost, as you seem to suppose. You shall go to meet your King – come, there is no time to waste.' She took him firmly by the shoulders, and steered them both across the room, still clutched together. From the door she looked back and said, 'Charles, I am sure, will speed you on your way.' Gilliam did not respond. Mrs Gilliam halted. 'Come, Charles, the strong box.' Then to Bell and Alistair, 'We have a hundred guineas in gold, on the premises, waiting to help convey you and the guns to your rightful destination – and to secure our business credit.'

There was a dead pause. Then Charles pushed past them and went into his library.

As they mounted the stairs, leaving Mrs Gilliam waiting to receive the money from him, Bell said, 'Alistair – Alistair, I may come too, mayn't I?'

'What?' He looked bewildered; she wondered what had happened to him in the three hours since he left the ball. Urgently, she went on, taking control. 'I shall come. It would seem suspicious for a young man to travel alone in a huge coach – I must come, to ward off prying eyes. Alistair!' She grasped his arms and faced him. He weakly shook his head; his eyes were blank. 'Alistair, listen. You are to go to Lancashire. That means travelling up through Shropshire. I will come with you, and I will stop at Castle Coldbatch. That will be best. You can go on with the guns from there, only a short way, and in friendly country. Wouldn't that be best? Listen to me, Alistair! I don't want to stay here any more. Take me to my mother's house.'

Alistair smiled now, a wan, helpless smile. 'Whatever you say, sister. I always said it would come to this. We'll go to Castle Coldbatch.'

They were in Alistair's room when Mrs Gilliam caught up with them. Having settled the coach and the cash, she came up to see to the passengers. She took in the situation with characteristic efficiency.

'I'll help your brother to pack,' she said firmly to Bell, 'while you go and put up your own things.' She looked searchingly into Bell's face for a moment, and seemed satisfied with what she saw. She put out a hand and touched Bell's arm.

'You are a good girl, Isabel Wiston, and a strong one. This kingdom is in the hands of such as you. God bless

144

you, and see you safe to the end of your journey.' Then she turned her attention to Alistair.

Was it true, Bell wondered? She did not feel at all strong. When her father was shot; when she had had to face the drunken soldiers; when Alistair needed her, then she had somehow found strength to carry her through. But now, as she climbed the dark stairs, her mind raced in terror, as if in a bad dream. Those same Hanoverian troops were here now, in the town; something dreadful had happened to Alistair, she felt sure, that he was not telling her; and behind these new troubles, the memory of her conversation with Hope that afternoon, pressing down on her like a great weight. With an effort, she pushed down the rising fear, and opened the chamber door.

Hope was not there. The room was lit only by the dying fire. Panic threatened to overwhelm her. Forcing herself to stay calm, she lit the candles on her dressing table, then slowly took off her now-crumpled ball gown and put on the plain, warm habit she had worn on the ride from Wiston. She laid the sparkling necklace carefully in its box. Still Hope had not come. Where could she be? Bell began to move agitatedly about the room, picking up and putting down articles of clothing, trying to keep her mind on the needs of the coming journey. It was no good; she could not think of it. She threw down the pair of stockings she was rolling, and started back down stairs.

Lights were still burning in the parlour; none of the household had gone to bed. Charles Gilliam was nowhere to be seen; the servants, intent on their own urgent errands, hardly seemed to notice Bell. Hope was not in the parlour, nor in the cold breakfast-room, nor in the library.

Bell tried not to think about their conversation before the ball; surely Hope had not really meant what she said about going away? The bad dream was turning into a nightmare; opening doors in a strange house, looking

145

for someone who was not there. Fear knotted her stomach; Hope's words drummed in her head. 'I'll go back to Wiston and get out of your way . . .' Surely she had not gone? Already? Please, thought Bell, please don't let it be true . . . By the time she descended to the kitchen, she was running and slipping on the stairs.

Bell had never been in Mrs Gilliam's kitchen before, and she hesitated for a moment at the door, peering nervously into the darkness. The small, high basement windows were just greying with the dawn; a long scrubbed table stretched palely away down the length of the room. At the far end of it, outlined by the glow of the dying fire, stood Hope. She had her back to Bell, shoulders hunched, looking into the embers. Relief flooded through Bell, followed almost at once by a new tension. She hurried forward, words spilling out of her: she hardly knew what she was saying.

'The soldiers are in the town, Hope – they could be here at once – we have to go. Mrs Gilliam has asked us, Alistair and me, to go north – to take the guns. We have to pack up and go, now, tonight, so as to get away before it is light –' she stopped. This was not what she wanted to say. Hope had turned at the sound of her voice, but she did not speak. Her face was in shadow, and Bell could not see her expression. She tried again, and the effort to keep her voice steady made her sound calmer than she felt.

'I have nowhere else to go now, you see. Except Castle Coldbatch, my mother's house. It is a very long way from here, and from . . . home. I know that you want to go –' She saw Hope flinch, and forced herself on, 'to go back, to Wiston, to your family, and I . . . understand why. And I have no right to ask you to come with me any further. So will you just help me pack, now, please, and then . . .' her voice faltered '. . . and then you can . . . go away.'

She stopped, appalled. Hope made a little noise, neither a cry nor a gasp, but something between, as if she had been struck. Still she did not speak. Bell could not

146

look at her 'What have I done? she thought. What have I done? Tears pricked her eyes, and a terrible sense of loss enveloped her. The silence lengthened between them, and Bell did not know how to break it.

It was Hope who spoke. She said, 'Is that your wish, then?' The violence in her voice was like a blow. Bell struggled to find words – anything that would stop the dreadful thing that was happening – but none came.

When Hope spoke again her voice was cold and deliberate. She said, 'As you wish, my lady.' Head down, she pushed past Bell and made for the door.

'No!' The cry was forced from Bell, 'No, please! Hope, don't – I didn't mean –'

Hope turned. Bell could see her face now, in the pale light: she looked exhausted, and Bell could see she had been crying. When she spoke, her voice too sounded weary. She said, 'What did you mean, then, my lady? What do you want? Let us have truth between us, Bell, if we have nothing else.'

Bell hid her face in her hands. Hope's voice went on, more gently.

'You have been deaf and blind ever since we came to this evil city. I lost you the day we came here – I see that now – but it seems to me sometimes that you lost yourself, too. What do you want, Bell? Is this the manners of Bath speaking to me again, or is it your own true voice? Tell me that this is your heart's wish, that I go away, and I will not question you again, but will do as you say. But tell me truly, Bell. What do you want?'

Bell was crying in earnest, now, the tears running between her fingers. She felt frightened and confused, unable or unwilling to answer, even to think. Hope stood silent, waiting. Nothing moved.

Suddenly, outside the kitchen window, a robin sang out its greeting to the winter dawn. In the dark back yard, under the looming shadow of the city wall, it piped its song of woods and fields and grass.

Bell thought, the robin still speaks in its own true

voice; it has not lost itself in this place, as I have. She looked up at Hope. Her dear, familiar face was drawn and pale, the eyes dark-ringed. I have done this, Bell thought. I have hurt her because I have been afraid. I have sent her away. And I cannot live without her.

She found she was shaking, and when she spoke her voice shook too. 'My heart's desire,' she said simply, 'is . . . you.'

Hope woke with a jolt. They had stopped. It was broad day; light filtered in through the little glass windows. She felt strange, lightheaded. She wondered how long she had slept. Bell, still asleep, lay wrapped in a quilt on the opposite seat of the coach, her hair coming loose and flecked with last night's powder.

Hope felt a great surge of love and happiness. She wanted to lean over and kiss the parted lips. Bell loved her: nothing else mattered. As they had rattled out of the city in the dawn light, she had looked into Bell's eyes and seen that it was true. And something else, too. Under Hope's gaze, Bell had flushed pink as a rose and looked away, with a sudden shyness that made Hope catch her breath.

She felt a great love for the world in general. Not only her beloved, but the ribbed cushion on which she slept, the arm rests and the nets and bundles and contrivances around, the very door handles of the amazing travelling coach, were outlined for Hope in a brilliant glow. The whole world glittered intensely with the bright light of loving Isabella.

Outside was a dense, yellowish fog. She lowered the window a crack, and there came in the most extraordinary sound: a powerful, sinuous swoosh and rattle, as if a giant were deliberately swirling dried peas round a pot as big as England. Then in the next breath, Hope took in a second marvel. The fog was not simply dank; it smelt; of sooty smoke, and fish, and – pickles? Vinegar? Or – no – it smelt of brine. That was it. Brine. Salt. Then she realised: we are by the sea.

But where? As far as Hope understood the hurried discussion outside Mrs Gilliam's house, the road east towards London was impassable, picketed by troops, and their only chance was to get away west and then north, and risk being pursued and overtaken, or finding the city of Bristol held against them. The breakneck drive through the dawn had been a nightmare, but they seemed to have been lucky – so far. Hope felt at this moment as if good fortune was theirs by right. She was here, alone, with Isabella – what could go wrong?

As it turned out, a hundred things could go wrong. For one thing, they seemed to be at a dead stop. She let the window right down, and stuck her head out. She could see a few yards of cobbles. Ahead, Hamish was standing by the leaders, hands in pockets, smoking comfortably.

'Hamish? Where are we?' she called.

He turned his head slowly, and slowly took the stub of a pipe into his hand. 'Orrst,' he said, and replaced the pipe in the invisible gap in his great red beard and whiskers.

'Are we by the sea?' she persisted.

He gazed past her for a moment, then spoke through clenched teeth, not deigning to shift his pipe for her again. 'Aye,' he said.

'Hope – where are we?' Bell wriggled up beside her to look out, then hurriedly pulled Hope back into the carriage. 'Who's that?' she hissed, 'Where's Alistair?'

'It's all right,' said Hope, 'It's Hamish – don't you remember? He's to be our coachman. He's on his way back to Scotland, from taking a message to France for his Lord.'

'Oh.' Bell sat down and pushed at her dangling hair. 'And where does he say we are?'

'Orrst,' said Hope. 'That's all he would say – 'Orrst.' Let me braid your hair.'

They remained at 'Orrst' by the sea for several hours. Alistair returned quite quickly. Hope was struck by how drawn and haggard he looked, his pale skin yellowed, his cheeks hollow and bristly, all the lines of his face sucked downwards, as if he were suppressing pain. She wondered if there was yet worse news of the Cause, more than he had told them. He had brought the ferryman, a ragged individual scowling and wiping his hand across his mouth. He stuck his hands in his pockets when he saw the coach and its four great horses, walked round it once, and shook his head.

'Never,' he said, 'Never get that thing on my ferry. Sink us all, young gentleman. No. Can't do it. Begging your pardon. No.'

'But surely –?' Alistair put his hand ostentatiously in his pocket, but the ferryman still shook his head.

Only thing,' he began, and paused; he touched his forelock as he took the coin Alistair offered. 'Only thing, I'd say, is get down to the Winkle House, and find a barge. Barge captains get in there, see – coalmen. They'm big boats, they barges. Take that rig, no trouble, iffen there was one empty. No trouble, young sir; thank you kindly.' He faded back into the fog.

Loading the coach onto a coal barge was no easy matter. Bell shivered with impatience as she stood beside Hope on the blackened, stinking timbers of the wharf. The men took so long over everything: Alistair twitching his knees and jangling his guineas, the bargee pulling ferocious faces and barking at the workmen, the mountainous man Hamish silently communing with his horses. She looked away, out into the evil-smelling fog. She must not think about the soldiers, riding, grimfaced, clattering, closing in on them moment by moment.

There was a crash and a shout. The coach had slipped out of one of its leather slings, and was dangling lopsided over the ship's deck, its shafts dragging on the stones of the bank. Three men threshed and swore as they laboured to haul the unnaturally heavy vehicle, with its hidden bellyful of guns, the final foot onto the slimy planks of the ship. Their master leapt on deck, hitting out with a rope's-end; they heaved the coach aboard by main force.

The horses were next. Alistair's mount, an ugly, rawboned beast from the Jacobite cavalry levies, curled its lips and rolled it eyes, and backed and reared away. Bell gripped Hope's arm in desperation as the man led it away and round again. At last Hamish took the bridle from the wharfinger. He passed his hands over the frightened horse's eyes, and seemed to whisper or blow in its ear; in a moment its panic drained away, and it walked quietly down onto the deck. Bell hurried down the shaking plank. The ship moved alarmingly as she stepped on it, as if the sea were a live thing pressing up under her feet; but she scrambled forward, only concerned to get away. She stood at the rail, gazing out along the riverside behind them, through the fog. It was thinning, she realised, swirling away in a faintly rising breeze. Away to the right stretched the endless, shifting surface of the sea, a moving grey ground marbled with black oil and pale curling lines of foam. A new creaking began, and she turned to see a great blood-red sail rising up the mast beyond the coach. It slapped, and filled with wind; a rope stretched tight and rose out of the water ahead of her; a barelegged boy ran up and flipped it free. The world heaved and slewed in front of her eyes; they were away at last. The line of the wharf slipped into the ragged fog, and soon there was nothing but grey sea, foamed with the line of their barge's motion. Even the dragoons could not follow that vanishing trail, Bell thought, staring until the bank faded completely from sight.

'Come inside, Bella,' said Hope quietly, taking her by the arm. They ducked under a roughened white rope and squeezed into the cabin. Along one wall was a shelf on which a palliasse and a grimy blanket made a comfortless bed. An unlit lamp swinging over a table and a single chair completed the furnishings. Everywhere there was a layer of blueblack grime – dusty in the corners, polished to a dark shine where it met hands and shoulders. There was a sharp metallic smell, overlaid with herrings and hard cheese.

Bell looked round and made a face. 'How long will the crossing take, do you think?' she asked, but Hope, who was trying hard to keep her feet against the dip and slide of the cabin floor, only shrugged helplessly. Neither of them had more than the haziest idea of what their journey entailed, or how far they had to travel. Somehow it didn't seem to matter much, Bell thought, looking out at the waves through the tiny barred window. She felt suddenly detached from all the fear and flurry of the last twenty-four hours. The soldiers would never look for them on a coal barge; they would reach shore again at some point – always assuming that this improbable vessel did not sink – and meanwhile the only two people she really cared about in the world were here with her, and safe.

She turned, feeling Hope's eyes on her. Neither of them spoke, but Bell's pulse quickened; and her stomach tightened in a little flutter of expectation, almost of fear. The rush of the sea, the creaking of ropes and timbers, seemed to ebb away to a faint lapping silence as they gazed at one another. They were suspended, stationary, in their own world.

There was a noise like a huge wet smack, and a volley of curses. Feet pounded past them outside; the floor beneath their feet slowly tipped over to the left, and failed to swing back again. They scrambled to look out forward. The barge had stopped – they were stationary, in the Bristol Channel. The sail was flapping empty overhead, and Mrs Gilliam's coach, thrown against its lashings, seemed about to break away and plunge overboard. Hamish had hold of all five horses' heads; he spoke to them in a strange, lilting tongue.

The wind failed them repeatedly all afternoon. At last, as real darkness began to fall, they saw the line of the Welsh coast rise out of the water. They ventured out on deck to gaze ahead down a splintering yellow path painted across the waves by the evening light. Ahead of them was a town of some size, broad wharves curving away to the right, and a great dark fortress – a castle – standing on the seaward headland; the town climbed up around and behind it from the riverside harbour. Westward windows blazed in the sunset.

'Here is Chepstow, Sir and Madam,' said the bargee, coming up behind them and speaking as proudly as if he had built it himself. 'No doubt you'll be glad to step back on terra firma, eh? Sea passage always turns the ladies' stomachs. Not long now.' He tipped his hat.

The wind had increased, and the lumbering barge began to run before it with a smoother, deeper motion that was quite exhilarating. Bell's spirits lifted; she almost laughed as she gripped the cold and dirty rail, and looked eagerly ahead.

They left Hamish to cope with the flurry caused by their unannounced arrival at Chepstow coal wharf, and set off to walk into the town. The fog had left the steep streets cold and dirty; darkness closed in. The stress of the last twenty-four hours was telling on them all. Alistair clung silently to Isabella's arm and Hope, as she watched them, had a sense of foreboding. They climbed slowly between tall, blank-faced warehouses. It was not like the playground of Bath, with its broad walks and little shops full of fans and perfumes. Here were chandlers and clothiers and rope-makers, merchants dealing in timber and fuel with yards full of covered stacks, as businesslike as barnyards. Passing through the massive town wall they found themselves in a broad marketplace; smoky torches glinted along tight rows of booths. The clanging of the market bell echoed off the walls of the tall houses. Some stalls were being dismantled or shuttered; at others, people jostled to buy from bawling traders selling in a hurry as the bell rang and rang.

They stood exhausted, until Alistair roused himself, and looking round said 'We are to put up at the sign of the Angel. I have told Hamish to bring the coach there. Can you see it?'

They found the inn filling the eastern side of the marketplace, its door and broad ground-floor windows already spilling out welcoming light. A smiling woman with a clean apron over a good woollen gown greeted them.

'We have a sitting room at the back, my lord, with a bedroom – or two – quieter than looking onto the market, more suited to polite company. Shall I find a closet for your girl elsewhere, my lady?' Her gaze was cool and polite, but appraising; Hope felt Isabella's grip on her arm tense. No doubt the woman was unconvinced that the Wistons were brother and sister and was suggesting discreetly that the young couple might want to be alone. Hope held her breath until Alistair intervened, assuring the landlady that his sister's maid would sleep in her room, and wait on them both. He smiled a little wan smile, and as they followed the potboy's candle up the stairs said to Hope, 'Look after her, won't you? These are hard times for us, and she will have much to bear.'

The little bedroom into which they were shown was much more homely than appeared from the grand front of the house; huge rafters and sloping shiny floorboards almost met around a low window. A sharp memory of the apple loft at Wiston came to Hope as she ducked under a great beam and hung their cloaks on a peg. She turned back. Bell had drawn the curtains of a bedstead that took up most of the higher part of the room, and was contemplating its pile of feather beds.

'Is it damp, do you think?' Hope said.

'I expect so – everything's damp. It feels as if these people live halfway under the sea! I never expect to be warm and dry again.' Bell sat on the heap of beds, having to take a distinct jump to get there. 'It's quite soft, anyway,' she reported. There was a tap at the door, and she sprang up as Alistair looked in and glanced round the room.

'Will you be all right here?' he asked. 'Quieter it may be, but I think they've put us in the garrets because their state rooms are all full of market folk. My bedroom has no window at all!'

'Never mind,' said Bell, 'We're only here for one night.

155

Hope and I will be quite comfortable, thank you.' Hope thought she was deliberately not looking at either of them; she blushed slightly as she spoke. Alistair smiled at her, and turned to Hope again.

'No doubt you will make the room as comfortable as you can – but first, please go down and order us some dinner, and bring it to the parlour. Whatever they've got; I'm not very hungry.'

Hope served them up the capon produced by the house, with a flagon of very pale wine; they were all quiet, constrained, and she quickly picked up Alistair's signal to take the tray away and leave them together. She sat on the top of the stairs to eat from what they had left. I really am a servant now, she thought; but the idea lacked the sting it had had in Bath. She was more concerned about what was going on. Alistair was not so much giving her orders, as asking her help. Something is very wrong, she thought – it has been in his face all day; something beyond the fiasco of the soldiers walking into Bath, and the scramble to save the guns. It must be bad news about King James's planned landing. It is hard for them, she thought, caring so passionately for this. She had tried to share the intensity which shone out of Bell when she was talking about the true king; but hard as she tried, it seemed to Hope that all kings must be very much alike, and none of them able to do any good in the lives of those she loved. Until she met Bell, of course; the Wistons would stand or fall with their king. Put not your trust in princes, she thought, grimly, standing up and shaking out her skirt. It was frustrating – infuriating – to be so powerless, to find out everything at third hand when someone deigned to tell her; never to know what was happening, even, let alone to be in control of it. She ran down the stairs and dumped the tray in the busy kitchen, evading cheerful greetings and enquiries, and slipped back up to the room where she was to sleep with Bell. She held up her candle, looking round. What would make it comfortable? She felt the bed – it certainly was damp; the thin linen was clammy and limp. She went downstairs again, in search of a pan of coals.

Struggling back up the narrow stairs with the warming pan and a large can of hot water, her spirits rose in spite of her tiredness. They could wash away the salt and grime of their journey, and climb into their warm bed – alone at last. And tonight . . . she felt warm already at the thought. She shouldered the door open. Bell had not come in yet. Although the little chamber had no fireplace of its own, it shared the heat of the great chimney stack from the room below, and it looked welcoming in the candlelight.

As she moved the hot pan between the sheets, she allowed herself to think about Bell. *Make haste, my beloved . . . let me see thy countenance. Behold, thou art fair, my love; behold, thou art fair . . .* She smiled. That was no part of her mother's Bible teaching, though a favourite of her great grandmother's. 'All manner of love is from God,' the old woman would say firmly, as Hope's mother set her mouth and banged the pots about on the fire. 'God made us for our own pleasure as well as for His. Pay no heed to those who hate and fear the flesh, child; perfect love casteth out fear.' Hope smiled wryly; perhaps her own love was not as perfect as she had thought, for she did feel nervous . . .

She heard Bell's step in the passage and the rattle of the door latch, and a spurt of joy leapt up in her, only to die abruptly as she saw Bell's face. It was white and blank, and Bell moved into the room like a sleepwalker. She did not speak to Hope, but walked straight past her and sat down stiffly on the edge of the bed, her hands gripped tightly together. After a moment she said, 'My father is dead.'

Stunned, Hope struggled to take it in. Then she went across and put her arms round Bell. There was no response at all, but she held tight, knowing no other way to comfort her. Bell went on speaking, in the same flat voice. 'He died in the prison, at Dover. Of a fever. He was never brought to trial. It was the messenger who rode in with the warning about the troopers who brought the news. He was on his way to Wiston, when he overtook them outside Bath. Someone told him Alistair was in the city . . .' her voice trailed away, but still she did not move.

Suddenly and clearly, Hope thought, 'So now you are mine.' Shocked, she pushed the thought away. She remembered her own grief when Anticipation died, and knew she would do anything to save Bell from that loneliness. She rocked and stroked the tense little body, until at last she felt Bell relax and curl against her. After a few more minutes, Bell suddenly spoke. 'I wish it was yesterday,' she said. 'Or last week; or last year. Then this would not be happening.' She curled up tighter in Hope's arms. 'Help me, Hope. I don't know what to do.'

Hope was suddenly drunk with exhaustion. All the tests and trials of the last forty-eight hours – and now this. With a great effort she made her voice calm and strong.

'I think we should sleep now,' she said steadily, 'and in the morning we can talk and think.'

Obediently, like a good child, Bell stood up to be undressed.

It was not as Hope had envisaged their bedding that night. Had she been less tired, she would have laughed at herself. But now she undressed Bell, and laid her in bed, with the care of a nurse rather than a lover. So that when she had snuffed out the candle and climbed in beside her she was unprepared for the fierceness of Bell's embrace, and her senses flamed at the touch of that warm softness against her. She felt, rather than heard, Bell murmur in her neck, 'I do love you, Hope.' Then, with the suddenness of the totally weary, Bell fell into a deep, peaceful sleep.

And Hope lay in the darkness, holding her lady in her arms.

A cart rumbling over the cobbles of the market-place woke Bell at first light. In her dream she had been at

Wiston and for a few panicky seconds she could not remember where she was.

Then she remembered: she was in a strange bed, in a strange town, and her father was dead. He had been in her dream; the soldiers were taking him away. She tried to picture his face now she was awake, and could not. Being awake was more frightening and unreal than a dream.

Hope stirred and mumbled beside her, and Bell felt a warm rush of comfort. Hope was real, her link with the past and her only certainty in an uncertain present. She shook her to wake her up, so she would not be alone any more. Hope wriggled luxuriously in some dream of her own. Then her eyes snapped open and she stiffened under Bell's hand.

'What's the matter?'

For a moment Bell wanted to say, my father is dead, and I'm frightened – of this journey, of not having a home any more, of loving you . . . But she said, 'Nothing. It's just time to get up, that's all. Alistair says we have to reach Monmouth today.'

She had no idea where Monmouth was. Neither she nor Hope could really imagine such a journey such as this. As they dressed, Bell passed on what Alistair had told her, that the main road ran straight to the north from Chepstow to Shrewsbury; that they would follow it to Waldon Hall in Shropshire, the seat of a Jacobite friend of brother James, where Alistair could get news of the state of affairs in the Northern Counties. Alistair thought that it would take about four days. From there it was a short journey north and west to Castle Coldbatch, up in the hills of Clun Forest.

'What is this Coldbatch like?' asked Hope curiously. 'Is it like Wiston?'

'No, I don't think so – no-one lives there. It was my mother's inheritance, and all the rest of her family are dead; it came to me because I am the only daughter.'

'It's your own house – yours?' Hope was amazed and incredulous.

159

'Yes, I'm sure about that. But I have no idea what it is like. When I was a child I used to think that it must be one of those ruined towers in the story books, where a lonely maiden yearned for the coming of her love, you know? Or where beautiful ladies waited for their knights to come home from the wars.'

'And we shall wait there for your brothers to return?' Hope looked up from packing the few things they had used overnight.

'I suppose so,' said Bell, uncertain.

They set off from Chepstow in driving rain, lurching up a steep road so narrow that tufts of coarse grass and dead brambles scraped past the windows. The coach slithered from side to side in deep liquid mud. Hamish, with the rain running from his hatbrim and the ends of his beard, coaxed the team between deep, axle-threatening pools and away from broken edges overhanging desperate slopes. As they climbed higher, the right-hand bank fell away, and they peered down over the tops of trees to a river running brown and sullen. Bell was beginning to ache from the harsh jogging of the coach, and the creeping cold. The greyness of the day and the dull wilderness around them were irritating and uncomfortable, but she felt she should be more upset than she was. My father is dead, she said to herself. She could not get the idea to mean anything. He died, far away, in Dover. I am very unhappy. But she was not. She looked out at the rain, and then across at Hope, sitting with her back to the horses. Their eyes met, and Hope smiled reassuringly. She means to comfort me, Bell thought, guiltily, because of my father.

A few miles north they came upon an enormous ruin: huge empty stone buildings, filling all the flat land between the road and the river. Broken arches stood out, curves soaring up, snapped off against the racing sky; heavy stonework lay cracked and tumbled under bramble brakes. Bell leant out to see better. One corner of the ruin

160

was patched and thatched over to house beasts, and people too, to judge from the smoke which oozed from the thatch. The wind that snatched it away buffeted the coach. Bell closed the window.

'I hope Coldbatch isn't like that!' she said to Hope, only half in jest.

Sixteen

The town of Monmouth loomed up in the gathering darkness across the river as a black-walled fortress.

In the hall of the Sun Inn, a fire of coals struggled in vain to dissipate the smell of mould. Hope waited at table, serving them the best the dirty kitchen offered, an underdone goose and a pie of mysterious contents. The Wistons picked at the food politely, with little appetite. They spoke briefly about money, and then conversed about the sights of the day's journey. Alistair knew the name of the ruin they had passed. It was called Tintern, and had been a popish abbey. They did not speak of their father; but Hope felt they had drawn together again in adversity, shutting her out. Alistair was very gentlemanly, helping his sister to her chair. Once, when their eyes met, he reached out and squeezed her hand. Bell sat with a little smile, attending only to him.

Hope was jealous, but even more than that she was baffled again by the ways of the gentry. They were riding desperately into unknown danger, likely to lose all they possessed; their father was dead. And they sat in the gloom of this miserable inn discussing architecture. She was almost relieved when Bell looked up and asked her to go and unpack. Perhaps in private they might at least behave more naturally.

Watching Hope stamp out of the room, Bell feared there would be yet more to cope with on this dreadful day. Alistair summoned the horse-faced landlord and asked for a bottle of claret. He turned back us her with a tired smile.

'I am grateful for your company, sister. But I'll not keep you longer from your rest.'

As she made to leave the table he rose with his usual courtesy and embraced her briefly. 'You show great courage, Bella. Our father would be proud of you. These are dark times, but I still believe we shall see a dawning, and that before too long. Goodnight!'

She found Hope wrestling with another reluctant fire in their imposing but chilly bedchamber. She did not look up as Bell came in. Bell pulled a face and gave an exaggerated shudder.

'Ugh! What a dreary place! But at least we are alone now. Are you ready for bed?'

Hope shot her a look which she could not read, then shrugged and turned back to the fire. 'If you wish.'

'Hope?'

'Yes?'

'Is something wrong? Are you angry?'

Hope applied the bellows with violence, and succeeded only in covering herself with smoke. 'No,' she said irritably, 'only tired, I suppose.'

They undressed in silence and climbed into the pompous bed with its dusty brocade curtains. Hope lay on her back, not touching Bell.

'Hope?'

'Yes?'

'Talk to me?'

A pause. 'I'm sorry. I don't know how to talk to you today. You seem such a long way away, at a distance, so that I don't know what to say to you.' Another pause. 'Is it because of your father?'

Bell thought for a moment. It was difficult to put her feelings about her father into words. 'I think that – that I didn't know him very well, really. His being dead is very shocking, and it has made everything very uncertain, and strange. But it doesn't' – she searched for the word – 'hurt as much as I expected.'

Hope said, 'When my grandmother died, I was desolate. I felt lonely, and angry because she had gone before I could spend more time with her.'

Bell remembered. 'No, I don't feel like that. I do feel . . . lost. And rather frightened, because it is as if I don't belong anywhere any more. Can you understand that?'

She thought that Hope opened her mouth to speak,

when there was the sound of a door-latch lifting, and a heavy step on the floor. Bell's heart thudded. The steps came nearer; and then she realised that it was Alistair, in the room next door. The wall between them must be only a partition. She heard the floor creak as he walked across the room, and then back again. She could picture so clearly the expression on his face as he paced and fretted, worrying about the things he could not share with her, and her heart went out to him. Their father's death had left him lonely, too. She shivered, and turned towards Hope.

'Hope?'

'Yes?'

'Would you . . . hold me, please?'

Wordlessly, Hope put out her arms, and Bell moved into them. As they touched, she heard Hope give a little groan, then her arms tightened round Bell, pulling her close. Bell felt the tremor that ran through both their bodies. Hope's breasts, hips, strong thighs pressed against her, then Hope's mouth closed on hers. Just for a second she resisted, shocked, before she felt her body melt. She had no words for the urgent warmth that filled her, overwhelmed her. Hungrily, her whole body returned Hope's kiss.

There was a sharp thud at the head of the bed. They froze, terrified, still clutched together. Bell was trembling; she felt Hope's frightened breathing on her neck. A second thump followed the first, as Alistair pulled off his other boot and dropped it on the floor. Bell let out a long, quavering breath, somewhere between laughing and crying. They rolled apart and lay without speaking.

After what seemed an age, Hope said, 'I am so sorry.' Her voice was shaky. When Bell did not reply, she went on, 'I have tried so hard not to . . . please forgive me, Bell. I am sorry, truly.'

Bell reached out and found her hand. 'You do not need to be sorry,' she said softly. 'I –' she swallowed nervously, 'I – liked you to do it.'

She felt Hope's fingers tighten round hers. Hearing Alistair's bed creak as he turned over, they lay side by side, holding hands. Bell fell asleep with the taste of Hope's kiss in her mouth; and it was the first thing she thought of when she woke next morning. She felt as if something momentous had happened; something from which there was no going back.

They were shy of each other that day: speaking little, avoiding touching. Intensely aware of Hope's presence, Bell could not look at her without remembering the night before. Every time she remembered, she felt the warmth rise in her belly; she dared not catch Hope's eye. As the coach lumbered up out of Monmouth and onto the wide, sheep-bitten pastures south of Hereford, the sun came out between ragged streaks of cloud. It shone in at the coach window, catching Hope's hair so that it brightened to gold. Bell gazed entranced, remembering the soft touch of that hair on her face. As if in answer to her thought, Hope looked up, and smiled with her eyes. Bell felt her colour rise, and looked quickly out of the window.

Later, when she thought back over their journey north, Bell could never clearly remember this day. Suspended between the memory of the night before, and the night to come, which she tried not to think about, she was only half aware of her surroundings; the flat green plain, the distant hills, the good stony road. To Hope, these things were the landmarks from which she dated all her future happiness, and she remembered them like beacons in the sky.

The day was only just closing in when Alistair came trotting back towards them with the news that their stopping place for the night was just ahead.

'We are close to Hereford,' he said, 'but it is best to stay here, outside the town – this is a village where the Cause is strong. I shall pay my respects to the local gentry.'

The wayside inn was a low, rambling building with an uneven face, warped into uncouth bulges when its timbers were green. Its name, painted on the wall, was The White Hart; over the door hung a set of antlers. Hope glanced up at them as she passed, and was pierced by a sudden thought of home – of Eli, and her mother. They were shown into the only private rooms in the house, over-looking the road: a little parlour off the twisting stairs, where their supper was brought to them, and three steps above that, two low bedrooms. With a connecting door. Hope's heart sank. But Alistair had said he was going out, and as soon as they had eaten he put on his hat.

'Hamish is below, if you need anything,' he said to Bell. 'I expect I shall be very late returning – I will say goodnight now.' He kissed his sister's brow, and with a smile for Hope as she gathered the dishes, he left.

She tidied the meal away, not looking at Bell. Her heart was pounding so hard she thought it must rattle the plates as she carried the tray out to the kitchen. She told them there that her mistress was tired, and they were on no account to be disturbed. Then, on an impulse, she went to their room, and rummaged in the depths of her bag. When she came back to the parlour, Bell had pushed the table away from the hearth, and spread Mrs Gilliam's thick travelling rug in front of the fire.

'There are no comfortable chairs,' she said. They sat down side by side, a little apart, stretching out towards the blazing logs; Bell gazed into the fire. Hope could not tell whether her face was flushed from its light, or from within.

'Shall I play for you?' Hope said. She produced her pipe, carried forgotten all this way; she hoped she had breath enough not to betray her shaking heart. Surprised, Bell nodded, and quickly turned her eyes back to the fire. Hope played the Mossmen's dance, that she had played to Bell almost exactly a year before, in the great hall at Wiston: a jaunty, self-sufficient tune, a

tune to defy the gentry and shame the hypocritical; a
tune of celebration, natural, unashamed. She ended on
a trill of grace notes. Bell turned to face her, and smiled
into her eyes.

'When I first saw you, your face was green, and you
wore breeches.'

'Yes,' said Hope, simply, and then, 'but that was not
me; that was Hobbinol. Hobbinol is the lord of the dance,
the free spirit, elfin, a fairy creature; from another world.
He comes to set mortals free.'

'And to give them their heart's desires?' said Bell.

Hope smiled. 'Not to give, perhaps; just to let them
know what they are.'

Bell blushed. 'Don't tease me,' she said. 'I think I fell
in love with you that night.' She looked away, into the fire
'Let's go to bed.'

The sheets were cold, but Bell's body through the thin
shift was warm and soft as Hope pulled her close, kissing
her throat, her lips, shaken by the strength of her own
need. She felt Bell's arms tighten round her, and her own
body moved urgently in reply, demanding, hungry. Her
fingers pushed aside folds of soft linen and skimmed the
smooth skin of Bell's thigh. No dream, no fantasy had
prepared her for this joy, or for the strength of this
excitement.

It was only then that she realised Bell was not
responding. Her body was rigid in Hope's arms; her
grip was one of panic rather than passion. Suddenly
sobered, Hope raised herself on one arm and looked
down at Bell's face, soft in the flickering light from the
fire. Her eyes were wide open; full of love and trust and
something very like fear. Hope thought, she really
doesn't know what is going to happen: she is
frightened. The thought made her feel responsible and
protective, and also very powerful. She smiled down at
Bell.

'Don't be afraid.'

'I'm sorry,' Bell whispered. 'I do love you.'

Hope slipped an arm under Bell's neck. Then she

bent her head and kissed her softly on the lips; she kissed her eyelids and her throat. With her free hand she began very gently to stroke Bell's hair, her cheek, her neck. 'I love you too,' she said, 'and I promise I'll not let you come to harm.'

Bell smiled, and some of the tension went out of her. Hope kissed her again, and her hand traced the soft curve of Bell's breast; she saw the brown eyes widen, startled, and then soften with pleasure. Very gently, she loosed the string at the neck of Bell's shift, pulling it wide open.

Seventeen

If Alistair had not been so preoccupied next morning he must have noticed something, Bell thought. It was a wonder no-one seemed to see how different she was, after last night. Her whole body felt changed: sleek and relaxed, like a cat in the sun, but full of new longings and sensations at the same time. They had hardly slept: her lips were bruised from kissing, and she could not watch Hope's hands preparing their breakfast without feeling them on her skin. She had an ache inside, too, that made her blush to remember how Hope's thrusting fingers had shaken her with wave after wave of shuddering pleasure, leaving her longing for more. She would do anything, anything at all, to have that pleasure again. She knew now that, whatever the world saw, Hope was no longer her servant; that the balance between them had shifted; and that Hope knew it too.

Bell felt as if happiness must be shining out of her like light, so that everyone must see the change in her and guess her secret. But Alistair was only interested in Hamish and the horses; the men walked about the yard all the time she and Hope were eating their bread and milk. Bell ate heartily; she was extremely hungry, she found. Eventually Hamish disappeared, and Alistair came in, paid the bill, and asked them to hurry.

'Last night – come out into the road,' he said, ushering Bell away from the curious gaze of the people of the house. 'Last night, I was told that Hereford is not safe – there is a company of German hussars there. We cannot avoid it, but we must take the utmost care. Our story is that we are travelling on urgent family business, over an inheritance.' His mouth twitched. 'I will ride in the coach until we are clear, and answer any questions. Your part is to look impatient, my dear, and say nothing. We must reach Totenbury, beyond Leominster, today; there is a safe house there, the Crown.'

The coach appeared from behind the inn as Hope followed them out into the sunshine. It was washed and sparkling; the horses were groomed to a shine, and even the tack had been given a surface polish. Hamish smiled at her, and raised his left eyebrow.

'Very fine!' Hope said to him, as Alistair handed his sister into the coach.

There was no trouble in the city, in spite of their fears. Lesser traffic, foot passengers and traders' barrows, gave way to them, a beadle touched his hat, and the only soldiers they saw were seated in a tavern, playing dice. This morning Bell found it difficult to believe that anything could hurt them; the memory of the night was more real than the tedious jogging of the coach or the threat of Hanoverian soldiers. They sat squashed in the coach in constrained silence; the sensation of Hope's leg pressed to hers from knee to hip obliterated all other thought. Bell looked resolutely out of her window, all her awareness concentrated on their two thighs.

Suddenly Hope, her face completely impassive, began very slightly to flex the muscles of her leg. A spasm of desire shot through Bell, leaving her weak. Her face grew hot; surely Alistair would notice? Hope did not stop, until Bell thought she must cry out loud. When they were a mile beyond the last houses, Alistair got down to ride and she drew a long shuddering breath.

'What are you trying to do to me?' she whispered furiously. 'You are wicked!'

Hope put on a grave face. 'Apologies, my lady, for my mistake. Only last night, I had the impression – forgive me if I was wrong – that I gave you pleasure.' She looked into Bell's eyes. 'Do I not please you, my lady?'

Bell felt as if she was going to faint. She wanted to lie down then and there in the bottom of Mrs Gilliam's famous coach and feel again the pressure of Hope's mouth and hands, the touch of her naked skin . . . She pulled herself together with difficulty, and said sternly, 'Hope, please. Not now.'

Hope grinned, unrepentant. 'When, then, my lady?'

Bell looked down, then up at Hope. 'Soon,' she whispered, 'oh, soon, please.'

She saw Hope's colour rise in response, and giggled.

'If you look at me like that again,' said Hope, 'it'll be sooner than you bargain for.'

'Goodness,' said Bell demurely, 'one is not safe even in one's own coach, in these wicked days.'

They drove on in the wintry sunshine for several hours. Soon they were restlessly tired of the coach; sitting so close that they could not keep their hands off one another, they were constantly aware that at any moment Alistair might appear at the window, smiling and asking how they did. After a couple of hours Hope shifted to the opposite seat and refused to come any nearer, and Bell was left to gaze out of the window and long for Totenbury.

They were passing through a straggling village, a dogleg street between timber cottages, when the coach lurched and Hamish's deep voice called out to stop the team. They looked out. He was down from the box, beside the rear off-side horse. After a moment he looked up. 'Cast shoe,' he vouchsafed. They were lucky to be in a village. There was no inn where they might sit, but at least there was a smithy; they walked about, strolling the length of the street while Hamish unhitched the mare and took her to be attended to. Alistair had been well ahead; it was ten minutes before he cantered back, looking desperately alarmed until he saw what was wrong

'Poor Alistair!' said Bell, 'He is so worried; but I'm sure we are perfectly safe.'

They had attracted a small crowd of children, edging closer, fists in mouths, eyes round with wonder.

173

'Is my purse handy in the coach?' Bell asked.

'Don't,' said Hope. 'we'll be overwhelmed; and it's not good for them. Please, Bell – no.'

Bell looked at her, holding her eyes again, shaking her to the pit of her stomach with desire; but then she bent her head.

'Very well,' she said.

They walked downhill towards the smithy, where the regular double chink suggested a shoe was making. There were more loiterers there, a small group of women, who dropped them bobbing curtsies, and two men leaning on the side of a stall behind the smith. They made no acknowledgement, but stared silently at the travellers. One had a lop-sided look to his face, with an old burn on his left cheek – perhaps he is the smith's assistant, Hope thought. She had seen such scars at her aunt's forge at Bassett Moor. Both men had an air of independence and indifference to the gentry that reminded her of home.

Alistair came up, leading his horse. 'Isabella, are you all right?' he said. He looked suspiciously round the circle of villagers. 'Come, Madam. Let us go back to the carriage,' he said rather loudly, taking her arm. Out of earshot, he muttered, 'I'm sorry – but did you see those two men? I think they were suspicious of us. This could be a dangerous village – we have no idea of their sympathies, remember. Men like that might easily set the troops or the magistrates onto us, if only for some paltry reward.'

Half an hour later, on their way again, Hope was wondering whether it was cold enough to give them an excuse to drape themselves in the travelling rug when Hamish drew rein, and they came to a trampling stop, with the brake blocks howling. There were at the foot of a hill, just inside a dark clump of coppice beech. They both looked out. Fifteen yards ahead Alistair, in his shirt sleeves, was standing amidst the branches of a fallen tree.

'I thought I might be able to clear it,' he called out, 'but

174

it will take two.'

Hamish thumped down from the box. Hope caught a glimpse of his face: wary, slightly frowning. It is odd, she thought: a fallen tree slight enough for two men to move, left lying in the highway. She could recall no recent storm or winds. Hamish checked the brakes, and walked to the other end of the tree. He looked at it, and looked around again. 'This is felled, not windblown,' he said. They all gazed around. The woods were dark and silent, close on either hand. After a moment Hamish bent to take the trunk in his hands, and Alistair followed his lead, grasping the biggest branch.

A pistol flashed in the trees ahead, and as the crack reverberated Alistair fell forward. Bell screamed.

Three men, two on foot and one on a big black horse, burst out of the wood. The mounted man had a second pistol, which he levelled at Hamish as he rode forward. The two footpads ran at Alistair, who was slumped in the branches, but threshing his arms – at least he was not dead.

Hamish straightened up, and as he did so his right hand came up in a swift, flashing underhand curve. The horseman let out a dreadful cry and fell backwards from the saddle. His stallion reared and flailed, catching one of the other men on the shoulder. He slipped and fell. Hamish gave a ferocious bellow, a warcry that sent Hope ducking into the coach, and lunged towards the third man, who turned and ran for his life. The man the horse had kicked also scrambled up and took to his heels, sobbing and cursing. Catching up with the black stallion, he climbed up and galloped away. There was a moment's dead pause.

Bell jumped out of her door, fell into the mud and picked herself up. By the time she reached him, Alistair was on his feet, swaying but upright, his face covered in blood. Hope grabbed the leather bottle of water that the coach carried, and a spare kerchief, and leapt down. Hamish took Alistair firmly by the shoulders and sat him on the tree. His hat and wig were lying in the

175

branches, and blood was oozing thickly from a furrow in his pale, cropped head.

'Scalp wound,' said Hamish, 'more blood than brains, lassie – always is. Dinna tak' on.' He took the water bottle and simply upended it over Alistair's head, then clamped the wad of cloth over the wound. 'Hold hard there, Master Wiston,' he said. Alistair put up a hand; Bell tried to wipe his face.

'I'm all right, Bell,' he managed, though her ministrations. Hamish went to the fallen horseman, who lay still, face up, staring at the first stars overhead. He bent and pulled out his knife, and wiped it in the grass. 'Miss Hope,' he called. Hope went to him, and looked. It was the man with the burnt face, from the smithy.

'From the village,' she said. 'Is he dead?'

'Aye, dead eno'' said Hamish. 'We'd best leave him here and get on. We've no call to go bothering the magistrates, I'm thinking – though these were no Hanoverian spies. Simple highway robbers. Can ye lift yon branches, think you?'

'Aye,' said Hope.

It was past eight o'clock when they reached the Crown at Totenbury, but at least they had been told it was a safe house. Alistair lay stretched in the coach, pale as a rag, shaken by every rut and stone in the road. At the inn friendly hands lifted him out and put him to bed; after a couple of hours he was recovered enough to eat a little, and take some claret, before he settled to sleep. Bell left his room relieved that he looked so normal, underneath his pallor.

'Hamish says his head will ache for days, but he will be all right, as long as he avoids a fever. He is not prone to fever; he was the one of us who never took the chickenpox, or any childish ills. I was delirious for days, Mistress Johnson says, when I had the quinsy –'

She looked round the room with a sense that she was becoming an experienced traveller. Hope had made it welcoming again: there was a huge flagon of hot water,

176

Bell's own dressing box stood open on a side table, and there were even two wax candles before it. She had made up the fire and turned down the bed. Hope herself had discarded her travelling dress, which was stained with the mud and moss from the tree, and had wrapped a big dark blue shawl round herself over her smock. She had loosed and brushed out all her beautiful hair so that it fell in glimmering ripples around her. Bell's spirits lifted; she ran across the room to Hope, eager for her strong readiness. Hope kissed her, and her hands moved swiftly to Bell's laces.

'You'd better get to bed, then,' she said into her ear, 'in case you take a cold.'

Next day Alistair insisted that he was fit to travel. With the help of the Jacobite inn-keeper, Hamish had worked out that they were some eighty miles from Castle Coldbatch; the best part of a day's drive north, to Onibury, then west and north to Waldon Hall for the night. After that they would venture into the wild Shropshire hills. They must get on, Alistair said; at least he did not attempt to ride, but sat in the coach, wrapped in a travelling blanket. There was room for them all, but Hope felt unbearably awkward. When they stopped to stretch their legs at mid-morning she said she would ride on the box with Hamish for a while.

Once she got used to the alarming sideways sway of the little perch, the sensation of travelling along in midair with a clear view over the hedges was quite exhilarating. At close quarters, Hamish smelt strongly of tobacco; but he was a reassuringly steady bulk beside her at the corners and over the bumps. Driving, for some reason, loosened his tongue. Looking steadily ahead, watching the path before the leaders' hooves and touching the team this way and that between low branches and deep ruts, he kept up a stream of talk. On a clearer stretch, he showed her how to handle the team, lacing the traces between her fingers. She ventured to praise his skill in getting the horses all safely onto the

177

coal barge and they talked about the ways of calming a frightened beast and of finding what ailed a creature that could not tell you where its trouble lay. 'Are you a farmer, then, Hamish?' she asked.

He shook the traces, and paused before he answered. 'Yes and no, lassie. A pasturer I have been, and a drover – of my own cattle, too, despite what yon bilious Welsh footman of Mistress Gilliam's may have told you. Not all clansmen are thieves; not even all Macgregors.' He shot her a gleaming sidelong glance.

'Is that your name?' she asked, innocently.

'It is, and I am not ashamed to own it though the infamous law against it is once more brought down upon us.' He looked at her again. 'You do not know it, then? Well, well – we are over hasty to see enemies in every bush, perhaps. I am of a proscribed race, lassie. My own laird, Rob Roy Macgregor, is even now following the standard of the Earl of Mar into battle, I hope, to the glory of King James the eighth of Scotland and in clearance of his name.' The out-thrust branch of a wayside oak made them both duck. Hamish crammed his hat down over his ears, and grinned ferociously. 'All Macgregors are outlaws – we are the most hated men on the borders, for our ancestors took no shame to defend their own hills even unto death; and every while and a while went out to remind the lowland stockmen to take good care of their cattle too, straying on the hills. And so the English government has seen fit to strip us of our right name, and turn us out landless and lonely; but we are like the Stuarts – we will remember our house and its rights, as long as the last of us bears his sword.'

His voice had deepened alarmingly, and the horses were fairly racing over the muddy road. He pulled them in, and brought out his tobacco pipe to stop his noise. After a moment's silence, he removed it again to sing a snatch of a marching song, under his breath. Breaking off, he asked 'You like a tune, lassie? I heard you playing upon a bit pipe, the other night, did I no'? A dancer's tune, it was?'

Hope had a moment of sheer terror, wondering what else he might have heard; but he smiled at her and began to hum the Mossmen's tune, in a complex triple time His singing voice was a strong bass, as she would have expected. She felt for her pipe, and gave him a descant. They progressed through a jig and on to ballads, and entertained themselves well for the rest of the morning.

Eighteen

Soon after midday, they passed through the wide streets of Ludlow, and then the landscape began to change around them. The open fields of Hereford and Leominster gave way to a more varied and hilly terrain; ahead, the horizon was mountainous, blue-grey. It was the middle of the afternoon when Bell leaned out, and asked Hamish to stop.

'Alistair needs to get out,' she said; and they were just in time to get him clear of the door before he was violently sick. Hope fetched the replenished water bottle, but he waved it away. He looked pale still, but with a hot spot on each cheekbone. He seemed only half conscious, and would have sunk to the ground if they had not lifted him to sit on a milestone. Bell had already removed his hat and wig; his wound had begun to ooze again, and she had made him a new bandage. She looked worriedly to Hamish.

'It's fever, isn't it?' she said.

Hamish nodded even before he had put a hand to Alistair's brow. 'We'll need to get him to bed. Has he been bleeding long?'

'Not very long. He slept for hours, until after we passed through the town; but then he woke and was agitated – he wanted to get out and ride.' Hope could imagine the trouble Bell had had keeping him in the coach; Alistair could be very imperious. No wonder his wound had opened.

'I'll come and sit inside with you,' she said.

'Aye – we must get on,' said Hamish, and picking Alistair up bodily, he deposited him in the coach. 'By my reckoning Onibury is only a mile or two down the road, and our turning is just beyond.'

The little town of Onibury was silent as they passed through and continued north, into a narrowing corridor in the hills, alongside a brimming river. Bell and Hope sat nervously watching Alistair as he lay with closed eyes on the opposite seat, gathering his strength. In less than half an hour they reached a widening in the road, where a ramshackle barn-like house stood back from the road. A tethered goat bleated plaintively behind the buildings; no other living thing was to be seem. The stream bent away westwards, and a beaten track branched off the road to follow it. A fingerpost indicated Shrewsbury ahead of them, but gave no clue what lay in the other direction. Hamish stopped, and climbed down to the window.

'We need a westerly road,' he said, 'but I am no' convinced this would be it. I'll mak' enquiry.'

Bell watched as he strode through the mud to the house. Alistair stirred, and she mopped his brow for the hundredth time, feeling the unhealthy heat coming from him. He smiled in thanks, without opening his eyes. Hamish returned. He looked at Alistair, and shook his head.

'We have need of haste,' he said. 'We mun turn here and again in half a mile by a great elm. And pray God the old loon that told me so had more wit than appeared.' He climbed back on the box and swung the ungainly length of the coach and horses left on to the riverside track.

As they turned at the elm – for sure enough a delapidated sign nailed to it directed them in faded letters "To Waldone Hall" – Alistair roused himself and opened his eyes wide.

'Where are we?' he said.

'We have just turned off the main road, heading for Waldon,' Bell told him. 'Try to rest. It should not be long, should it? It's not very far?'

It was not, perhaps; but their progress was very slow. The track was narrow, and deeply rutted by heavy carts whose wheelspan was just less than that of the coach: they continually lunged sideways into axle-deep hollows with one set of wheels or the other, struggling out only to tip again ten yards on. Alistair clung to the left-hand window, gulping air; he was sweating heavily, the moisture running off his face. After half an hour, the track began to climb steeply uphill and then its surface improved; their wheels bit on flint and rock. Alistair seemed to Bell's anxious eyes to breathe a little easier.

'How is it now, brother?'

He turned and patted her hand. 'I shall do, Bella, never fear. I think it cannot be much further. Look out this side – a paling begins by the road. That must be Waldon. Sir John is a friend of our brother's and loyal to the Cause: he will be our friend in our need.' He leaned back and closed his eyes.

A few minutes later they were clearly driving along the neatly-fenced edge of a great park. Bell looked anxiously for the first glimpse of the house. But it was an hour, even on this good road, before the house came into view, and then they were upon it almost at once. They passed down a short avenue of young trees and drew up before a large, old-fashioned stone house with a mossy paved court at its doors. Hamish climbed down to hold the horses' heads. Alistair roused himself, but he was so ill that Bell, without any difficulty, stopped him getting out; she jumped down herself, and Hope followed. They stood looking up at the house. It was shuttered; and Hope saw that no smoke rose from the massive chimney stacks.

Bell drew herself up. 'Would you knock at the door, please, Hamish,' she said. He moved to obey, but the horses shifted and dragged the coach against its brakes. We are not cutting much of a figure, Hope thought; she went quickly and took hold of the near-side leader by the bridle. Startled, it pulled away.

'Hush, then, beauty,' she said, experimentally, in as deep a voice as she could manage. The horse blew down its nose, and looked at her out of a deep yellow eye; but she held on, and the team all more or less stood still.

Hamish knocked once, twice, and a third time on the doors; nothing happened. Then there came a sign of life:

a deep-throated barking, somewhere away in the distance. Hope took a firmer grasp on the bridle as Bell, smoothing down her habit, stepped forward towards the door. But it did not open; instead, the dog appeared, still barking ferociously, round the side of the house. It was a brindled hound, with an ugly pushed-in face, slavering from huge jaws and pulling with all its might against a chain held short by a fat man in a livery waistcoat and breeches of a dirty green. His periwig was pushed back on his head; over his left arm he carried a musket. He stopped, pulling the dog onto its haunches. He stood and glared at them, slowly choking the dog into an eye-popping, rasping silence.

Hamish took a step towards the man – or more likely, Hope thought, towards the dog – but Bell raised her hand, and he stopped.

'Good afternoon,' said Bell, 'I desire to see Sir John Waldon.'

There was a dead pause. The dog's wheezing could be plainly heard. Then the man said roughly, 'Want may be your master, then. Sir John's not here.'

'Then we will wait for his return. I am Miss Isabella Wiston, my brother –'

'No.' The man's voice was full of stony certainty. 'All the family is away. My orders are to admit no-one – unless they come with a warrant from King George. I am sorry to deny you, madam, but the house is closed up, and the folk abroad, and there's an end of it.'

Bell took a step towards him, and Hope could hear the desperation in her voice as she said, 'My brother is very ill – we cannot go further tonight.'

'I am very sorry for it, madam,' the man said, 'but my orders admit of no exceptions. No-one may come here – especially, as you say, those who are – sick. Or wounded, belike. The house is shut up. Sir John, please God, is in London; my lady, his mother and all the household besides have gone away. And there's an end of it.' And he actually turned his back on her, and walked a few paces in the direction he had come.

184

Before Bell could try again, Alistair's voice broke in, faintly, from the depths of the carriage. 'The house is suspected, Bella – they have fled from arrest. Is it not so, goodman watchdog?'

The man stopped and turned, his face twisted with emotion; the dog gave a strangled yelp as his hand twitched. 'Suspected? It is ruined. Drink, debts and disloyalty –' He choked his own words in something very like a sob, and the dog howled. Bell's nerve gave way; she scrambled quickly into the carriage.

Hamish, who had stood all this time near the house door, moved forward. He walked deliberately towards the man, and as he did so he slowly loosened the neckcloth knotted at his throat. Hope stood frozen: was he going to fight? The watchman obviously thought so; his eyes never left the huge Highlander. Hamish stopped a couple of paces from him, and looked down at the dog. He put out his right hand to the beast's muzzle: it sniffed him, and gave a whimper. Hope held her breath. Hamish sank slowly on his haunches and ran his hand along the animal's back.

'Fine dog,' he said, in a conversational tone, 'good guard, na' doubt. Pity about his eyes.' He cupped his hand under the slavered jowls and tilted the unresisting beast's head, to catch the evening light.

'Eyes?' the man said, his voice harsh with surprise, and with anxiety. 'What about his eyes?'

'He'll no' see much wi' the left, I'm thinking?' Hamish said, and pulled down the red-rimmed socket with his thumb. The dog shook its head, and Hamish scratched its ear.

'Well,' the man said, thoroughly shaken now, 'now you mention it – what's wrong?'

'It will no' be stone-blind yet-a-while. You could try eyebright. Might help him.' Hamish stood up and ran his hand deliberately down the animal's length, bending over him. As his did so, his jacket fell back, and the loosened neck-cloth released something that was hanging round his neck – a necklace of beads, ending in

185

an ornament. Hope's fingers froze onto the bridle. It was a cross – a papist crucifix. He straightened up, and stood with the thing lying outside his shirt, as if he had not noticed. She bit back a cry of alarm.

'Well, now,' he said to the man, and his hand went quietly to his throat, to tuck the charm inside his shirt, 'are ye quite sure there is no refuge here, for the weary and heavy laden?' the voice was light, almost casual, but he held the man's eyes. The guard changed colour, but he shook his head.

'I cannot – I would help you if I could; but it is forbid, especially forbid for those of our faith . . .' his voice trailed off.

'A pity,' said Hamish. He walked deliberately past him, coming to Hope, and taking the bridle out of her hand. They were ready to go, Hope back inside and Hamish on the box, when the man cried, 'Wait! Wait there!' and going to the corner of the house shouted out. In a moment a little boy came running to him, looking at them with big eyes.

'This is Matt – my son,' he said, 'He will show you a place to go.'

It was another three weary miles, over roads no better than a pair of sheep-tracks in the scrub, before the boy called a halt and scrambled down to knock on the door of an isolated house. It was a narrow, dark stone building, with a slate roof sweeping down low over its little door. Eventually, after what seemed an endless wait, they were admitted. Hamish lifted Alistair unconscious from the coach, and carried him indoors. A silent man showed them into two low rooms at the far end of the house, sparsely furnished. There was little besides a bed and a small table in each. To Hope's relief Hamish, when he had put Alistair to bed in the inner room, went off to feed the horses and look to the coach himself.

'It must be got out of sight,' he said, 'it would provoke comment – and we shall be here some time, I'm thinking.'

Hope drew Bell out of Alistair's room. 'Did you see?' she burst out. 'What shall we do, Isabella? A papist! Hamish is a papist – they all are – and they take us for papists, too!'

Surely everyone knew that the Pope was the devil on earth and that Rome was the whore of Babylon? But even after she had explained again about Hamish, Bell did not seem to understand her horror.

'So he's a Macgregor, and he wears a crucifix? He well may do – many of the highland Scots hold to the old faith, I believe. Surely it is our good fortune that the watchman saw it, if it meant that he relented and sent us here? We should be grateful to Hamish Macgregor. What would we have done, otherwise?'

'But – this is a Papist house!' repeated Hope, her eyes wide with fear.

'They mean well towards us – what harm can it do? You are foolish, Hope, and more superstitious than you accuse them of being! Do you think they are going to baptise you in your sleep, or take your Bible from you by force and carry you off a slave to Rome? In Bath –' a moment's wistfulness flickered across her face – 'there were lots of Catholic gentlemen. After all, they have more reason than most to long for the return of King James.'

Hope frowned. 'Why?'

'Why, because the King is of their faith, of course. Did you not know?'

Hope lay half the night awake, struggling with the events of the day. She lay most of the time alone: soon after they had settled, Alistair became delirious, and twice appeared at the door between their rooms sobbing and shouting for candles, because it was too dark to study. There was black blood on his forehead. So Bell went in the end and sat up beside him, bathing his head and soothing him throughout the night to keep him in his bed.

Nineteen

The next day Alistair was worse. In the morning, he dropped into a heavy sleep for two hours but woke raving and terrified them with his incoherent shouts and urgent, meaningless demands. Eventually, they called Hamish who enquired of the household for something that might give him relief. He came back with a bottle of brandy.

'Some say spirits is the best specific for all ills,' he said, 'but in my observation it isna' so. Just keep him quiet, my leddy. I'll spell ye, if ye need to sleep yoursel'.'

But Bell would not leave her brother. She knew that he was going to die. She sat beside the sour-smelling bed, watching his breath come and go heavily, and the demons within swell and distort his face into masks of terrifying anger or pain. She held on to his hand and felt the dry heat, and the sudden fits of shaking that would only stop when he snatched at her fingers like a drowning man. He did not know her; when he opened his eyes, his gaze was far away, and what he saw frightened her as much, perhaps, as it did him. She was glad when his eyelids dropped, and released her from sharing his visions of horror.

But in his quieter hours, she had time to think. She thought not only of their childhood together, in the other world of Wiston, but of more immediate matters, such as what they were going to do next. What could she do if he died? She tried not to feel lonely. She had Hope; it was disloyal to feel so frightened, so bereft. They were to stay at Castle Coldbatch without Alistair, after all, that was the plan; but Alistair away, and Alistair dead, were two very different things. Women alone – a single woman – how could she be safe? What could she do?

'There is nothing you can do for a little while, Bella,' Hope's voice chimed in, startling her. She had brought a tray of food – coarse black bread, but there was a little dish of eggs, and the milk was fresh. 'Come and eat, now,' Hope said. Bell obediently tried to force some of it down her constricted throat, but without much success. Hope was trying to distract her, talking, bustling round; she should try to concentrate, to respond, but she did not want to wash, or to have her hair done. She felt only Alistair's needs, his closed eyes drawing her to him, all the time. With an effort, she brought her mind round to what Hope was saying.

'. . . so you see they are not all papists. She says the Lawrences are good people, good to her, and . . .'

'Who?' Bell broke in, 'I'm sorry, I was not listening properly. Who are you talking about?'

'Her name is Mercy Lewis.' Hope, obviously pleased to have got through to her, sat down beside Bell and took her hand. 'She's the maid – I talked to her in the kitchen. She says this is a safe house for all sorts of people passing by – Mr Lawrence and his wife are very brave and generous, she says.'

Bell squeezed her hand. 'That's good. I'm glad you have talked to her. We do need friends, Hope, don't we?'

Hope could not keep Bell's attention for very long from her desperate concentration upon her brother. Satisfied that she had at least made her eat something, she went back to the kitchen. Mercy, a sturdy, blackhaired, rosy girl a bit older than herself, was knitting by the fire and very glad of a new face and company to talk to.

Strange 'bout they hens,' she said, for the third time since she had brought in an unexpected laying of eggs that morning. ''Twas like they knew the need – poor lady, and she so pulled down and pallid. She et 'um up?' Hope smiled and showed the plate – she had taken care to finish it herself.

'Thass good. You sit here wi' me, take a pot on ale.' She talked on cheerfully, and Hope sat on the settle opposite and allowed herself to relax. Mercy showed a great interest in Isabella's fine clothes and pretty possessions, which reminded Hope that both their cloaks needed sponging and pressing since the encounter with the highwaymen's mossy roadblock. She would do it in a moment. The fire was beautifully warm and Mercy's lilting voice soothing and friendly, almost familiar; she was a bit like Dolly. Hope drifted near to sleep.

The door burst open. Hope stifled a scream as Bell crashed into the kitchen.

'Please come – help me – he's very bad – please.' Bell was in tears. Hope beat Mercy to the door, where Alistair's raving could be plainly heard. They ran together to his room. He was sitting up; he had torn off his bandage and was striking out with it at something only he could see, his voice sobbing hoarsely in his throat. When Bell went to him, he grasped her in his arms; Hope went and pulled his desperate hands away before she should be stifled. They had to wrestle with him to keep him in the bed. Then, just as suddenly as it must have begun, it was over. He slumped in their hands and slid back onto the pillows, his eyes closed, his thin, sweating throat working so that his adam's apple bobbed convulsively. Bell reached for the cloth and wiped his face once more. They all three looked up at the same moment and read their own fear in each other's faces.

It was Mercy who spoke. 'Poor gentleman – he do need some help, surely.' She stood back, and turned to pick up the bowl. 'I'll bring some fresh water,' she said. Then she looked at them again, from one to the other. She spoke to Bell. 'You could go to the old Dame,' she said.

'Who? Where is she?' Bell stood up, ready to go at once.

'Up the bank, Brynsquilver. 'Tis a bit of a step. I could show the way, but she'd need to know all about him – poor gentleman.' She looked at Alistair again, and quickly away. 'Needs must go soon, I'm thinking,' she said.

Hope took Bell's hand. 'Let me go,' she said, 'you stay

with Alistair. He's quiet now –' She could not go on, but Bell understood her, as the tears welling up in her eyes showed. He was not strong enough to put up any more resistance, either to his nurses, or to his affliction.

'I'll stay with him. I am not frightened,' Bell said. 'I want to be here.'

They left the lane and climbed up a steep rocky cleft, a running rivulet as much as a track. Hope's steps reached out from rock to rock; she breathed the clean, damp air. It was warm; before long she pushed her cloak back over her shoulder, and dropped her hood on her back. Ahead the path plunged straight uphill, to a distant cresting of the ridge. Something a bit more than a 'bank', she thought, feeling the unaccustomed pull in the muscles of her thighs. But she had not been out in the sunshine, honestly walking on her own feet, since she left home, more than a month ago; she could not help her body's enjoyment. She breathed deeply.

Mercy ran a few steps to catch up. 'We'm three-four miles to go, up-along,' she said, 'Take 'en easy, now.' Hope slowed a little, and Mercy took her arm. 'I'm a bit afeart of th'old dame,' she said, 'She do have a keen eye, that one. I mind once, I went up to her about my William – he were bewitched by that Sal Hamer over Three Gates, that had the wall-eyed baby. She witched him to go to her, and she put the evil eye on me so I was covered in sores and blains. The old dame say to me, here's a potion, girl, but t'aint for him, 'tis for you; and she say, if you want 'en back, my girl, you got to lay this potion to your face every blessed morning. And she say, you eat nothing but greens. Greens! Truly, thass what she say. And she looked at I like I was a little child gone wrong in its alfabetty, the criss-cross-row, and she say, 'Have you understood me?' Thass what she say, 'Have you understood me?' and she promise in a month, he come back.'

'And did he?' said Hope, shifting slightly to loosen Mercy's eager grip on her arm.

192

'Oh yes, he come back inside a fortnight, more shame to him, wi' a great welt across his face, said he fell over wi' a hurdle. She'm a witch, that Sal Hamer.'

They came over the top of the rise, and stepped full into the westering sun. Hope stopped. Before her lay a secret valley, silver-gilt in the late winter light. Lines of small trees stood etched against the sun, clear as patterns on a glass; the long shadows of oak and elm and wooded knoll lay like velvet on the sparkling slopes. Little hills, linked and interlaced, cupped the woods of the valley bottom in gentle fingers. The air was calm; away to the south of them, a skein of mist wound softly between the trees.

'Tes pretty, 'tes.' Mercy pulled at her arm. 'Down along this way.'

They began to drop down into the woods of the eastern slope, their feet crunching on a clean brown carpet of leaves and husks laid down by some well-grown beeches. There was no open ride or logger's drag, but the footing was easy. Hope stepped confidently on familiar woodland ground, striding between rocky outcrops and the fingers of beech-root, noticing that where the soil lay deeper it was a kindly amber, both rich and loose. Someone tended or at least used the woods here. They were not choked with windfallen trees and spindly saplings. But it was not an order kept up by forester's rules: a great beech lay where it had fallen years ago, still alive along one side, making a hedge of itself; they walked through random pools of sunlight where the aconites were getting ready for the spring. Talking over her shoulder to Hope, Mercy plunged unwarily into a patch of dense reeds and sank overshoe into the bog around a spring.

'Bydam, look at that! This path is deceiving: some say no one finds their way to the Dame's cottage save them she wants to come there.' She wiped out her shoe with a handful of grass, and crammed it back on. They climbed a stile and crossed a small cleared field, an intake from the woods, putting up a hare that struck out a flashing circle of spray from the long grass. They re-entered the woods and began to descend a little. Mercy nodded to a small flat space surrounded by hazel and the slender grey-green trunks of ash, their black buds waiting; Hope saw that there were the first inchings of little daffodils all around.

'Th'old Dame lies there,' Mercy said, 'my mother tell me thass where they laid her, to go back where she came from.'

Hope looked at her, amazed. 'They buried her here?'

'Thass right.' Mercy broke off an encroaching bramble shoot, careful of her hands on the thorns, and poked another back into the brake. They went on. It is his only chance, Hope told herself; it is for Bell's sake; but she was shocked to the core at what she was doing in this wild, Godless place, protected by the charity of papists, and now visiting a wise woman who made witch potions, and seemed no better than a wild beast, burying her mother under a bush.

'Her own mother?' she said to Mercy, unable to suppress her horror.

'Mother? No, bless you, 'twasn't her mother. She'm not from round here. No kin, at all. They do say she were found on the road, down by Lawrences', a toddling babe with not so much as a rag to cover her, after the wars, when masterless folk passed by, and th'old dame took her in. There's others say her parents was tinkers, sold her to the old dame for a servant girl; but she'm an outsider, whatever; and so was the old one before her. No church round here would hold her bones, and she'd have none of them.' She shrugged. ''Tis but the way of things,' she said. Hope followed her in silence.

They passed six goats in a long sliver of a field still surrounded by woods, and then, crossing a stile, they entered the old woman's garden, and Hope saw her. She was sitting at her door, her face turned up to the sunshine, her eyes closed. Her flesh was fallen with age, but she was not pale: her skin was richly coloured by wind and weather, more richly than the washed-out tints of her draped shawl and skirts, which were the same grey-brown as the winter trees and the low thatch of her cottage behind her. She opened her eyes, composedly, but gave no sign of welcome; she waited. Mercy suddenly thrust Hope forward from the stile, in front of her.

'You go now,' she said, 'I's'll bide in the wood. Call when you come outby. Wait – take this for her.' She lifted her skirt and delved in her pocket, bringing out the two remaining eggs, wrapped in a wisp of wool. Dumping them in Hope's hand, she crashed away into the trees.

Hope walked into the garden. As she skirted a great bush of rosemary and came face to face with her, the Dame slowly stood up. She was old, but she stood easily, her feet apart, hands hanging by her sides. Slightly stooped, she still matched Hope's height; her shoulders were broad, and she had carried some substantial weight, Hope thought, from the drape and hang of her clothes on her wide frame.

'Welcome,' she said. 'You are welcome, at the last.' She made no move, but stood looking at Hope, as one might look at a relation who had come back unhoped-for from the wars, or a child long parted in anger and returned to make peace. She drank her in.

'I am Grace,' she said at last.

'Hope,' said Hope, as simply. She put out her free hand, and Grace took it in a warm grip.

'Come.' She turned and went in by the door at her back. Hope took a deep breath of the green hillside before she followed.

'Your errand is for medicine.' It seemed more of a statement than a question. As well as she could, Hope described Alistair's state. Grace asked minutely about the nature of the wound, its colour and its smell, the look of his eyes, the heat of his hands. Hope was struck by her stillness, a concentration of the whole body through the mind, like a thrush listening. Finally she nodded, and turned to reach for bags from the low rafters and a bottle from a basket behind the door. A large pestle and mortar stood on the table under the only window. She began to work in deft silence. When it was done she stoppered the bottle and held it out to Hope, who discovered that she still held the eggs. She set them on the table.

'Mercy Lewis,' said Grace; another statement. 'Give her my thanks. She should marry soon; William Jones-the-Mardu will be a good-enough father for her children.'

Hope received this as a message to carry; she nodded.

'Give the boy – he is eighteen and some months, and slight, you say? – give him half now, and half in the morning. It will work overnight, and again, and the fever should break within that time. Do not fear it. Then he will sleep.' She did not say, 'Have you understood me?' She stood looking at Hope again, almost as if the unimportant business were now over, and they might begin – begin upon – what? Hope felt strangely stirred; she tried to shake off the complete absorption of the woman's gaze, but it held and handled her.

She roused herself to say her thanks. Grace shook her head slightly, and smiled a small smile 'When he sleeps, Mercy is safe to mind him. Then you may bring her here, to me.'

'Bring – her?' Hope was startled; she felt herself flush.

'Your – lady. Bring her here, to me. There is a great deal to say.'

Hope gave Mercy the message about William Jones as soon as she found her, and it served to occupy her mind and her tongue all the may back to the Lawrences' house; which was just as well. Hope could not have said anything of the thoughts that were in her own mind, as they hurried back to Alistair and Bell.

196

The fever broke around midnight, and half an hour later Alistair fell into a sweet and natural sleep.

'He'll do, my leddy,' said Hamish, turning down his cuffs with an air of satisfaction. 'His sleep will heal him now. And you may sleep yoursel'.' He turned to Hope, as he left the room. 'Get your mistress to bed, lassie. I will keep all from your doors, until midday on the morrow.'

Bell stood up, swaying. She had nothing left; but at last she could let herself go. There was a sensuous luxury in allowing Hope to lead her to their chilly little room, and put her to bed like a docile child. As they lay down, she heard herself say, quite stupidly, 'You won't leave me, will you?' and before she even heard Hope's reply, she fell into sleep with the suddenness and finality of walking over a cliff.

She woke at first light, with a sense of relief, of newness so strong she had to remind herself that Alistair was not recovered yet. She slipped out of the bed quietly, and went to look at him. He was still sleeping, but as she put the blanket back from his face he quietly woke, and smiled at her, and turned onto his back. He knew her. She knelt by him and kissed his brow.

'How do you feel?'

'Like the nether millstone – ground quite flat,' he replied, and then looking at her with concern, 'but I have been worse, have I not?' He still looked deathly tired; a worry crossed his face. 'What day is it?' He asked. 'Have we lost much time?'

She assured him that he had not been wandering in the mists for more than twenty-four hours, and then she gave him the other half of the wise woman's draught. He pulled a face at it, but swallowed it down; and after a very few more sentences, he began to drift back into silence. She sat beside him until he was sound asleep again, breathing evenly. After half an hour in which he did not so much as move, she crept away.

Hope's eyes opened as Bell came back into their room.

'What is it?' she said. 'Is he worse?'

'Oh no, he is better! And thanks to you.' Bell sat down on the edge of the bed. 'The medicine you fetched has broken his fever. He is well.' She took Hope's hand. 'I did not believe, but you did, and you have saved him.' She bent down to kiss Hope's mouth.

'Oh – you are so cold,' said Hope, 'come back to bed.'

Bell slid under the blankets. Two days of desperate struggle were over, and she had slept well. She felt her blood run like fire as they embraced. Hope made to rise on one elbow, but Bell pushed her gently down. 'I love you, and you please me so; now I want to please you.' She found the hem of Hope's shift and slid her hand under it. 'You shall tell me if I have learned my lesson well.'

Before midday they were up and dressed, in case anyone should come. Alistair was still sound asleep; they were speculating how long it would be before he would he able to go on when Mercy came tapping at their door with a tray. Hamish looked in, and pronounced that Alistair was mending, and would no doubt sleep on all day.

'The old woman's draught did him good,' said Hope, as they sipped at the salt fish soup Mercy had brought.

'Oh yes, it must have been that, don't you think?'

'She might even have saved his life, then?' Hope persisted. Bell nodded slightly; she did not like to think he had been so near to death.

'She said I was to go back again. This morning, when he slept.'

'Why didn't you say so before? You must go straight away.' Bell dropped her spoon in the soup, and put it aside. 'Is it to get another medicine? We must do everything for him that she says.'

'I don't think it was for Alistair, exactly,' said Hope, looking at her spoon. 'She said he would be asleep by now, and could be left to Mercy; and then I was to take you to see her.'

Bell realised why Hope was so hesitant. 'She wants payment, that's all it is. Well, we are grateful; I will come. I have silver of my own, or it would even be a proper use of one of Mrs Gilliam's guineas, to see us on our way.' She felt the importance of correct management of the situation. Hope was shaking her head; but Bell had never known working people refuse payment. She would see to it.

It was not so sunny this morning; Hope was pleased she had got Bell to come, on whatever terms, but she wished the valley would show itself off for her. They toiled up the stony path in a clammy drizzle, and found the view lost in low cloud. The beechwoods dripped. The goats were huddled in a corner of their field, under a hurdle shelter.

'Goats are such soft creatures,' Hope remarked as they passed, 'You don't see sheep trying to keep themselves out of the rain, do you?'

She turned to Bell as she spoke, and saw a glimpse of her ankle as she lifted her skirts, vainly trying to keep them clear of the long wet grass. She felt a distinct trickle of excitement in her stomach: Bell looked at her, and Hope saw her eyes slide down over Hope's own kilted skirt and bared legs. She reached out, but Bell slipped out of her hand, smiling, and climbed up onto the stile.

'I will tell you a story about goats, one day,' she said.

Hope caught her round the waist as she sat on the wooden bar, and nuzzled in the kerchief at her throat. 'Oh?' she said, coming up for air, and sliding her hand into Bell's placket. 'I look forward to it.'

Eventually they went on, and climbed into the old Dame's garden. She was waiting, again. This time her hands were occupied, stroking a small tabby cat that lay stretched down her lap. Her hands moved slowly from ears to tail, hand over hand – a gentle flow of pleasure and communication, that did not engage her eyes or her full attention. This she turned on them; but she did not get up. The cat raised its head and slipped to the ground and away. Hope felt Bell beside her stiffen, as Grace did not acknowledge them. She sat, and watched; Bell began to bristle.

'She is an old woman,' Hope said, in a whisper; but Grace's mouth twitched slightly, and she dared not say any more. She walked down the path, ahead of Bell.

'Welcome,' said Grace. Her eyes stayed on Hope.

'This is my Lady,' Hope said deliberately, half turning and holding her hand out to Bell behind her, 'Miss Isabella Wiston, of Wiston Hall, Somerset.'

'She also is welcome,' said Grace, and added, 'And it needs not to name her father's house; she is welcome without that.'

Bell stepped up, ahead of Hope; she said, 'Good morning, Dame. I am greatly indebted to you, for my brother. He is much improved by your good offices. Please you to accept this, in acknowledgement.' She held out the little bag of silver she had extracted from her purse. There was a tiny stillness, and then a pause that lengthened and lengthened, until Hope wanted to scream, and Bell's hand finally wavered and fell. She flushed, but her chin went up in defiance.

'Surely, goodwife,' she began, in her voice of command.

Hope took her wrist, and spoke over her to Grace. 'Accept our thanks, if you please. The young man is sleeping, as you said; and I have brought her here.'

Bell turned an amazed and outraged face on her, and her mouth opened; Hope, aware of a moment of crisis, held her eyes and her wrist very hard. 'Be quiet, Bell,' she said.

Grace laughed. A low, amused laugh, brief but warm.

'Do not squabble, my chicks,' she said. 'Madam,' she went on, standing up and then sinking ever so slightly and slowly, as if in the most courtly of curtsies, 'I thank you, but here where I live, and where I am going, I have no need of money. I am glad of your brother's fortunate recovery.' She motioned them nearer, standing still at her door.

Bell was flustered. She realised she had been too prickly; she saw now that she could not treat the old woman as a petty person in trade or an old pensioner on the estate. She had stature of some sort; a personal dignity. But Hope – why had Hope shouted at her like that? She was sorely puzzled, and a little alarmed. But she kept her countenance; she returned the curtsey, and met the old woman's eyes.

It was a gaze you had to meet squarely; a searching, assessing stare. Bell stared back, tilting her head back a little. The face was beautiful: a clean brown skin, large bones inside the folded, softly-ageing flesh, and a network of lines that spoke of good humour, calm, and an absence of bitterness. But there were also signs of patience and pain; and round her shrewd, alarming eyes there were blue marks, the bruises of great weariness.

Bell summoned up her blood. 'I am glad to meet you, Dame,' she said, 'and to be able to thank you myself.' The stare did not leave her face.

'Grace,' the old woman said.

Isabella felt rebuked again, and then compelled to reply in kind. 'Isabella,' she said.

'Sit down.' The tone was firm, not to be gainsaid. Bell looked around; the old woman reseated herself on the only chair, but there was a bench beside the door. She took it, as coolly as she could. Hope sat on a rock beside the path, near the old woman's feet. The cat leapt onto its mistress's knee.

'You have come very late,' Grace said, 'but that is not your fault.' She stroked the little dappled head.

I'm glad something isn't, Bell thought. She felt completely at sea; but Hope was regarding the old woman with entire trust; she must be patient.

'I came early; I have been here since I was less than your age; it is long enough, too long, perhaps,' She stopped, but Bell did not feel it was an invitation to respond. She waited. After a moment the old woman went on, 'Long enough to learn and to unlearn too; to simplify. You will have little to go on, but perhaps there is not so much that one needs to know, after all.' She stopped again.

She's rambling, thought Bell. I have no idea what she is talking about. She raised her eyes from the demure downcast pose she had adopted, high enough to pull a face at Hope, sitting at the old woman's feet; but she was not looking at her.

'Go down, Parsley,' the old woman said, and the cat jumped off her knee. She stood up; they followed her. 'You are welcome, both of you, to this place. You will go on soon, on your journey; but there are things to see first, and to remember. Come.'

She led them first round her garden, a sloping plot well enclosed with hedges of alder and willow, where the first fluffy catkins were showing their tips. She named the indistinguishable clumps of wintering plants as she strode by them; Bell hardly heard. She took them out at the top of the enclosure, above the cottage, through a belt of hazel coppice, and stopped by a black pool below a rock.

'The spring has never dried up, in my time,' she said, 'but there is need to tend the pool. Sarah Jones-the-Castle and another dug it for me ten years gone; it will do a year or two more.' She looked at them in turn, and spoke to Hope. 'You saw where the old dame lay, beside the path?' Hope nodded. Bell swallowed hard. 'Good. Then we may go back.'

She led them at a swinging pace down the hill, and in at her door. The house was quite bare, but not in poverty, like some Bell had seen in dutiful visits with her Aunt

Patten. The floor was cleanly strewn, and the walls whitened last summer; only over the fireplace was a black stain. There were cooking instruments there, a single great pot and a series of skillets and small pans, and it was a substantial stone hearth, with a turf fire glowing and a stack of logs to one side. Parsley sat on top of it, watching. At the opposite end of the room, a six-step ladder led up to a half-floor, not much more than a broad shelf hung to make use of the upper part of the gable end. It was low and dark, but Bell could see a deep pallet, neatly draped, and a cloak and other things hanging on the far wall. The window's light fell on the table opposite the door, showing an array of mortars and flat stones for mixing; there was a high stool before it, and ranged along the rafters on either side were bags on pegs and wrapped bundles pushed into hollows in the thatch. The dame – Grace – went to one of these and drew out two books from behind a bundled cloth. She laid them on the table and waited for Hope and Bell to come beside her.

'Here is Master Culpeper,' she said, 'A good enough account, with some rare plants described in case you should meet them; overly ordered, of course, and set out like a regiment of soldiers. The green world will not march to his design or any man's; but with discretion, you may learn what to recognise and use.' She flipped its pages with her seamed and scarred thumb, a familiar gesture of one who knows their book, like Alistair with his hand on his beloved Euclid, Bell thought. Then she put it aside, and opened the other volume, a rough sheepskin binding rubbed brown and shiny at the corners, sweated and bubbled with age and use. It was a manuscript: pages of black, crabbed script at the beginning, and then a larger, lighter hand, maybe two, making the patterns of lines and half-lines that mean a book of receipts. Bell leaned forward to see what they were for; Grace smiled at her.

'You know your letters? You will read here without difficulty; I doubt you will understand a great deal, at first. But it cannot be helped. Perhaps there will be some time for us, after all.' She looked from Bell's face out of the window, where the sun was showing a momentary gleam as it set beneath the clouds over the westward hills. 'But I do not think so. I do not think that I can wait.' She closed the book, then reaching out she took a hand of each of them. They stood so for a moment; Bell, looking sideways under her lashes, saw that Hope was crying.

They were through the woods and onto the stony path before Hope came back to the present enough to talk to Bell. Until then she struggled silently with the awakened memory of Anticipation. Her sharp grief at missing her, missing her parting, not having her blessing and farewell, had been painfully called up, even as the unaccountable words of the old woman had seemed to give her a sort of substitute for those last moments. She replied to Bell's last question.

'I did not tell her where we were going. Of course I had to say we were travelling – how else could I account for Alistair lying at the Lawrences' house with a bullet hole in his scalp? But she knows what she knows without telling.'

'She knows what she chooses to suppose, more like. She came here from outside a lifetime ago, as you say Mercy tells you, and now she is in her decline she thinks you are sent to her, as she was a sending, a foundling of the old dame – isn't that it?' Bell's voice was sharp. Hope caught her hand, and pulled her to a stop.

'Bella – my love. There is nothing to fear.'

'What do you mean? I am not afraid.'

'Look at me.'

Bell sniffed, and then raised her head. Standing in the hillside path, where anyone might see, Hope drew Bell into her arms and kissed her very slowly.

'I love you,' she said, 'I shall never leave you. Wherever you go, I shall go.' The Bible echo rang in her head; but there was a difference, now. The landscape had

204

shifted and changed; whatever came of the encounter with the old woman, if she never saw her again, now she saw in a slightly different light.

Back at the Lawrences there was a new guest. Everyone was crowded into the kitchen, watching breathlessly as a muddy young man ate a slice of pie and downed a tankard of ale. He looked up at them furtively as they entered, and Hamish burst out, 'Come, man, you've broken your fast – tell us what you know. You held out at the town of Preston, you say?'

'Preston in Lancashire,' the man said, reluctantly putting down the tankard. 'For a week, or thereabouts; I was at a barricade, night and day for three days. Then General Carpenter came up, and that was the end of us. Mr Foster sent out a parley, and the next day they marched into the town. Not many got away.' He looked down at his plate.

'Who was there?' said Mr Lawrence. 'Foster was in command, you say?'

'If you can call it command,' the young man said, 'My Lord Derwentwater would have been a better choice. I saw him with my own eyes, take off his coat and help to build a barricade. He fought like a lion; men would have followed him. As it was . . .' He trailed off; tears welled up in his black-rimmed eyes.

'Lord Derwentwater is of the faith,' said Lawrence, bitterly. 'No doubt they thought him too dangerous a choice for leader.'

Hamish put a hand on his arm. 'And who else?' he said to the fugitive. 'Were, there Highlanders there?'

The man looked up at him. 'There were: a thousand men, with not a word of English or a pair of breeches between them. They drew them up in lines in the square,' he said, 'and made them lay down their arms.'

Hamish swore, and was silent; the men all gazed at each other, their faces white.

The runaway Jacobite knew nothing at first hand of what had happened further north, but he was clear that the Earl of Mar's Scottish army was much greater than the small group of Lancastrians who had been defeated, and was still in arms, somewhere north of the River Forth. 'The clans will be there,' said Hamish.

'And so will the King, I make no doubt,' said Alistair, 'so we must take our cargo further: into Scotland.'

They prevailed upon him to wait one more night. Even then, weak as a baby, he had to travel in the coach; Bell could have ridden his horse which needed exercising as much as she needed to be active, but there was no lady's saddle. Hamish reckoned they had forty miles to go; two days, on roads like these. For most of the first day's travel Hope sat on the box again, though a sleeting rain lashed her face and dripped down into her cloak. They wound their way west and a little north, by the gaps in the hills, using steep tracks and deep lanes that threatened to engulf the carriage at every boggy dell and overflowing stream.

'It sounds a gae lonely place, this Castle Coldbatch,' said Hamish. 'Master Alistair and I must make better speed when we leave you, if we are to come to Scotland in time.' They swayed up out of another muddy hollow. 'So far from the highroad folk must be always ready to welcome strangers. They expect your lady, no doubt?'

'I don't think so.' Hope looked round at the desolate place with some anxiety. 'It must be many years since any of the Wistons visited them. Bell – my lady speaks of the steward and his wife as her mother's faithful retainers. She has never been there herself, even though it is her inheritance.'

Hamish raised his eyebrows and said nothing, but peered ahead into the driving sleet.

The rain persisted. It was at noon of the next day, under a dark and murky sky, that they finally reached Castle Coldbatch. It was Christmas Eve.

Twenty-one

Hope was wrong in thinking they would not be expected. Word had obviously been sent out to Coldbatch from Castlebridge, the dirty little town where they had stayed the previous night. The lodge gates that loomed up through the driving rain were standing open, and on the threshold six figures waited, motionless. They stood in the mud, with sodden sacks over their heads and shoulders, to welcome the mistress they had never seen. As Hamish drew rein, one man ran forward to take hold of the two leaders; a second, the smallest, ran towards the carriage as it shuddered to a halt, and opened the door. The rest stood still, in the pouring rain; when the carriage door was opened, they made their obediences dumbly, like stupified children, then stood still again, dripping. The rain lashed into the carriage.

Bell found her voice. 'It is Mr Malpass, I think,' she said kindly, and held out her hand. To take it, he was forced to let go of the door. As soon as he released her hand, Bell drew the door firmly closed, and rolled down the window. 'Thank you all for your kind welcome,' she said in a clear voice, putting out her head. 'But please, all of you, find some shelter now. We should like to drive in and dismount at the door. I look forward to speaking to you all later; for now, my brother is weak and weary; and we need rest. Lead on, Mr Malpass.'

The coach was led, with some trouble, through the muddy gateway, then into a narrow passage under a tall gatehouse, and out into the courtyard of Castle Coldbatch. Bell surveyed her inheritance, and her heart quailed. The sea of mud around them lapped at the walls of what looked, at first sight, like the ruined castle in the old story. How old it was, she could not guess. Over to the left stood a round tower, roofless, and in ruins above about twenty feet: its walls were striped white with bird droppings and stained with the blood-red trickle of rust from rotted iron fittings. The tower stood at one end of a great barn-like hall. Its windowless bulk loomed before them, pierced only by crumbling arrow slits and by a massive oak door, tall enough to admit a man on horseback. At the other end of the hall, to their right, a second tower, in better repair, sported incongruous modern windows, leaning out on flimsy struts from the failing stone.

She looked at Hope. 'It's like the ruined abbey, do you remember?'

Hope nodded. 'Above Chepstow – yes, that's what I was thinking of . . .' Her voice trailed away.

But this is worse, thought Bell, there is nowhere in this crazy pile where you could shelter a pig. She was wrong about this, as she quickly discovered when they climbed down from the coach. Mr Malpass was there again to push open a little wicket in the heavy oak door, and his wife, a breathless old woman on monstrous wooden shoes, ushered them into the darkness of the great hall. The smell of pig was unmistakable. Bell peered around. The sty in the far corner was empty, as far as she could see in the half-dark: perhaps, she thought, the poor creatures had been turned out in honour of her state visit. She stifled an almost hysterical urge to giggle, and followed Mistress Malpass through the draughty gloom to a staircase which rose at one end of the hall. It clung at a crazy angle to the huge stones of the wall; each step was a single massive baulk of oak, twisted and black with age. There was no handrail.

Like a sailor at ease on a rolling ship, the old woman stumped unperturbed up the dizzying structure; Bell gritted her teeth and followed, then Hope, then Hamish supporting Alistair.

'Maister Wiston, yours is the first room.' She pushed a door opening off the stairs into what Bell realised must be the second tower. 'Come up, my lady, if you please.'

The room was at the very top of the tower: the light from two huge casement windows made them blink after the darkness of the stairs. However odd the windows had looked from outside, they made the room more welcoming than anywhere else in the castle. Bell looked around the wide, irregular chamber with pleasure. An effort had been made for her: the floor was swept, and if some black cobwebs still lurked about the rafters, it was only in the inaccessible corners and crannies. The ancient smell of wet stone was almost defeated by the camphor that wafted from the folds of old-fashioned wall-hangings. They were obviously just out of storage and newly re-hung; not all perfectly straight, but very bright and cheerful in the flickering warmth of a good fire.

As they entered, Mistress Malpass bent to put on more logs. The fire-place was of a date with the windows, thought Bell: comfortable additions to the old house by some not-long-departed ancestor who wanted a home rather than a fortress. She recognised the arms of her mother's family, the Bembertons, over the mantel. The sides of the great stone hearth were carved in the likeness of the supporters to their coat of arms: a comical heraldic bear with long back legs and pussy-cat paws, and a mythical lizard with scales the size of dinner plates. At the other end of the room, opposite the door, squatted a huge bed: four black, bulbous posts each a yard round, framing a lumpy expanse of red damask that must be eight feet square. She saw Hope staring at it, amazed. Behind the old housekeeper's back, Bell caught her eye and put out the tip of her tongue, just for an instant. She saw Hope's colour rise and looked away to regain her own gravity.

'Tis your own grandmother's room, my lady,' said Mistress Malpass, in the delighted tone of one who gives a present to a child, 'and her good things are all here still.' She waved her arm at the room, but it was unclear to Bell what she meant.

Suddenly she wanted very much to be alone with Hope. She smiled back at Mistress Malpass. 'I should like to wash off the dirt of my journey; and I expect my brother would like to do the same. May I have a can of hot water?' Before the old woman could reply, she went on, 'My maid shall come with you to fetch the water back and save your legs on the stairs. Go with her, Hope, and tell my brother not to disturb us for a while. I think I may lie down for an hour or so on this fine bed. Be quick.'

There was much to be done over the next few days. The Malpasses and their four sons occupied the gatehouse, and unless called on made little contact with the Wistons, beyond providing their meals. It was midwinter, and the food was scanty, but willingly offered. The old woman left an ashy-crusted loaf and a quart pot of small beer on the staircase each morning, and in the afternoon scuttled across the yard with four bowls and a canikin of cooling soupy stew. She did offer to wait on her long-lost mistress, but took no offence when Bell told her that she did not require personal service. The Malpasses had served the owners of their house and lands at a distance all their lives, and seemed unusually free from the consuming curiosity which Bell had found to be the chief characteristic of so many servants.

Mistress Malpass did, however, have a clear idea of what Bell's role in the household was: to be decorative, and do nothing. She was startled and worried when, the second day after their arrival, she saw Bell shaking a duster out of the tower window. Between them, she and Hope had scoured out the chamber, hanging the bedding before the fire in an attempt to drive out the mouldy smell that had gathered in its depths over the years, and opening the wide windows to the southern wind whenever the rain stopped. Hope borrowed a broom and swept the high beams; dust billowed into the yard like smoke. Bell did what she could in the face of the old housekeeper's scandalised disapproval, but when Mistress Malpass caught her carrying logs upstairs on the third morning, she was so outraged that Hope had to persuade Bell to stop.

'I thought she was going to burst,' Hope grinned. 'I think if she catches you at any more 'maid's work' she will lay about me with her broom for an idle slut. You must play the lady for her, my love, or she'll be up here waiting on you herself to show me how it should be done.'

That was the last thing either of them wanted. They had not had so much time alone since the old days at Wiston, and they were greedy for it. Bell spent some of her time amusing Alistair, and keeping him company while he gathered his strength to continue the journey to Scotland; but as soon as he slept, they shut their door and took to the great red bed.

Bell had never imagined that she could want anything so much; every inch of her body cried out for Hope's hands and lips. In the mornings, when Alistair rode out for exercise, a glance from Hope as they sat either side of the hearth, a twitch of her heavy blonde eyebrows, was enough to make Bell drop the tapestry she was stitching and reach out for her love.

Alistair rallied daily. His morning rides quickly lengthened, and by the end of the week he was ready to set out; but first he wanted to be sure that Bell would be provided for.

'Malpass must render his accounts,' he said. The old man was summoned, and came prepared, with a great ledger bound in black like a family Bible. He stood before them at the far end of the long table in Alistair's room. He addressed himself only to Bell.

'I took up my duties here in the year of the Glorious Revolution, young Madam; and I have faithfully carried out my stewardship and kept my account, yearly and half-yearly, as is written here, for a matter of twenty-eight years.' He struck the book softly with his fist, and set it upon the table before him. He laid his gnarled hand upon it, protectively, as he went on. 'Your grandmother, my lady, the Lady Alice Bemberton, was inheritor then, and she said to me, Jeremiah Malpass, that I was to keep Castle Coldbatch for her and her heirs – that is your mother, that I never saw but twice in my life, and now your honoured self. And so I have, indeed. It is all written here. You will find it fairly set down, regular in all dealings.' He patted the book. 'It is all written here,' he repeated.

And so it was, they found. So far as anyone could keep a record of the unending effort and daily tribulation of a bleak hill farm, lean sheep on hungry slopes, with more frosts than fair weather, he had done so. They read of his lifelong struggle with diseases, floods and chancy harvests; of a little farm lumbered with the upkeep of a monstrous old house, unused and falling inch by inch into inevitable decay. Malpass had sold the lambs in the autumn, and cossetted the ewes through the snows; he counted each pig that was littered, and wrote it down as butchered or reared or sold, for the village or for the kitchen; he went yearly to the great fair in Shrewsbury and sold the yarn, and the few small fleeces that his wife did not spin; and he wrote it down, in a spluttering, fading, painful penmanship that spoke of the midnight candle and the sufferings of the faithful steward.

'This is an honest man,' said Alistair, when he had shown them his work, and gone. 'God knows how he has kept so honest a path; I honour him, truly. He has done right by you, Isabella. What there is here that is yours will be rendered up to you.' He paused, gnawing his lip. 'But it is so little. A beggarly trio of bare fields, a bleak sheepbitten hillside and an old man with four surly sons who never thought to see you come back and claim what has seemed to them their own birthright . . . it is so pitifully little for you to live upon now, let alone to be the basis of the rest of your life.' He turned away to the window.

Bell was distressed by the pain on his face, much more than by the picture he painted of her own future. She went and slipped her arm through his. 'I am very well,

Alistair – I am very happy here, and will thrive like the hillside heather until you return. Go to the king: that is where your duty lies.'

He squeezed her arm.' You are the bravest of us all, Isabella. I will do as you say, and do my best for us. Wiston –' but he stopped, and did not say what was in his mind about their lost home.

Twenty-two

Alistair left two days before the New Year, driving away into a bitter wind that carried hailstones in its teeth. They stood outside the gates to wave goodbye; Hamish flourished his whip as they turned the bend in the road and vanished between the whitening hills.

After he had gone, Hope and Bell explored the secrets of their new home. They found that Lady Alice's 'good things,' so prized by Mistress Malpass, were contained in four coffers, blackened oak chests carved with initials and dates ranging back to 1555 and decorated with yet more versions of the comic Bemberton bear. They were not locked, but the lids fitted tight; levered open, each one breathed out camphor and lavender.

'She must have tended them – look,' Bell said, lifting out a cloak of deep blue wool, folded smoothly round linen rags. 'It is perfect, all pressed and clean – look, underneath! How lovely!' It was a silk bodice, a delicate green ground embroidered at every seam with a tracery of tiny flowers. Bell held it up to herself. 'Lady Alice was my size, or thereabouts, do you think?' she said.

'Try it on,' said Hope. 'Just take off your dress . . .

There were many more beautiful clothes: damask petticoats, slashed sleeves with silken insets of flame or blue or green, and long bodices stiff with golden thread. The fine old lace was a wonder to them, even to Bell, who had had a taste of modern French work at Bath. They found useful shifts and smocks to replace their own scanty linen, and they each chose a new petticoat and a cloak. But there were strange garments, too, that begged to be tried and made them helpless with laughter: great high collars and ruffs such as they had only seen in the old portraits at Wiston, and hats like velvet plates. The third chest contained mostly men's clothes, some very odd. Hope put on a shirt with a high neckband and extravagant wide sleeves, and a pair of short velvet breeches with a monstrous jewelled pad at the front.

'The hero of the story!' she cried. She leapt on to the bed and struck an heroic attitude. 'Thus noble Guy, at last disengaged from love's cruelty, arms himself like a knight of Chivalry,' she quoted, striding up and down the counterpane, hands on hips. 'Crossing the raging main,' she went on, swinging out at arm's length from one of the great bedposts, 'he hears of the Emperor's fair daughter, Blanche . . .'

Bell attempted haughty beauty, and ruined it by laughing.

'. . . and makes her his prize!' declared Hope, leaping from the bed and grabbing her.

Bell squealed but yielded to her fate most becomingly. 'Have mercy, sir knight,' she panted, falling backwards onto the bed, 'at least, dismount that monstrous weapon!'

It was lucky that they were not actually naked when Mrs Malpass arrived. At the sound of her clogs on the top stair, Bell sprang up, pulling her bodice together and shaking down her skirts. Hope, still wearing the Elizabethan shirt but nothing else, rolled off the far side of the bed and crouched behind the curtains. The old lady seemed not to notice anything but the mess they had made spreading the revered 'good things' around the room. Hope, squeezed between the bed and the wall, could hear the disapproval in her voice.

'I am sure I'm sorry to disturb you when you are busy, my lady,' she said, sniffing, 'but since you have not mentioned it yourself I needs must let you know that the ewe is killed and hung, and ask who your ladyship would have us bid to the feast.'

Hope heard the stillness as Bell stopped picking up the scattered garments on the bed and turned round. 'Take me with you, pray?' Her voice was bewildered.

'Why, New Year's,' came the reply. 'Your ladyship has forgotten that today is New Year's Eve? I have swept the chamber below, and folded away the bed, and it looks decent; the table will not take more than sixteen, but there are not many gentle families within journeying distance.' Hope felt the tremor as Bell sank down, silent, on the bed. Mistress Malpass, full of her business, went on without pause. 'Sir Lucas and the Lady Gwyneth will expect to be asked, no doubt, and the Morleys; and Mr Chester, and Mr Dear the vicar. That makes a neat dozen. Or fifteen, if the young Morleys are to come? It is for your ladyship to decide.'

But was it Bell's choice? Hope wondered as she dressed Bell for the feast next day. Perhaps the housekeeper really thought she was following her lady's wishes: but to Hope it was as if the old crone had suddenly grabbed Bell out of her arms and turned her into someone she thought they had left behind in Bath – Miss Wiston the heiress, the fine lady, the smiling, hateful, untouchable puppet. She finished the last curl on Bell's ceremonial coiffure, and plucked away the napkin that covered her bare neck and shoulders. Bell was wearing one of the beautiful old dresses, stiff with blue and green stones: they had had to lace her stays agonisingly tight to get it on. Bell rotated slowly, using Hope as her mirror, since Coldbatch did not seem to boast one. Hope nodded without speaking: she knew Bell wanted to be reassured, to be told she looked well, but the words stuck in her throat. She wanted to tear off the dress, the unyielding stays, and carry Bell in her shift to the bed, to make her remember where her life's centre lay. She wound her hands in the napkin. She would not quarrel; she would not let these things come between them. She said gruffly, 'You are more beautiful than they deserve Now I must go and be kitchen maid to the old mother hen.'

Bell looked round her dinner table, her first attempt at being hostess in her own house, with growing dismay. I must not cry, she told herself firmly. I must not cry, however hateful they are. She deliberately took another mouthful of mutton. It helped. She chewed slowly; it was surprisingly sweet and tender. There was not much of it left, nor of anything else that Mistress Malpass had so plentifully provided. Castle Coldbatch would be on even shorter rations than usual in the coming weeks. Her guests seemed to have satisfied both their appetites and their curiosity; for the moment they were ignoring her completely. That at any rate was better than the insolent appraisal to which she had been subjected for the last three hours, until she felt like a heifer at market. She looked warily down the table. The oaf sitting two places down on her left – Benedict Morley, was it? – looked up from an improvised game of knucklebones with his brother and raised his tankard to her, grinning and greasy. She put her face into a polite smile. The boy's mother spoke to him sharply – Bell could not hear what she said for the general hubbub of conversation, but he dropped his eyes, smirking.

'So, mistress.' It was the dreadful Sir Lucas, on Bell's right hand. He had finished his third attempt to explain her genealogy to the vicar, on his other side, and now turned to torment her again with his commentary on her present situation. 'So. You are come to live on your . . . estate here, alone?' The sneer was thinly veiled; his long upper lip pulled at the grey bristles below his mouth, and his eyelids drooped as he glared coldly into the top of her bodice. She felt as if she were breaking out in goose-pimples.

'I shall stay some time, at least, sir,' she said, as levelly as she could. She had resisted their prying and speculation all this time, and she was determined not to give anything away about her brothers' situation, or about Wiston. This man clearly assumed they were ruined; or perhaps that she had run off from her family, in some disgraceful way, and so put herself at everybody's mercy. She deliberately looked away from Sir Lucas, nodding down the table to Mr Morley, who took the foot. He raised his tankard in a perfunctory salute and glared at her down the length of the table. He had declared his loyalty to King George in the first minute of being introduced, and obviously put her presence in Shropshire down to what he called 'this wicked and bloody rebellion.' He looked as if he expected the king's troops to arrive in pursuit of her any day, and was angry that he had not forced her to confess it. Mrs Morley had been far less hostile. She had let Bell know, by way of introduction, that the larger and more prosperous of the two farms her husband worked had been part of her marriage portion; she had been a Miss Alliband – here she had paused as if to receive congratulations – and would be charmed to welcome Miss Wiston to her family's ancestral home. Pulling her two lumpish sons significantly closer, she added archly that she, for one, would be delighted to see Miss Wiston settled here in the valley permanently. Now she simpered at Bell, and nudged the nearest son.

Bell put down her drink, and picked up the ancient two-pronged fork to clear the remains of her dinner from the dented pewter plate. She had reserved the most battered of the old tableware for herself; but she need not have troubled; her guests were not particular. At that very moment, the Morleys' other son was hammering his overturned plate with the butt of his knife to emphasise some point in his argument. At his shoulder, his sister made sheep's eyes at young Mr Chester, a leering provincial cavalier with the frogged red coat and long moustaches which had been the height of fashion some ten years ago. He had kissed Bell's hand and breathed hard down her neck before dinner; now he sat with his boots on the table, sunning himself in Miss Morley's admiration. *She seems pleased enough with him, at least,* thought Bell. *Well, she shall find no rival in me, that's certain.* She looked down at her plate. The loud, coarse conversation swelled around her, fuelled by the New Year ale; the laughter seemed not only heedless but cruel, so that she had to remind herself they were not laughing at her. She wondered suddenly what Hope was doing; a great wave of loneliness and longing swept over her. If only the people would go away, she thought, or if only I could. Her throat ached again with the threat of tears.

'Hush, sweetheart, hush, they are gone. All's well now, all's well.' Hope filled her voice with as much calm as she could, rocking the forlorn little body in her arms. Bell's tears subsided, but she still clung on tight.

'Don't ever leave me, will you? Promise you won't.'

'Of course not. You know that. Besides,' Hope teased, 'where would I go? No-one else but you would have me.'

Bell turned away out of her arms, and stared into the darkness. 'Where can either of us go?' She spoke in a tight, desperate little voice that frightened Hope. 'If Alistair does not come back – and he may not, I know – if he does not come back, I don't think I can stay here. You saw them, Hope, how dreadful they are, and I have nothing, and they know it. I shall be the poor neighbour, to be pitied – no, not even that, they don't seem to have any pity, or Christian charity. They sneer and laugh at me, they look at me as if I was a – a pony they had come to buy and they had found it was broken-winded. Good for a short trot round the fair, but not worth taking home.' Her voice shook, but there was no stopping her. 'And they expect me to be looking for a husband – any husband, since I'm in no position to be fastidious, being poor. That dreadful Chester thinks I would come running if he so much as crooked his little finger – the conceit! And it's not just the young ones. The vicar, too – did you see him? A horrible old man, with greedy eyes. He positively drooled when he said goodbye; he does so much look forward to seeing me in church . . . his wife died last year, Mistress Morley says, and he's only – only fifty-five –' She turned convulsively, grinding her face into the pillow.

Hope knelt up and began to rub Bell's back, squeezing the clenched shoulders until she could begin to smoothe the knots away. Then she knelt astride her, smoothing the beautiful back down and down and down. In truth she did not know herself what they were to do. If King James returned in triumph – and she had less and less faith that he would – even then it did not follow that Alistair would be safe and well, or that they would regain Wiston. And even if they did – she switched to long strokes outlining Bell's shoulder-blades with her thumbs, stretching the taut muscles outwards – what would that mean but a return to a place where they were known, where Bell might, in the end, be happier to do what was expected of her? She dragged her mind away from the thought of Bell married; it would be better to stay here, in this wilderness, and be together somehow. She swept both hands down the length of Bell's body, shifting her own weight and bringing her fingers inwards; after a little while, Bell turned over with a sob that had nothing to do with her anxieties about the future.

In the days that followed they found a kind of intense peace. To be together was enough luxury; they did not look to the future. As Bell had predicted, food was shorter than ever after the feast, but at least Mistress Malpass seemed satisfied that Bell had done her social duty, and left them alone. Bell did not even have to explain why she did not go to Mr Dear's church services; the Malpasses were absentees themselves. Hope thought they were probably Dissenters – there was something about their sturdy independence which reminded her of Bassett Moor – but she made no move to find out, or to discover a chapel for herself. She and Bell lived in a charmed circle, all alone at the top of the tower, concerned only with food and firelight, each other and the great crimson bed.

It was on a bleak morning in February, when the snow-filled clouds hung low over the northward hills and a gusty, chilling wind was rattling their windows, that Hope looked out to the east and saw a rider in the distance.

'Someone's coming,' she said.

Bell got up from the nest of rugs by the fire and came to see. 'One rider? Oh, I hope it's not a visitor. I can't bear any of those dreadful people now.' Hope put an arm round her. They watched the rider disappear on a bend; but he was clearly heading for Coldbatch. They stood suspended. In a few minutes he reappeared; as he rode out of the trees he raised his head, looking up at the castle. Hope felt Bell go rigid in her arm. Then she said, 'It's James.'

'No!' Bell flung off James's hand and stormed across the room. She stood staring out of the window at the snowy hills. There was a silence.

'You had better listen to me, Isabella.' He walked towards her but stopped without touching. 'Isabella –' his voice was low and apparently controlled, but a lifetime of his bullying had taught her that he was most dangerous when he went quiet. He moved away, back to the table, and began again.

'I will tell you the whole story. There is only one chance of regaining Wiston. I must go to the King –' King George, he means, Isabella thought incredulously, the Hanoverian usurper, and he calls him king so easily; it slips out of his evil mouth like spittle. His low, insistent voice forced her to listen.

'I will go to his feet, with our contrition and submission; and with a suitable gift for the attorney general, who has charge of the cleaning up –' Cleaning up! she thought, as if the stand they had made for the rightful king were some sort of mess on the kitchen floor. She turned on him, but he held up his hands; his dark eyes glittered.

'Listen, Isabella, listen to me. We could be not only forgiven, but welcomed. My information is that English gentlemen who go back promptly to London now, and bring their mouths to the right ears, will be pardoned, and the example made of them will be one of generosity.'

'Mouths! Ears!' she broke in, hardly able to believe what she thought he was saying. 'You mean that you will go to London as an informer – to speak against others, who will suffer at your accusation?'

He heaved a theatrical sigh, hunching his shoulders and rolling up his eyes. His coat is threadbare, she thought suddenly; and where is his diamond ring?

'No no, you mistake me. I have only to be properly

contrite, properly zealous to make amends for the damage we have done to the realm, and all will be well.' He had moved out from behind the table, where he had spread out the document he had brought on the uneven oak. She stepped back as he cane towards her.

'And that is why I must have a little money. Something to offer, to show how sorry we are for our errors. It will not be easy to convince Walpole, what with father's recalcitrance – you know he attacked his gaolers, and died cursing the king? It told against us, I do assure you; and then Alistair and his damned coachload of French guns.'

'Alistair is a loyal gentleman, and a hero,' Bell said, gulping to bring down the shrill fury in her voice.

'Alistair is a fool.' James slammed his hand on the back of the big chair she had sat in for the New Year feast. 'He rides across the border, bold as a dragoon, with an outlawed highland ruffian at his shoulder and four dozen proofs of treason under his arse, straight into the rearguard of Argyll's forces. How he got away I shall never know – he is as slippery as an eel, and about as much of a gentleman.'

'But he did escape?' Bell could not stop herself asking for reassurance again, despite James's contempt. He would tell her whatever suited him; but how else could she find out? At this moment, obviously, it suited him to make sure that she understood that Alistair was far away, and unlikely to return. He smiled.

'Alistair is in France, madam, as I told you. I do assure you of it. You will not hear from him for some time. Look.' Thrusting his hand into his pocket he brought out a dog-eared packet of papers. Sifting through them, he selected and opened a letter. He folded it to show only the foot of the inside page, and held it out to her. 'Look. Go on, take it, read. It is from a friend in the regiment, who went to the court in exile months ago, fell ill and so has never returned, the lucky dog. Read what he says.'

Bell took the soiled page, and focussed with difficulty

224

on the sprawling handwriting. *I have to report that your respected brother, Master Alistair, arrived here last week with the latest batch of crestfallen cavaliers, all intact except for his humbled pride and most villainously dirty linen, and is this day gone east, to* – a place name, she could not read it – perhaps Lorraine? – *in the hope of meeting there with certain French gentlemen after his own mathematical mind, and one supposes, joining in their philosophical games. The brandy here has run low, and* . . . She scanned to the foot of the page, but there was no more about him. She read it again. When she looked up James had seated himself at the table, and was staring at her with an unsmiling, brooding gaze.

'So you see, Isabella; Alistair has gone to ground in some hole in the distant parts of France and will in all likelihood never be able to return. We must do without him, you and I.'

She tensed, expecting another demand to sign the papers, to mortgage Castle Coldbatch. This was what he had come for; for three days, now, he had been cajoling, threatening, asking her to let him raise money upon her estate, the only property they had left in the world, and at her sole disposal. She braced herself to refuse again. But he looked out of the window, and said, 'How is young Jos Chester? An amusing fellow is he? Quite the lady's man, I hear. Do you find him – agreeable?'

'What? Who?' She was taken aback.

'Chester, my dear; don't pretend you have not met the local rake, in all your weary weeks here so far. You must have sifted all the available society in this – secluded spot. Or perhaps you prefer graver company? I hear the Reverend Mr Dear is eager to see all young ladies, and not too concerned about their . . . other possessions. Charmingly unworldly, very appropriate for a clergyman. Of his years. Not all established gentlemen are so easily satisfied with nothing but a pretty face.' He stood up. 'Understand me, Isabella –'

Furious, she broke in. 'I do understand you, brother, all too well. But you will not frighten me into signing away my mother's inheritance. I can stay here, if need be, and live contented. Whatever you say, I know that there is no real alternative. We will never return to Wiston, and we are poor.' She turned on him, not bothering to conceal or modify the scorn and loathing she felt – that she had felt for him all her life. 'We are both poor, and now you are the poorer, James, because your wants and desires have ever been in excess of mine, and indeed in excess of honesty. I am content to be poor. I shall live and die a lady, come what may. I do not need an eligible marriage. I do not need the favour of a usurping king. And I do not need you.'

Upstairs, Hope clenched her hand in the shift she was sewing as she heard their voices rise, and the door slam; when James's steps descended the stairs, she went to the door. Bell came running up and slipped into the room. Hope took and held her; they leaned silently together.

Ten minutes later they were sitting by the fire when James barged unceremoniously into the room. Ignoring Hope completely, as he had done ever since he arrived, he announced to Bell, 'I shall ride into Montgomery; I have business. Do not expect me back until tomorrow.' Then as he reached the door, he turned to them again. 'But do expect me then. I shall be back – have no fear.' He smiled a nasty little smile, a mere lifting of the corners of his moustache, and was gone.

They watched from their courtyard window as he mounted and rode off, trampling the Malpass chickens out of his way. One of the four sons stopped shovelling dung in the corner to watch him, sullenly, without moving a muscle as James rode out under the gatehouse.

'You don't need to hear to know that he is cursing the hens, and the Malpass boy is cursing him,' Bell said. 'He inspires hatred almost without trying.'

226

'Has he always been like that?' There was no chance of changing the subject completely, Hope thought; at least she might deflect it from the immediate present.

'Always.' Bell sat on the broad window ledge. 'One of my earliest memories is of James beating a dog until he broke its back, and the boy it belonged to attacking him; father refused to punish the boy, but he had to leave the village – he went for a soldier, in the end. I expect he's dead now. James had a few followers – the other sneaks and bullies, I suppose – but no one chose him for a friend. Our mother used to try to make us play with him, lest she should seem a cruel step-mother, but he did not care for us any more than we did for him. They say his mother, that was Lady Belinda Felthorpe, was as cold-hearted as he is; only my father would never hear a word against her. I suppose I ought to be sorry for him, in a way.'

'He has no right to Castle Coldbatch, though.'

'No.' Bell sprang up. 'It's freezing hard, and the sun is coming out – look. Let's go out for a walk.'

They crossed the rutted courtyard, and doubled back round the outer wall below their southerly window, into the valley. They had walked this way before; you could make a circle, cutting into the high road where it crossed the river to come back. The sunlight on the snow filled the air with spirit-lifting brilliance.

Bell said, 'So it is all over.'

Hope glanced at her quickly. Her chin was up; that look meant she had something important to say. Perhaps James had told her more than she had shared so far. 'You said James had brought news of the end of the war – the Jacobites are scattered, the King has gone back to France.' She looked at Bell, who did not reply. 'Will he never return?'

Bell sighed. 'I suppose he may; next time perhaps he will be better supported, or we will be more ready.' She shrugged. 'I don't know whether I care about him any more. There is something more important.' She paused.

227

'This morning James showed me a letter from a friend of his in France, saying Alistair is there.'

'That's good,' said Hope, glad that Bell sounded so sure. 'He's safe, then.'

'Yes. Yes, I think he is. But he won't be coming back, Hope. We are on our own.'

'I wish we were!' Hope said. The sooner the better! Just as soon as we are rid of James, everything will be all right.'

They walked on in silence. There was deep snow heaped under the hedges and walls; the landcape was strange, transformed by the distorting, uneven white blanket. It was very cold; the bridge seemed a long way ahead. Hope looked across the river.

'I have never noticed that long mound before,' she said, 'it looks like Somerset.' She could have bitten her tongue.

Bell shook her head. 'I don't recall it, either.' she walked on. 'Do you miss home, Hope?' she asked.

'Not at all,' Hope ran a step to catch Bell round the waist. 'Not at all. All I need is you – you know that.'

Bell turned her head and kissed her, very quickly. 'I'm terribly hungry,' she said. 'Let's see whether that path ahead is a short cut – it goes in the right direction.' After a hundred yards, though, the path bent away from the line they wanted, and led them up a little rise to a broken wicket gate in a high hedge. They peered in.

'An orchard!' said Bell. 'This must be ours – Malpass spoke of an old orchard. Come on.'

She wriggled through the gate and plunged in, heedless of the deep snow that crunched into jagged holes where she trod. They stood amid ancient apple trees; gnarled branches sparkled with patterns of frost. Hope held her breath at their beauty; her boots, however, were letting in freezing water.

'Look!' Bell pointed at a tree in a corner, sheltered by the highest part of the surrounding hedge. On its silvered branches hung golden fruit. They both waded towards it.

'An applejohn tree,' said Bell, 'and not properly picked. There must be two dozen apples left.' She reached up and pulled a fruit. Hope took one too; it was cold as a stone in her hand, damp and wrinkled, but still heavy. She bit into it, and was amazed by its sound sweetness, wonderfully fresh to taste despite the rubbery sag of its ageing skin. She ate it all, spitting out the inedible skin as she went. Bell was on to her second. The tree was quite tall, and the missed fruit was mostly high up, in its inner branches. They had to climb, adding a layer of wet black moss to the already wet outer folds of their clothes. Hope pulled off one of her petticoats and they knotted it into a bag to carry all the fruit.

'They'll be lovely when they are not so cold,' said Bell, 'and they would be nicer peeled. We'll have a feast tonight.'

Bell cried out Hope's name, and thrust upon her outstretched fingers. Hope rode her raised thigh, calling in response, sliding on the wetness between their legs. Bell began to laugh, the bubbling spring of joy that had startled and delighted Hope the first time it had happened. They rolled over, Bell still breathlessly calling Hope's name as the pulse of her pleasure crested and broke. She was full of power and fire; her hand slid down Hope's back, parting her legs. Hope gasped and Bell bent towards her.

'Enough.' James's voice cut across the room like a whip.

Bell screamed and twisted away from Hope, whimpering in panic.

He was standing in the doorway. God knew how long he had been there, watching them; they had heard nothing but the sound of their own lovemaking. He spoke again, slamming the door and stepping into the room; his voice was thick and violent.

'So this is it. I thought there was something. Slut. Whore. So calm, so self-satisfied. She's well-fucked, I thought: who's been at her? Not poor little Chester. One of the studs about the farm? I did wonder, but no. Too refined for that, my little sister. Quite up to the latest fashion in fornication. I should have guessed sooner. Back home, when you were so eager to keep your kitchen drab to yourself.' He was upon them; he grabbed Hope's plait, that lay half-unravelled on her shoulder, and thrust his face in hers. His breath stank of brandy.

'Hope, isn't it? Hope! Good, is she?' He spoke to his sister, as he threw Hope across the bed. 'Well, we'll see. You can't afford to be so selfish now, little sister, slut.'

Hope balled up, and rolled herself off the bed onto her feet. She was cold as ice, and naked. Out of the side of her eye she could see Bell, kneeling, holding the bed curtains wrapped round her; she was pale, her dark eyes huge.

'James –' she began.

'Be silent.' He deliberately stepped back, into the firelight, confronting Hope. His face was darkly flushed and ugly as he dropped his cloak. Holding his leather riding gauntlets in his left hand, he began to unlace his breeches.

As he stepped forward, Hope lashed out, but her bare foot did not stop him; he grabbed and lifted her, slashing her across the face with the heavy gloves. She staggered. The bed caught her behind the knees and she fell sprawling. Bell flew at him, but he came on, pinning Hope down as he fended off his sister with a thrust of his right arm.

'No, Bell, you won't stop me this time, you bitch!' he panted. 'Stand off, or it will be the worse for you both.' He paused, his knee driven excruciatingly into Hope's thigh, and turned to look at Bell. 'Now I'll show you how it's really done. Then we can try it, if you like, sister dear. I am good for two, I promise you.'

Hope wrenched her eyes away from his fumbling hand. Her arm was over the side of the bed; she felt the little table beside her pillow; and on it the dish of apples they had been eating only an hour before. And with the apples – she stretched out her fingers – her hand closed on her hunting knife. James pushed Bell contemptuously away, and his knee slid off Hope's leg. She arched herself violently towards him, rose up, and stabbed him.

He was big, and she was still partly pinned down so that her flailing arm did not reach far. The knife went in, but swerved and slid towards her own wrist She jerked her hand away, and the blade ripped out of the side of his waistcoat. He grunted and stopped dead, as if in surprise. Then his balance gave way and his weight crashed down, crushing the breath out of her.

Bell screamed again, and pulled at him. James recovered, dragging himself violently to his feet and raising his hand to strike Hope again, a murderous glare swelling his face to twice its normal size. He looked unhurt and very angry.

Hope twisted away from his blow, and ducked under his arm, scrambling out of range. He came after her.

Naked, she ran for the door and burst out of the room. Swinging round on the door-post, she raced safely down the treacherous stairs, only to trip and sprawl in the frozen mud of the great hall. Above her, James burst out onto the stairhead; but before she could stand and face him, his curses turned to a shout and then a scream, cut off by a heavy, damp thud.

She stood up. James lay silent in the darkness beside the stairs. All Hope could hear was Bell, crying wildly in their room.

He was obviously dead. Bell brought a candle; they stood looking down at him, unwilling to touch.

'He has broken his neck,' said Hope, in a small voice.

Bell looked at him. She felt nothing for him, nothing but disgust; she put her arm firmly round Hope's waist. 'Good,' she said. 'You are freezing cold. Come, we must dress ourselves before we call Mr Malpass.'

231

'No – no, Bell, think a minute.' Hope bent over James and pushed his arm aside. His shirt and waistcoat were sodden with his blood. 'Look,' she said, and drew a shuddering breath, 'the stab wound shows. No one will believe this was an accident.'

'But it was!' She felt almost impatient with him, for giving them all this trouble. 'It was the fall that killed him.'

'But I stabbed him first.' Hope's voice was low, desperate; Bell tried to look into her face, but she held her head away. 'I stabbed him, Bell. That is a hanging matter.'

So they dragged his body across the ancient hall, and tipped him into the empty pigsty, and covered him with straw. Then Bell took Hope by the hand and led her back upstairs; they washed off the filth. 'Come on,' she said, 'Back into bed. We have to get you properly warm.'

They huddled together, and she stroked Hope's hair and would not let her talk. They lay shivering, and Bell began to plan what they should do. One thing was clear; they had to get away. Eventually Hope relaxed into her arms; after a little while longer, she whispered, 'I'm sorry, Bell.'

'Sorry? Why ever should you be sorry? You must not say such a thing. You did nothing wrong. Don't let me ever hear you say you are sorry for it; I am not sorry; I'm glad, do you hear?' She grasped her hair, and shook her. 'But we must decide what to do.'

Hope was quiet for a moment. Then she said, 'I – we must get away.'

'Yes. I was thinking – shall we go to France?' it sounded as incredible out loud as it had in her head; but it was the only place she could think of.

'How?' said Hope.

'I don't know. There is a little money left. But I don't know that it would be enough.'

'We could try to get home.'

Bell was sure this was wrong. 'That is where they'll look for us,' she said.

Hope did not speak.

'I know,' Bell said suddenly. She lifted herself up, to look into Hope's face. 'Brynsquilver – your old wise woman – that's where we'll go. It's only two or three days journey, even on foot. She'll look after us until it – all dies down.' She laughed, and said as lightly as she could, 'She will be expecting us.'

There was a pause. When Hope spoke, Bell could hear tears in her voice. 'If you are sure,' she said. Bell bent her head down and kissed her. 'Come,' she said. 'Time to get dressed.'

They did not set off at once, but waited until the Malpass family would be asleep. James must have stabled his horse; so Joseph would find it when he went to fodder his plough team in the morning, but he was not likely to go looking for James. Mrs Malpass would leave their breakfast on the stair; they would not be missed until later in the day, when she found they had not taken it.

Bell had another idea: they dressed in men's clothes, from her grandmother's coffers. 'No one will be looking for a couple of lads, tramping for employment,' she said sturdily, belting in the smallest pair of breeches they could find. Suddenly Hope was heaving and gagging; Bell moved swiftly, and took the hunting knife that she was tying to clean out of her hand. 'Let me,' she said. 'We may be needing this.' She wiped it carefully and sheathed it, and stowed it in her bundle.

Some time around ten o'clock, when the waning moon was shining on the snow and the cold was intense, they opened the southerly window in the lower room and let themselves down onto the field path. They looked up at Castle Coldbatch. Bell shook herself. 'Let's go,' she said.

Twenty-four

At first they were very cold, walking with heads bent along the beaten road, the moonlight shining off the surrounding banks of snow. The highway was the only way out of the hills; they were concerned that they were leaving tracks. Then towards dawn the moon clouded over, the temperature rose, and it began to snow – huge, wet flakes that filled the air.

'At least this will hide our traces,' Bell said, pulling the good blue cloak tighter round her neck.

'Outside, anyway,' Hope answered.

They could not keep going: the swirling snow in the black darkness confused them; it would be easy to stumble into a ditch and break a leg, or stray from the road completely. They passed a wayside cottage, and at a field's-length from it found a little cart shed. Inside were a wagon and the remains of a straw stack. They threw most of the straw into the cart and lay down, wrapping themselves together in both cloaks. They still had little to say; but they made a little warmth around themselves, and fell asleep.

Sunlight was needling through the boards of the shed when Bell woke. She pulled the cloak up to her nose, sleepily trying to keep it out; but her feet were on fire: she had to sit up, in the end, and take off her boots. The chilblains on her heels were angry and weeping and her left toes were a swollen red pulp. The boot was sodden.

'I have some fresh stockings.' Hope's voice was flat as she sat up and dug into her bundle.

Bell turned to her, and was alarmed by her face – her right cheek and the side of her brow were reddened, puffy, and her eye was almost closed. She bit back a comment, and accepted the stockings with a smile.

They talked about practical things only, that morning. They had not come more than eight or ten miles from Coldbatch, and could not risk being seen in daylight.

Hope stared into the distance, withdrawn and silent.

'We can keep warm in the straw,' Bell said, altogether too brightly. 'No good risking a fire.'

Hope did not reply.

'Breeches are good for walking,' Bell tried, 'Your legs are freed, and they don't get wet and heavy.'

'Mine are heavy to start with,' Hope said. They were made of ancient leather, stiff and thick, with the remains of a rich red colour in their deepest folds. Bell thought she looked rather fine in them, truly like a forester; but she did not dare say anything so lighthearted this morning.

There was no more snow, and enough frost to hold off a thaw; they were aching with cold by the afternoon, as they lay wrapped in the soggy straw. Hope was still silent. Bell wondered fleetingly if they would ever make love again, but she drove the idea away, and burrowed into her side. Hope put her arm across her, saying in the same flat voice, 'I'm sorry you're so cold.'

In the gathering dusk of the afternoon they prepared to go. They ate up all that remained of the food they had brought – the end of yesterday's loaf, and a small piece of hard cheese. There were also the two apples. Bell had hidden them in her bundle when they had eaten earlier on, but now she brought them out, and Hope's knife with them. In silence, she peeled one, and held it out. Their eyes met; then Hope reached out to her, and took, not the apple, but her hand that held the knife, closing her own larger fist round Bell's fingers as they clasped the hilt. She lifted Bell's hand to her lips, and kissed the cold knuckles; her lips were dry and cracked.

'I love you,' she said.

'I love you too.'

As soon as it was fully dark they set off, making as much speed as they could along a completely deserted road. No-one had passed the shed all day; the country side seemed empty, all sensible people keeping their own firesides and wishing away the winter. Bell was in such pain from her feet that she had little attention to spare for Hope's brooding silence. It was five or six hours before they topped a rise and saw the first sign of life – a few house lights, strung out up a slope, with the denser blackness of buildings along the skyline.

'That will be the market town we slept at on our way here, do you remember?' Hope said. 'We would probably not be sought there. But we had better wait – we can't walk into a place this late at night without everyone wondering who we are. Is that a barn, over there?'

It was a barn, a large stone building, and inside it was hay, stacked high – a great improvement on the previous night. They made a nest deep in the midst of it, disturbing other uninvited guests that squeaked and rustled as they settled down. Bell was even able to take off her boots before they slept. She was glad it was so dark. She could tell her feet were bleeding and she didn't want to see them. She woke first, forced herself to look and quickly put her own stockings over the blood-stiffened rags of the pair Hope had given her, before pulling her boots on by brute force and willpower. She did not think she could walk more than another day at the most but said nothing as they set off, hoping for breakfast in the town.

The road was not deserted this morning. It was already eight or nine o'clock; they joined a steady trickle of hill farmers, carrying baskets or driving a couple of sheep, and even a cart or two, with stacked wood or a tethered calf behind the muffled drivers. As they walked into the town, it was obvious that they were in luck – it was market day. They would not be so conspicious, two tramping lads coming into market, and there would be food to buy, even at this hungry season. They walked up the length of the steep street, looking at what was on offer. At the top of the town they drank at the street pump, and then walked back, as casually as possible. They stopped at the baker's stall for a quartern loaf and found a woman with a little basket of withered but sweet goat's cheeses, and, the best of all, a huckster selling hot pies. They sat down under the wall of the church, and ate.

'You boys!' A big voice, from the direction of the church. After a moment's blank surprise, they scrambled to their feet. It was a dark man, in clergyman's bands; he was shaking his stick at them.

'Be off with you – none of your wicked games in the church-yard. How many times – be off!' He took a step, brandishing the stick; they gathered up their things and ran.

When they stopped, round the corner, they found they were laughing for the first time since leaving Coldbatch. 'I quite like being a boy,' Hope said.

Things continued to improve when their stomachs were full, and they could walk in the daylight. There was no more snow, and Bell thought perhaps her feet were hardening; the pain was less. She cared less about it now anyway. Hope was coming back to her. They talked about the road and their route as they walked along, reckoning they might complete their journey that day. When they stopped to rest, Hope got out her pipe and played cheerfully. They were sitting on a stile, almost warm in the sun, when a drover came by, struggling to control six jostling heifers.

'Good morning,' he said to them, and turned his beasts unceremoniously into a small paddock whose gate stood open beside them. He slammed the gate. Hope and Bell looked at him with some apprehension, but he only watched until his animals settled in a huddle and quieted, before he turned his back, leant on the gate, and brought food from his pocket.

'I thought yon was a bargain, nine o'clock this morning,' he said, biting into his pie. 'Damned if I wouldn't give 'em back now, and be thankful.' He scanned them, and spoke to Hope.

'You for hire, lad? I could do with a hand to help me home – only over Clun, nobbut a day beyond thisn. Give you tuppence. And your keep, the day.' He flourished the pie temptingly.

Bell looked anxiously at Hope; but she stood foursquare in the road, her feet apart, left hand in her breeches pocket, and touched her cap to him. When she spoke her voice had dropped an octave, Bell could have sworn.

'Thankee, goodman, but we cannot.' Bell looked up the hillside, to keep her face straight. 'We'm hired to go South and overdue by days as 'tes. Ben here, blast him' – she punched Bell in the upper arm, unexpectedly and so hard that she staggered – 'fell ill at Chester and lost us a week. We mun hurry, man.'

The drover nodded, resigned; to avoid more conversation, Hope touched her cap again, and taking Bell's arm, all but dragged her away; entering into it, Bell shoved her off, and they ran down the road, jostling like boys. When they were well clear, Bell pulled up, laughing but winded, and Hope came up and put an arm round her. 'Don't I make a good peasant lad?' she asked, grinning.

Soon after noon, they drank beer at a crowded inn on a cross road and set off again quickly to use the rest of the daylight. They thought they knew where they were.

'It's soon now that we strike off west again, into the hills,' Hope said.

'I remember a junction of three lanes with a great oak,' Bell said.

Hope nodded, 'And that was quite near the Lawrences' house, just north; the lane to Brynsquilver is the next turning.'

But they never seemed to come to the triple junction; the light was already beginning to thicken and dim when they came upon an uphill path, and decided to risk it. They climbed quickly, tired now, and anxious; beyond an empty byre, a hundred yards up, the snow lay deep and undisturbed. In places they were wading thigh-high. But at last they came over the brow, into the teeth of a sharp wind that stung their eyes; Bell pulled her hood tight round her aching ears.

'This is the valley,' Hope's voice was full of relief, and perfect certainty. 'Yes. Here we are.'

Walking and climbing along the wooded hillside on sheep tracks and no tracks at all was desperately hard work. They both fell more than once, twisting their feet on hidden ruts and undergrowth. The low slanting sun glinted off the snow and played tricks on them, burning their eyes, but when it sank behind the opposite hills darkness gathered alarmingly fast. They were soaked in snow-melt outside and sweat within when they struck into the bottom of Grace's goat field, and recognised the shed, and the stile into her garden.

She was not there. They knew as soon as they came round the rosemary bush, in sight of the cottage: the fire was out, and the windows were shuttered. They shouted. There was no reply. The door yielded to the latch, and they went in, alone.

Hope climbed quietly down the ladder. In the dark disappointment of the previous night, they had lit no fire; the cottage was icy. But she found logs stacked in the hearth, and kindling to hand. She took flint and tinder from her bundle and got a small fire of sticks alight. She squatted, watching the little flames flick round the twigs. For a moment, when she woke, she had thought that she was home in her father's house, where her slopey beam came down across her pallet and the thatch was close to her face, as it was this morning. But she was far from the forest. She piled on more kindling. The hearth was cold; smoke billowed into her face, repelled by the heavy, damp air above. She flinched. But it was a good chimney, and soon there was a crackling blaze. An she watched it, and began to feel a tiny tickle of warmth, she thought somewhere deep inside that this might, after all, be the end of the road. They had perhaps come home to Brynsquilver.

She looked round. The room was bare and clean in the morning light, carefully emptied out, it seemed, of any incidental odds and ends, but otherwise exactly as they last saw it – only Grace was missing. Hope shivered. She turned back to her bundle and extracted her skirts, glancing at the breeches that lay where she had dropped them, stretched out like half a man, unbending, resisting the wear of the world. She burrowed in her bundle for her stays, but after a moment discarded them, beside the breeches, and tied on her skirts over her shift. A picture of old Grace had come to her, standing sturdy and unconstrained in her earth-coloured layers of clothes. I will not wear the breeches, she thought, but they have shown me that I do not need to truss myself like a chicken. My back will be strong enough, like hers. She crossed to the window and looked out, but a thick cloud lay all about them; in the garden, leaning stalks dripped. She shivered again, and went back to build up the fire; then she began to move about, touching things.

The table was rigidly tidied, the three mortars lined up, their pestles laid in them straight, from back to front. She opened the little cupboard beside the hearth: a crock of salt, damp but clean, with a cloth laid over it She walked to the other end of the room, under the sleeping platform, and found a low door. Inside was a narrow room partitioned off the width of the cottage; bins and sacks stood on the floor, and above them hung a forest of thin cloth bags that bounced lightly away from her hand. She lifted the first lid: a bin, about a quarter full, of flour – wheat flour. The next was peas, a third barley flour, almost full. She hesitated; Grace was not here, but she would be happy to give them a meal. She took up the deep pot that was standing by the door, and went out to the spring.

She had the griddle heating, and was moulding flat barley cakes when a movement outside the window caught her eye. Her heart jumped. She could see nothing when she looked out; she went to the door. Before she had it well open, a cat slipped in past her feet – Grace's cat, thin and muddy-footed, but with only a sprinkling of icy drops on her coat. She looked up at Hope, once, and went to the hearth where she sat composedly, and began to clean.

'Parsley?' The cat allowed herself to be stroked, even arched to Hope's hand for a moment, rubbing a purposeful face on her skirt. Hope bent down, loving the lithe, dense back and pushing head.

'Parsley, where have you been? Where is your mistress? You're thin, poor girl.' But the fur was dry; she had not been wandering in the open. Cats find themselves places to hide, to lie up, she thought, when they are left on their own. She straightened up, thinking. Parsley washed behind her ears.

There were steps outside. The cat crouched, but then sat up, indifferent. It could not be Grace. Heart in mouth, Hope turned to the opening door.

'Oh, you're come!' It was Mercy, carrying a basket, stamping snow off her boots. 'She said you'd come. But it's been a while.' She put her basket down on the table. 'You best have these, then. I been bringing bits up, just in case, each time.' She lifted out a jug, covered and tied down. 'This morning's milk, 'tes.' She brought out a little loaf. 'Mrs Lawrence say I'm wasting my time with the food, until the spring, but I tell her, Dame say Hope be coming, and naught about springtime.' She put her basket down, and crossing purposefully to the corner behind the door took hold of a broom and began to sweep the hearth. 'Oh, her cat! Kitty, Kitty?' Parsley removed herself from reach, up the ladder. 'You been back days, then? Where did you find the cat? They always know what's good for them, cats.'

'She came in, just now,' Hope said, finding her voice. 'Mercy, what do you mean – where is Grace?'

Mercy stopped sweeping and looked a her, just a little sideways. 'Dame died, Epiphany time. Don't you know that? You must know that. She said, you'd come. And you have.'

'Died? No, I didn't know, I –'

'Hope?' It was Bell's voice, calling her. 'Hope, where are you? Here's the old woman's cat.' Bell's face appeared above them and then disappeared again; she came down the ladder backwards. Hope watched her knuckles whiten as each red and swollen instep met the rungs; there was fresh blood on her heels. Mercy's wince of sympathy was followed by a look of complete shock as she recognised Bell. She dropped a stunned curtsey.

'My Lady. . .' words failed her.

Bell smiled. 'It is good to see you, Mercy. Oh! and you have brought our breakfast. That was kind.' She frowned. 'But how did you know we were here?'

Mercy groped for words. Hope could see she was struggling to make sense of Bell's presence, to connect this tousled and travel-stained figure with the beautiful lady she had so admired only a few weeks before. 'What – what chance have fetched you here, m'lady? How come you all hurt and bloody?'

There was a moment's awkward silence. Mercy hurried on, 'Well, whatever. You bring me some warm water, Hope, and let me see to her poor feet.'

Bell sank into Grace's chair by the fire, and submitted gratefully. Hope finished making the barley cakes, and put the bread and milk on the table. 'Breakfast now, both of you,' she said cheerfully.

Mercy looked awkward, but when Hope sat down beside Bell she perched on the bench that faced them and broke the bread.

Bell ate little. Sipping at her milk, she looked over the brim of the wooden bowl. 'Mercy,' she began.

'Yes, m'lady?'

'Does everyone know that we are here?'

'Oh no, bless you, only the old Dame told me Hope

243

would come back, and bade me look out for her. The Lawrences know I been coming up here, but they keep close, never says a word to no-one.' She frowned. 'Is there danger, then?'

'There may be, I think.' Bell paused. 'We must not stay here long, but we must be careful. People will soon know someone is here, for news travels faster in the country even than in town, but you must tell no-one who we are. Especially, you must not call me 'my lady' any more. My name is Bell: do you think you could call me that? It is of the greatest importance. Will you be my friend in this?'

Mercy nodded. 'Dumb as any stone.' she said firmly, and smiled at them both.

Twenty-five

Hope sat beside the Dames in their graves, thinking. She looked out across the valley, flooded now with the brilliant light of spring, touching new leaves with a hundred different greens, and here and there sparking on lace-white blossom. Troubled, she let her eyes rest on the far hills as she fingered the old pipe in her pocket. It was May morning.

How soon had she known that they would stay here – that this was their destined place? That first morning, when the cat came home? No, even before that, she thought; she had known and not known – Bell had seen it in her before she was aware of it herself, when they had first come up here together; and already then Bell had been afraid.

And that was the problem. For the first few weeks after they came here Bell had seemed afraid of the place, and even of being seen; she would talk to Mercy, but if Mercy brought William or one of the young women of the neighbourhood with her, Bell would disappear until they had gone. Their frank interest in her had no hostility in it, Hope thought; her speech, her manners were alien to them, and it was not their habit to veil their curiosity. But Bell shrank from their open stares, and went silently away. 'I do not belong here,' she said bitterly to Hope.

Then, late in February, Mercy's William's littlest sister, Nance, had been taken with a flux, shitting and puking hour after hour. On a raw afternoon as it was getting dark, Mercy had come hammering on their door. At her shoulder loomed William, his broad face furrowed with anxiety, carrying the child in a blanket 'Th'old Dame would have helped her,' pleaded Mercy. 'Can you not maybe tell us what to do? She'm gone, else; look,' and she pulled away the blanket. Hope blinked in alarm at the stinking child, shivering and sweating in William's arms. But before she could gather her wits, Bell had

245

broken in, calm and quick. 'Bring her here, by the fire, while I find what she needs.' She set water on the hottest part of the fire, then went quickly to Grace's store of herbs, and set to work. Hope knew better than to speak her surprise, but Bell, looking up suddenly and catching her eye, said shortly, 'I do have some usefulness, Hope. Mistress Johnson was not of the opinion that even ladies should grow up a burden on the world.'

They had kept the child that night, so Bell could watch her. In the morning she was still weak and pale, but the flux had abated and when Mercy returned Nance was asleep. 'You must give her nothing for another whole day and night,' Bell told her firmly, 'except this clean water from our spring – here is a jar – William can come for more if you need it. And keep her warm, and quiet, and give her the medicine three more times, at noon, dusk and morning. You understand?' Mercy nodded, shining with relief, and something very like worship.

Of course, after that, others came, from up and down the valley, for medicines. Bell dispensed, from Grace's ample stock; and when it was a matter of bonesetting, or of a sick beast, Hope did her part. Many would have asked for charms, too, but Bell would have none of it. 'There is no magic here,' she said in her most queenly voice to one slattern girl who dared to ask her for a love potion. 'If you were to wash your body and comb your hair he might feel more drawn to you.'

But expectation had been stronger than all her efforts. 'Gwennie says to thank you and to give you this pot of curd,' said Mercy the next week. 'She did wash herself seven times in clean water like you said, and combed her hair under the full moon, and Evan Griffith did kiss her behind the cow byre, Tuesday. That were a rare charm.'

Bell would not touch the curds. She spent more and more time at the work bench with pestle and mortar, and, as the evenings began to lighten, she would sit after supper reading Grace's books; but when their patients brought gifts, of eggs or bread or firewood, she grew tight-lipped. On the evening of Lady Day they came home from a long walk in the hills, and found a beautiful quilt, neatly folded on a chair.

'It's from the Joneses-at-the-Bryn,' said Hope delightedly, 'Where I helped with the cow. Look, this piece is from Mary's sprigged gown, and that's the baby's old dress he left off only last month.'

Bell was furious. 'I do not want their things,' she cried, 'We do not want to be – paid!' And she threw the quilt from her.

Hope felt her own anger rising in response. 'Why should they not pay us back? Who are we? We are as poor as they are, and why should they rest beholden to us? You are not their Lady, Bell, you are no more than they are, now.' She was sorry as soon as she had said it; Bell had turned away, silent, and said nothing.

For her own part, things had come to her hand here as smooth and familiar as an old hoe handle. Soon after they came, she had found a little box in the storeroom full of neatly sewn and labelled packets of seeds – potherbs and peas, even three different kinds of cabbage – and had heard Grace's voice speak to her through them as clear and matter-of-fact as the day. The first peas were up now, and three good rows of carrots; it was high time to think of a place for the cabbage. Bell had said nothing to stop her while she dug and raked and sowed, and Hope's spirits had risen as she thought of watching the vegetables grow through the summer. But then came the business of the goats, and everything seemed in doubt again.

It had been just two weeks ago. Startled by the noise of the beasts, they had come rushing out to find a tall, raw-boned young woman they did not know just fastening the door of Grace's goat shed on her loudly protesting charges. She turned slowly when she heard them, wiping her hands on her old sheepskin jerkin, and

247

said briefly, 'All safe. You were ready?'

Hope felt Bell freeze by her side. They were Grace's goats, come home. This weather-beaten young woman must have kept them through the winter.

While Hope struggled for an appropriate response, the stranger spoke again, more awkwardly. 'You were ready? She said to bring them to you in the Spring. I fetched them all, but if you have need of wool maybe, or sheep's meat, I could take the old one's second kid?' she paused, looking from one to the other.

Without a word, Bell turned on her heel and went into the cottage.

Hope rallied herself and smiled at their visitor. 'Thank you,' she said, 'I had forgotten all about them; but I am glad to have them. You will sit and eat before you go?'

The young woman looked towards the firmly closed door of the cottage, and back at Hope; and flashed her a brief, dazzling smile. ''Tis a fair step,' she said politely, 'I must go. But thankee. 'Twas no trouble.' She turned and walked away, down the track, pausing only once and half turning as if to speak again; but she changed her mind, and vaulting over the stile, raised her hand, and was gone. Leaving Hope to manage both the goats and Bell.

In the row that followed, all that was clear was that Hope's glad acceptance of the cottage, the cat, the obvious need to plant vegetables and the commitment of tending a growing flock of beasts irked and frightened Bell; she was not ready to accept the place in the rural community that was so firmly thrust upon them. She still hoped that Brynsquilver was a temporary hiding place She could not think of a hut in the woods as her home.

'I feel as if I had walked into a cage,' she said, her knuckles whitening in her lap. 'we stumbled blindly in here, creeping into a crack for refuge, and before we could turn round, crash, the door falls shut, there is no way out. And I have no room to stand, or sit or lie down,

Hope – almost I feel as if I cannot breathe!'

How could anyone be short of breathing space, here on this most lovely hillside, under the May morning sun? Hope sighed, and took out the pipe she had been fingering; she played a little tune, a new tune that had been in her head; it would be nice to get it right. But after a few moments she put the pipe down, and turned her mind, at last, to yesterday.

The news had come from Mercy, of course. She had come running up, as she always did, with a basket of things she thought they might fancy; and a handbill, all rubbed and folded, and ripped at the top, where William had pulled it off the church door at Castlebridge. He had told Mercy they should have it, and though she had not understood why, you could tell from her solemn face that she knew it was important. ''Tes about the – rebellion,' she said, awkwardly. 'My William say, no need to have that stuck up for all to see, when good folks have suffered enough already over their blamed wars and tribulations.' And he had bravely torn it down, and brought it home for them to read.

It was a long bill; no simple proclamation of victory, but a detailed list of those who 'did in a traitorous and hostile manner take up arms and levy war against his present most Gracious Majesty' and the pains and penalties to be meted out to them; and near the foot of the paper, the name of Wiston, of Wiston Hall, Somerset. It declared that Sir James Wiston and Alistair Wiston Esquire were proscribed traitors, not having made their submission within the time of grace allowed by a merciful sovereign; and furthermore, that all their lands and rents were declared forfeit to the offended sovereign, and none should succour or harbour them, on pain of his displeasure.

Hope wondered again what it might mean that James was named. News of his death could not have reached London, that was evident. They themselves had never heard a word of any hue and cry after him. Malpass might never have found his body; or if he had, perhaps he had simply buried him, quietly, at Castle Coldbatch, and said nothing, but carried on his faithful service to his absent lady. That was fanciful, she thought; more likely his sons had got rid of the body, reckoning it the last service they would pay, to secure an inheritance that nobody would ever dare claim from them again. Well, they were rid of him. Strange, she thought, I really do not care; I feel nothing about him at all. But as for Alistair – Sir Alistair, he should be now, of course – she shook her head, and lifted her pipe to her lips; and let it fall again. Bell had wept for Alistair, and said she must go to France, and be with him; and then that she could not go, and she would never see him again, and her heart was broken. And Hope had realised that it was the thought of Alistair that Bell had kept secretly in her mind all this time – of the moment when Alistair would come back, and find her, and take her away, back to her old life, the life of a lady. And I? Hope thought; what of our life, together? Only last night, she had kissed away the self-pitying tears, and Bell had turned passionately to her, making love eagerly, greedily, until they were both exhausted. They had been asleep for scarcely more than an hour or two when the dawn chorus had woken Hope, and she had crept out into the woods. The sun rose over the treetops, and fell hot upon her face, and she was suddenly in another May morning, a lifetime before, but not so long ago. She lifted her pipe to her lips, and began to play the May Day carol, for her love.

Bell woke and stretched. Her body was still heavy with the pleasure of last night's loving, and she let the memory of it warm her. Lazily, she stretched out for Hope, but her place in the bed was cold. Bell opened her eyes. It was broad day. She listened for the little noises of Hope moving in the room below, but there was nothing. Suddenly she was cold awake, and the memory of yesterday's news hit her like a blow.

Gone; all gone. Wiston, where she had grown up; her

father, dead in the prison; James – her mind flinched from the memory of his heavy corpse. And now Alistair: Alistair was gone too. For he could never return from France; he might as well be dead for all she would ever see or hear of him again. Tears gripped her by the throat; she rolled over into Hope's place, sobbing, burrowing for comfort, pulling the quilt over her head to shut out her trouble like a little child. But it would not go away. She bit into the rustling pillow, and then suddenly opened her eyes. Nothing ever stays the same, she thought. And Wiston had changed for me before I left it; everything changed, when Hope came. She drew breath, and rolling over again sat up, clutching her knees.

What if things had been different? If the King had come into his own, and her father had lived, and they had all gone home, to Wiston. What would she have done then – what would they have done, she and Hope? When they were children, it was all very well; but now? She knew now what would have been said, what she would have been expected to do. Could I have refused it? She shook her head, appalled at her slowness, her stupidity. Why have I never thought about it before? Did I really want to go back? Back to what? To marriage, and the life my mother led? How long would Hope have borne the strain of being servant and lover? Not long, she thought, remembering Bath with a startling new clarity of understanding. Not long. She began to get up; but another thought struck her, and she sat down on the edge of the bed.

So perhaps I have chosen this, without knowing. It is all of my own doing, after all. I chose her; everything follows from that.

She got up, pulled on her shift, and began to climb down into the house; and faintly, from a distance, she heard the notes of Hope's pipe, calling her out into the daylight. She thought, why am I so slow to know my own heart? The only place in the world for me is where she is; and we are here. She looked round the simple, workaday room. Hope's great grandmother had believed in a new world where all were equal in love; they would build it again, here; in spite of all the kings. She snatched up her shawl, and wrapping it over her shift, stepped out into the sun. The pipe called to her, led her, a clear strong thread of sound; Hope was playing the May Day carol, the sweet, insistent heartbeat of the spring, just as she had played it a year ago.

The sun was hot on Bell's face as she ran down between the garden rows; a bumble bee hummed loudly by the lower hedge. A good place for beehives, she thought, smiling; it is nearly time for swarm-catching, and if we had good luck there would be honey for cough-syrups this year and maybe more the next.

She climbed the stile, and set off towards the sound of the pipe.

Historical Notes

In 1715, the year in which *Rebellion* is set, the soldiers of King George put down the followers of James Stuart. The Jacobites hung on for another thirty years, organising and plotting, especially in Scotland. See Sir Charles Petrie's classic account, *The Jacobite Movement*, first published 1932, revised 1959, for details.

Although Anna Liddell and her utopian colony are fiction, they had many historical counterparts in the 17th century among the Diggers and True Levellers who believed in universal equality and universal love. Those radical politics were violently supressed by Oliver Cromwell's dictatorship. For information about them, see Christopher Hill's *The World Turned Upside Down,* first published 1972.

A few of the Onlywomen books available:

What Night Brings
by Cárla Trujillo

Altogether Elsewhere
by Anna Wilson

Hatching Stones
by Anna Wilson

Bulldozer Rising
by Anna Livia

The Vinland Sheep (Historical novel)
by Helen Shacklady

Stoppage Time
by Helen Sacklady

Something Wicked
by Jay Taverner

All In The Game
by Eleanor Hill

Passionate Friends: Mary Fullerton, Mabel Singleton, Miles Franklin
by Sylvia Martin

A Passionate Development
by Eleanor Hill

Beyond the Pale
by Elana Dykewomon

Love Ruins Everything
by Karen X. Tulchinsky

Incidents Involving Warmth: collection of stories
by Anna Livia

Mosaic of Air: collection of stories
by Cherry Potts

A Noise From The Woodshed: collection of stories
by Mary Dorcey

Mouths, Tigers' Mouths: poems and prose
by Sophia West

Onlywomen Press website is
www.onlywomenpress.com

We also do mail-order. Write for a free catalogue to:

ONLYWOMEN PRESS
40 St. Lawrence Terrance
London, W10 5ST
England